EXPLORING THE COSMOS—
IN A MICROCHIP . . .

I was floating, spinning, tumbling with no control. Pulsating waves of blinding light pounded me. I was falling into the infinitely small, and there was no halting my descent. I would shrink and shrink and shrink until I slipped through the realm of matter entirely and was lost. A mob of contemptuous glowing things—electrons and protons, maybe, but how could I tell?—crowded close around me, emitting fizzy sparks that seemed to me like jeers and laughter. They told me to keep moving along, to get myself out of their kingdom, or I would meet a terrible death. . . .

—from "Chip Runner"
by Robert Silverberg

D1780487

Books in This Series from Ace

ISAAC ASIMOV'S ALIENS
edited by Gardner Dozois
ISAAC ASIMOV'S MARS
edited by Gardner Dozois
ISAAC ASIMOV'S FANTASY!
edited by Shawna McCarthy
ISAAC ASIMOV'S ROBOTS
edited by Gardner Dozois and Sheila Williams
ISAAC ASIMOV'S EARTH
edited by Gardner Dozois and Sheila Williams
ISAAC ASIMOV'S SF LITE
edited by Gardner Dozois
ISAAC ASIMOV'S WAR
edited by Gardner Dozois
ISAAC ASIMOV'S CYBERDREAMS
edited by Gardner Dozois and Sheila Williams

ISAAC ASIMOV'S
CYBERDREAMS

**EDITED BY GARDNER DOZOIS
AND SHEILA WILLIAMS**

ACE BOOKS, NEW YORK

If you purchased this book without a cover, you should be aware that this book is stolen property. It was reported as "unsold and destroyed" to the publisher, and neither the author nor the publisher has received any payment for this "stripped book."

This book is an Ace original edition,
and has never been previously published.

ISAAC ASIMOV'S CYBERDREAMS

An Ace Book / published by arrangement with
Bantam Doubleday Dell Direct, Inc.

PRINTING HISTORY
Ace edition / July 1994

All rights reserved.
Copyright © 1994 by Bantam Doubleday Dell Direct, Inc.
Cover art by Peter Gudynas.
This book may not be reproduced in whole or in part,
by mimeograph or any other means, without permission.
For information address: The Berkley Publishing Group,
200 Madison Avenue, New York, NY 10016.

ISBN: 0-441-00073-8

ACE®
Ace Books are published by The Berkley Publishing Group,
200 Madison Avenue, New York, NY 10016.
ACE and the "A" design
are trademarks belonging to Charter Communications, Inc.

PRINTED IN THE UNITED STATES OF AMERICA

10 9 8 7 6 5 4 3 2 1

We are grateful to the following for permission to reprint their copyrighted material:

"Nearly Departed" by Pat Cadigan, copyright © 1983 by Davis Publications, Inc.; reprinted by permission of the author;

"Computer Friendly" by Eileen Gunn, copyright © 1989 by Davis Publications, Inc.; reprinted by permission of the author;

"Night Win" by Nancy Kress, copyright © 1983 by Nancy Kress; reprinted by permission of Virginia Kidd, literary agent;

"Realm of the Senses" by Geoffrey A. Landis, copyright © 1990 by Davis Publications, Inc.; reprinted by permission of the author;

" 'Forever,' Said the Duck" by Jonathan Lethem, copyright © 1993 by Bantam Doubleday Dell Magazines; reprinted by permission of the author;

"A Hand in the Mirror" by Sonia Orin Lyris, copyright © 1993 by Bantam Doubleday Dell Magazines; reprinted by permission of the author;

"A Coney Island of the Mind" by Maureen F. McHugh, copyright © 1992 by Bantam Doubleday Dell Magazines; reprinted by permission of the author;

"Synthesis" by Mary Rosenblum, copyright © 1992 by Bantam Doubleday Dell Magazines; reprinted by permission of the author;

"Chip Runner" by Robert Silverberg, copyright © 1989 by Davis Publications, Inc.; reprinted by permission of the author;

"Dreamwood" by Cherry Wilder, copyright © 1986 by Cherry Wilder; reprinted by permission of Virginia Kidd, literary agent.

All stories have previously appeared in *Asimov's Science Fiction*, published by Bantam Doubleday Dell Magazines.

For
Cynthia Manson

ACKNOWLEDGMENTS

The editors would like to thank the following people for their help and support:

Susan Casper, who helped with the wordcrunching involved in preparing the manuscript; Shawna McCarthy, for having the good taste to buy some of this material in the first place; Ian Randal Strock, Scott L. Towner, and Adam Stern, who did much of the thankless scut work that was necessary; Constance Scarborough, who cleared the permissions; Cynthia Manson, who set up this deal; and thanks especially to our own editor on this project, Susan Allison.

CONTENTS

NEARLY DEPARTED
  Pat Cadigan   1

A HAND IN THE MIRROR
  Sonia Orin Lyris   19

COMPUTER FRIENDLY
  Eileen Gunn   49

CHIP RUNNER
  Robert Silverberg   67

A CONEY ISLAND OF THE MIND
  Maureen F. McHugh   83

DREAMWOOD
  Cherry Wilder   91

REALM OF THE SENSES
  Geoffrey A. Landis   125

NIGHT WIN
  Nancy Kress   129

"FOREVER," SAID THE DUCK
  Jonathan Lethem   153

SYNTHESIS
  Mary Rosenblum   165

NEARLY DEPARTED

Pat Cadigan

*"Nearly Departed" was purchased by Shawna Mc-
Carthy, and appeared in the June 1983 issue of
Asimov's, with an illustration by Odbert. In the
decade since then, Cadigan has gone on to be a
mainstay of Asimov's, and one of our most popular
authors. Many of her stories have appeared on major
award ballots, and one of them, "Pretty Boy Cross-
over," an Asimov's story, has recently appeared on
several critics' lists as being among the best science
fiction stories of the 1980s. Born in Schenectady,
New York, Cadigan now lives in Overland Park,
Kansas. She made her first professional sale in
1980. She was the co-editor, along with husband
Arnie Fenner, of Shayol, perhaps the best of the
semiprozines of the late 1970s; it was honored with
a World Fantasy Award in the "Special Achievement,
Non-Professional" category in 1981. She has also
served as chairman of the Nebula Award Jury and as
a World Fantasy Award judge. Her short work has
been assembled in the landmark collection Patterns.
Her first novel, Mindplayers, was released in 1987*

1

2   *Pat Cadigan*

to excellent critical response, and her second novel,
Synners, *won the prestigious Arthur C. Clarke Award.
Her most recent books are the novel* Fools *and a new
collection called* Dirty Work. *Coming up is a new
novel, tentatively entitled* Parasites.

*"Nearly Departed" is one of a series detailing
the adventures of Deadpan Allie, who is also the
main character of the novel* Mindplayers—*a sort
of high-tech psychoanalyst of the future, who can
hook directly into another person's mind to seek
out the root causes of their psychological troubles.
In the jazzy and multifaceted story that follows, she
suggests that stock phrases like "the privacy of the
grave," "quiet as a tomb," and "rest in peace" may
soon be marked "obsolete" in the dictionary. . . .*

"Three things," I said, and held up a matching set of three fingers.

Nelson Nelson looked tolerantly amused. "Run 'em."

"One—" I curled my index finger. "I don't do empaths. Two—"
I bent my ring finger. "I don't get physical. Three—" I pointed the
remaining finger at the old fox on the other side of the desk. "I
don't rob graves."

The couch creaked as NN rolled over onto his back and folded
one arm behind his head. "Is that all that's bothering you? Kitta
Wren hasn't been buried."

"I don't do dead people. If God had meant me to pathosfind
dead people, he wouldn't have invented the Brain Police."

A broad smile oozed over NN's saggy features as he reached
for a cigarette. He was smoking those lavender things again.
They smelled like young girls. "What's the matter, Allie? Are
you scared of a dead person's brain?"

"I'm scareder of some live ones I know. Fear isn't the issue.
I just have certain beliefs and this job you're asking me to take
goes against every one of them."

"Such as?"

Sighing, I shifted position on my own couch and scratched my
forearm. The vulgar gold lamé upholstery NN was so enamored

NEARLY DEPARTED 3

of was giving me a rash. You can dispute taste but you can't stop it. "Such as, death is the end. The end means there is no more. Dead people should be allowed to rest in peace instead of having their brains plundered and looted for any last bit of—of treasure, like Egyptian tombs."

"Eloquent. Really eloquent, Deadpan," NN said after a moment. "You're probably the most eloquent mindplayer this agency has ever employed. Someday you might talk your-self out of a job, but not this time." He winked at me. "Actually, I respect your feelings. Those are good feelings, especially for someone who trades on the name Deadpan Allie."

"Being deadpan doesn't mean you don't have feelings. You just don't show them."

"I personally don't share them. I feel there's a lot of validity in, say, going in and getting the last measures of unfinished music from a master composer who dropped dead at the harpsitron, or mining the brain of a gifted writer for the story that was unwritable in life. Postmortem art is highly regarded and a large number of artists, including Kitta Wren, signed postmortem art contracts. It's a sort of life after death—the only one we know about for sure."

I scratched my rash some more and didn't say anything.

"Kitta Wren *wanted* a postmortem. It's not grave robbing. If she hadn't signed the contract, it would be different."

"Kitta Wren was a five-star lunatic. She had a psychomimic's license and when she wasn't writing her poetry, she was bouncing off the walls."

"Ah, but she was brilliant," NN said dreamily. I blinked at him, astounded. I'd had no idea he liked poetry. "When it came to her work, she was totally in control. Somehow I always thought that control would bring her down. In a thousand years, I never would have guessed anyone would kill her."

I wanted to tear my hair and rend my garment. "NN," I said as calmly as I could, "I *hate* murder. I am *not* the Brain Police. If they want to find out who did her, let them send in one of their own to wander around in her mind."

"Oh, they will," Nelson Nelson said cheerfully. "Right after the postmortem." A cloud of lavender smoke dissipated over my head as NN flipped his cigarette into the suckhole in the center of his desk. "The Brain Police can't do anything until that's taken care of. Otherwise whatever poetry is left in there could be fragmented and irretrievably lost."

The rash had crept up past my elbow. I kept scratching. "There are mindplayers who postmortem for a living."

"I'll pardon the expression. Wren's manager hired you. Come along, now, it'll take you somewhere you've never traveled."

"I've never been to the heart of a white dwarf star and I don't see why I should go."

NN exhaled with a noise that was almost a growl. "Do you want to work for me?"

"I'm thinking."

He gave me that oozy smile again. "Deadpan, this is important. And you might learn something." He raised up on one elbow. "Just give it a chance. If you can't do it once you're in, fine. But try it."

I sat up, scrubbing my arm through my sleeve. "Don't make a habit of signing me up for postmortems."

My eyes popped out. I held them in my palms until I felt the connections to my optic nerves break and then lowered them gently into the bowl of solution. The agency's hypersystem would have removed them for me, but I've always preferred doing that little chore myself.

I lay down on the slab and felt it move me head first into the system. Even blind, I could sense the vastness of it around me as it swallowed me down to my neck. It was the size of a small canyon, big enough to spend the rest of your life in just wandering around. All I wanted at the moment was some basic reality affixing and reassurance. If I was going to run barefoot through a dead lunatic's mind, I needed all the reinforcement I could get. After an hour of letting the system eat my head, I almost felt ready.

I hadn't been gassing Nelson Nelson as to how I felt about postmortems just to cover a corpse phobia. To me, you ought to be able to take something with you—or at least make sure it goes the same time you do—and if it's your art, so be it. Hell, there were plenty of living artists with a lot to offer. Stripping a dead person's mind for the last odds and ends seemed close to unspeakable.

I supposed the appeal of postmortem art was partly what Nelson Nelson had said—life after death. But there seemed to be more than

NEARLY DEPARTED

a little thanatophilia at work. Art after death made me think of sirens on rocks, and I wasn't the only one who heard them singing. Occasionally there'd be an item in the news-tube about some obscure holographer or composer—holographers and composers appeared to be particularly susceptible—found dead with a note instructing that an immediate postmortem be performed because the person had been convinced that the unreachable masterpiece he/she had been groping for unsuccessfully in life could be liberated only by the Big Bang of death.

So there'd be the requested postmortem and the mindplayer who hooked into the brain, which was all wired up and floating in stay-juice like a toy boat lost at sea, would come out not with a magnificent phoenix formed of the poor deader's ashes but with a few little squibs and scraps from half-completed thoughts that had turned in on themselves, swallowing their own tails for lack of substance, vortices that had gone nowhere and never would. Some people aren't happy just with being alive. They have to be dead, too.

At least Kitta Wren hadn't been one of those. The information Nelson Nelson had dumped into the data center in my apartment was freckled with little details, but rather sketchy taken all together. I punched her picture up on my screen and sided it with her bio.

She'd been a very ordinary woman, squarish in the face with a high forehead and medium brown untreated hair. Her only physical affectation had been her eyes. Since the advent of biogems, everyone had at least a semi-precious stare. Jade and star-sapphires had always been popular choices and moonstones proliferated among entertainers of the more mediocre stripe. I hadn't seen very many people with my own preference for the shifting brown of cat's-eye and it takes a certain coloring to carry off diamonds effectively, but Kitta Wren had gotten herself something I'd never seen before.

Her eyes seemed to be shattered blue glass, as though someone had deliberately smashed the gems before putting them in. Her pupils were spiderwebbed with white cracks. I enlarged them for detail and paused, staring at them. I was wrong. Her eyes weren't spiderwebbed with cracks—they were spiderwebbed with spiderwebs, thickened as though coated with dew or frost. "Come into my lunatic parlor," I muttered, wondering if the webs had been a manifestation of her psychosis, or some kink she'd always wanted to indulge, or if there was any way of separating her own ideas from her psychosis.

She'd gotten her psychomimic's license at nineteen and spent the five years after that almost continuously crazy, with a few months off here and there for extended periods of writing. Later she had begun limiting her psychotic times to summers while she worked on a cycle of poetry. The result, a long series called *Crazy Summer* had given Wren her first major recognition. From there, she'd gone to being crazy only at night, then only during the day, and once she'd spent six months orbiting the moon in high mania.

When she died, which had been—I punched for the date—just the day before, she'd been a week into a general schizophrenia no one seemed to know anything about. Cause of death—I blanched a little—disembowelment. There was a photograph of her office where she'd gotten it. She'd been strong all the way to the end, going clear across the room before collapsing. Dead just under an hour when her manager had found her. Not too bad—five hours was about the limit for an untreated brain. After that, it's not worth trying to hook in with it. No suspects and no murder weapon; the Brain Police were holding off their investigation of her brain until after the postmortem was performed. Standard procedure—their technique tended to wipe a mind clean.

Under Miscellaneous, I found a small picture of Wren's manager, a gold-skinned androgyne named Phylp with fan-shaped eyebrows. The request for a pathosfinder was entered as well. It seemed Phylp wanted someone who wouldn't treat her like just another deader. Sounded to me as though Phylp were hoping Wren hadn't left behind as little as he/she suspected.

A morgue is a morgue is a morgue. They can paint the walls with aggressively cheerful primary colors and splashy bold graphics, but it's still a holding place for the dead until they can be parted out to organ banks for burial in the living. Not that I would have cared normally, but my viewpoint was skewed. The relentless pleasance of the room I sat in seemed only grotesque.

The other two people in the room didn't see it that way. One had introduced himself as Matt Sabian, postmortem supervisor. The other was unmistakably Phylp. He/she overshadowed Sabian despite the latter's silver hair, garnet eyes, and polished skin. Phylp was the flashiest androgyne I'd ever seen—most of them

NEARLY DEPARTED

preferred no higher an appearance profile than anyone else, but Phylp handled major talent. It was probably advantageous to have such a memorable manager. If anyone could remember the talent after seeing the manager, the talent must be pretty major. Show biz.

"I understand this is your first dead client," Sabian was saying. The absurdity of the statement made me want to laugh, but they don't call me Deadpan Allie and lie.

"Up till now, I've worked only with living minds, yes." I sneaked a glance at Phylp, who was more arranged in a chair than seated in it.

"You shouldn't have any trouble," Sabian said. His voice had an odd hint of disappointment. "Your own mind will have to provide a good deal of visualization, except for her memories and the like, so I hope you're not given to bizarre symbolism. Other than that, everything in a living mind is present in a dead one. Except life, of course. We leave this world as we come into it— without thoughts, personality, memories, talent. When life fades, it leaves these things behind, just like any other material item we have. You'll have to actively stimulate the mind to obtain any of them. It can't offer you anything voluntarily. It takes life to do that." He pulled his left ankle up onto his right knee and played with the elastic cuff of his pants. "It'll be very much like hooking into a computer program of Kitta Wren's identity, actually."

I sat up a little straighter. "But it's not really that simple, is it?"

Sabian opened his mouth to answer but Phylp spoke up for the first time. "That's why I wanted a pathosfinder for her."

"Pardon?" I asked.

"Someone who would understand that it's not just a matter of searching out data." The throatiness I had momentarily taken for emotion was Phylp's normal speaking voice. "I want whatever it is that comes out to come out sounding alive. Because she was alive when she created it."

Sabian pointedly did not look at Phylp, who returned the favor. It clicked for me then. Sabian, postmortem supervisor. If Phylp hadn't insisted on hiring a pathosfinder, Sabian would have been doing this job. A nice sweet plum of a job, too, doing a postmortem on someone of Kitta Wren's stature. I did a sight reading of his Emotional Index, but I couldn't tell who he was angrier at, me or Phylp. I supposed I

8   Pat Cadigan

could understand how he felt, but it was still extra stress I
didn't need.

"How well did you know Kitta Wren?" I asked Phylp.

"Not at all. I managed her, but she was a stranger to me."

That was a lot of help. "What about family?"

"Only two brothers. One is at the South Pole. The other is
under the Indian Ocean in a religious trance."

"Do you know anything about her early life?"

Phylp almost looked sheepish. "Only that her parents gave
the children to the state and vanished." He/she spread his/her
hands gracefully. "That's all anyone knows. In the five years
I've handled her, she never showed the slightest inclination of
opening up to me or anyone else. It was a major disclosure if
she told me she liked her contracts."

"That sort of self-isolation isn't exactly normal behavior for a
poet, is it?"

"Nothing about her behavior was *normal*." Phylp frowned at
me. "She was crazy. All the time she was crazy, and when she
wasn't, she wanted to be. God knows what she got out of it. I
don't."

Her poetry, apparently. I turned my attention back to Sabian.
"What about the psychotic dead mind? Is the psychosis still
operable?"

"Very much, though in a strictly mechanical way. And it probably doesn't know it's dead.

I hesitated. "Which do you mean—the psychosis or the mind?"

"Both, I would think."

"How does a mind not know it's dead?"

Sabian's chin lifted defensively. "How does yours know it's
alive?" I didn't answer. "It's the same question, really." Not the
way I saw it, but I let him go on. "Minds contain information,
but it takes the presence of life for it to *know* anything. What
does a computer program *know?*" The polished skin stretched in
a tight, triumphant smile, as though he'd given me a glimpse of
Big Truth.

"And where is the brain?" I asked after a moment.

"Here." Sabian pointed his toe like a dancer and pressed a
panel in the floor. A section of the far wall slid back and there
it was. What had waited behind Kitta Wren's spiderwebs in life
now hung in a tall, clear canister of stay-juice, trailing wires
like the streamers on a Portuguese man-of-war. The wires went

NEARLY DEPARTED

down through the bottom of the canister of the maintenance box, which kept a minimum number of neurons firing. Two more wires leading from the visual center were coiled on top of the canister.

"We're still within the optimum time to go in. In another day, the neurons will begin to cease firing efficiently and after that deterioration will be rapid. I hope you'll be able to get everything on the first try."

I hoped so, too.

They left me alone so I could sct up my portable system. Assembling the three large components and five smaller ones was a kind of busy work. There are comparable systems that need no assembly, but there's a lot to be said for the ritual of preparation as relaxation therapy. I never needed it more than I did just then.

I worked in silence, rolling the system over to the brain and then fitting the pieces together until I had the familiar unbalanced-looking but actually quite stable quasi-cubist structure. Nothing showed in the way of circuits, wires, or guts of any kind. Good equipment, NN was fond of saying, doesn't have to show its guts.

Pulling out the drawer with the connections and thermal tank for my eyes, I paused. A living client I would have hooked into a relaxation exercise such as making colors, building landscapes, or running mazes, but what could I do with a dead one? It couldn't get much more relaxed. Or could it? I wouldn't have thought. On the other hand, I wanted it functioning a little more than minimally when I made contact.

In the end I decided on some abstract moving visuals since I would be connecting directly with the visual center anyway. I dragged over one of the chairs and made myself comfortable.

Despite the apprehension I'd felt about the job from the beginning, something like professional reflex took over. It didn't take any longer than usual to calm myself into a smooth, alert state of receptivity. I had positioned the thermal tank on the maintenance box next to the canister, where I could reach it easily. When I was absolutely sure of its location, I thumbed my eyes out and let them down into the solution. It never ceased to amaze me how well I could function blind, but most mindplayers had superior short-term eidetic memory.

I had only to hold the system connections under my eyelids; they crept in and found their way to my optic nerves by themselves. After a few moments, awareness of my body faded and I was through the system and in Kitta Wren's mind.

Every mind is different. Every mind is the same. Those are the first two laws of mindplay. Recognition in an unfamiliar land always came as a surprise to me no matter how often I met clients mind-to-mind. I was even more surprised to find that the initial impressions and sensations of contact with Kitta Wren's mind were not dissimilar to those I associated with living minds.

Normally I would have made my presence felt gradually so as not to startle my client by bursting in like an invader. But this client couldn't know that trauma and I was coming directly into the visual center instead of the less abrupt route through the optic nerve. After the usual slight disorientation of passing through the barriers of personality and identity, I found myself in the thick of random pictures and arbitrary memories. Around me, the mind seemed to tense as it felt the addition of something new and unpredictable. Then it ground on as before, accepting me as just another thought.

The abstract visuals programs was still running and I was awash in lazy spiral rainbows and harlequin rivers. I set it for gradual fade-out. The program's wane uncovered more of the brain's own pictures, some of them mundane objects remembered for no reason, some of them vignettes from Kitta Wren's life. I let them swirl around while I decided on the best way to go about the postmortem. Hitch a ride on a memory? Follow a random thought? Get hold of some false starts or blind alleys and reconstruct them?

I had caught a false start when the mind tried to think me. There was almost no warning. The false start was in my grasp and I was receiving multiple over-and undertones accompanied by the memory of its creation and the frustration Kitta Wren had felt before finally giving up on it. A walk in the rain in the middle of the night during late summer. Taste of rain dissolving on lips and tongue and the first line. *Do I drink the rain or does the rain drink me . . . drink? think?* I was searching it for possible salvage when the mind clamped down on me and Kitta Wren's old, unfinished poem together.

NEARLY DEPARTED

It thought the poem piece by piece, starting with the memory. It remembered the night and then the season (why not the season and then the night, I wondered), and then moisture, pausing to associate it with varieties of wetness. I was overwhelmed by the smell of the ocean, followed by a brief image of a coffin covered with barnacles lying on the sea bottom. The taste of rain returned more strongly, eradicating the picture of the coffin (*my brother, that's all*) but not quite managing to suppress a fleeting thought of snow. *Do I drink the rain . . . I drink the rain and the rain drinks me . . . Drinking the rain I am drunk and am drunk by drunken rain . . .* The mind niggled and gnawed out each variation from the original line (what was it about rain that fascinated poets, anyway?). When it was through, I was next.

I made a mask of my face and then took it off. The mind reached down for me in its purely mechanical probing and I threw my face into its processes. Traveling at the speed of thought, my face was everywhere as the mind tried to find the correct association for it. Curiously, I saw it materialize on the smooth, blank surface of a writing slate before I slipped through a half-remembered dream—images of cold stone carvings on a cathedral wall and a quick impression of *I should write about a mad cathedral*—and found myself down in Kitta Wren's back burner.

There isn't a mind in the world that doesn't have a back burner and it was usually a lot more difficult to get a client to open it up. Sometimes the incomplete puzzlements and notions stewing there were capable of growing into full-fledged ideas; other times they changed into false starts or shrank away into un-existence. Kitta Wren's back burner was so full of images that some of them were teetering half-dissolved on the edge of forgotten, as though she had deliberately pushed every idea that occurred to her to the back of her mind and then tried to forget all of them. Not the most productive way to work. I propelled myself through them to see what I might be able to salvage, which, I thought, would yield more results than looking at material she'd given up on. I was learning.

It was like holo-collage, the self-indulgent beginner's exercise for holographers who aspired to feature-length work, with her inner voice fading in and out where she had found words to go with the pictures. In quick turn I was looking up from the bottom of a deep, narrow hole at a circle of innocent blue sky, staring across the surface of a bed at eye level, watching two people, their faces in shadow, touch hands and listening to the indistinct murmur of their low, womanly voices (each was Wren). I was caught in a storm in the desert with rare rain beating straight down (there was that rain again, she seemed to return to it over and over), observing a street scene populated only by machines with my cheek pressed against the pavement, tasting an empty cup and pretending there was something in it. I went back and reviewed that last one to see where she'd gotten it.

Something from nothing, Kitta Wren's intelligent inner voice said. *Something from nothing*. I saw a chrysanthemum in the bottom of the cup; it metamorphosed from live to painted on. The center of the flower was an eye. *Something from nothing. I fill me with something from nothing.*

I had almost focused on what she had meant to taste in the cup when I began to get the feeling I wasn't alone. Which was absurd—even *she* wasn't there anymore. I turned my attention from the cup and waited. Possibly what I had felt was the mind reaching out for me again. Lowering my energy level as much as possible, I moved in among the jumble of unfinished ideas and waited. Rain punched dents in the sand. The sideways view of the street shimmered in the soggy desert sky like a mirage.

The mind spasmed. I had given it a new combination of thoughts to think by the way I had juxtaposed her old fragments. It fixed on me just as the madness hit.

That was what I had felt approaching, her psychosis, and it struck like a concentrated, highly localized storm. I thought my perception of it had been colored by my exposure to the desert scene, but it remained stormlike even after the mind separated me from its own familiar concepts, and I realized the nature of what Kitta Wren had done to herself.

Had she still been alive, I would have been witnessing a localized psychotic episode, a variety of seizure meant to produce not a convulsion but an altered state of consciousness. Except there was no consciousness. The seizure tore into her ideas and images and they flew up, dropped, rose again and fell flat with no one to pick them up and use them. The rest of the mind seemed to come to a standstill while the storm raged on. She'd been hoping for a literal brainstorm, a creative madness that would tear through her mind, stirring her thoughts into new and better patterns, giving her the stimulation she had refused to seek outside of herself. The mind seemed to shimmer and its perception of me grew vague. I

NEARLY DEPARTED 13

slipped away down to an area of learned reflexes and automatic behavior to wait things out. As soon as the seizure had passed, I would go back, collect her ideas, memorize them and get out. Phylp had been wrong. I would have to treat this strictly as a data retrieval operation, I couldn't deal with the mind as though it were living—

Reaching for a cigarette with only a dim awareness of the act I/she felt the first pain. I/she looked down at the slate on the desk and the stylus in my/her hand. It gleamed like a knife. (Memory run; it was a go; humans keep memories packrat style, who would have thought this one would be in Habits and Mannerisms?) But it couldn't cut away the blankness of the slate to reveal the words that should have been there. Stuck in my/her brain.

Then I was past the memory pocket and the mind had me again. Tropism. I should have known. Minds were meant to live and be conscious. Except there was no consciousness but mine. And if mine was there, then the mind must be alive.

Alive. It pulled at me and I passed through the psychosis like a kite in a high wind. The madness clutched at me, searching for a way in almost as if it were a separate, living intelligence as alien as I was. I tasted anger and spat it out; it came back to me distorted, a sea of strange faces registering disappointment, confusion, and hate. Kitta Wren's view of the world, vinegar laced with poison. The mind dragged me onward and I went, trailing the madness and the memory and the madness of the memory through the fireworks display of her emotional life.

Something from nothing. I looked to see who she was speaking to but there was no one. Just an affirmation. *Give me nothing, I take nothing. Offer me nothing; thank you. His eye may be on the sparrow but the Wren looks out for herself.* She had worked hard for her unhappiness and her mind showed her efforts to me as though they were trophies and prizes. A coffin under the Indian Ocean, something she'd never seen, an image invented and embellished for her own meditation. A silhouette in a blizzard at the bottom of the world. Empty pedestals labeled *Mother* and *Father* and an arena of thick, sweaty faces demanding a show, their greedy voices orchestrated by a golden-skinned androgyne. *Give them what they want. Something from nothing. Give me nothing. You take something.*

In her office, she faced the invisible, hungry multitude. Her mind tried to push me back into the memory but I clamped down and kept out of her perspective. The seizure had leaked into her visual center and the slate on the desk swelled to enormous size. She backed away from it, hallucinating patterns on the slate. Faces again. *Give them what they want.*

The pain doubled her over. She straightened up slowly, both hands on her belly. There was a dark stain on the stretchy material of the secondskins, just below navel level. *Something from nothing. Give them what they want.* Her fingers gripped the cloth. Psychotics frequently displayed extraordinary physical strength. And then there were those with a touch of telekinesis, unusable until a moment of crisis. It didn't matter if the crisis took the form of an hallucination brought on by an anxiety attack.

Her hands fell away. She didn't explode, or convulse, or even scream. She simply opened up and thirty years of misery poured out.

The memory went black, along with everything else. Then the mind stirred itself again and wrapped around me. Kitta Wren may have died, but her mind wanted life. Any life. Mine would do just fine.

Listen, she said. The memory was so worn only her words remained. *All they want is the show. Give them what they want, but never ask anything of them. Something from nothing. The Wren looks out for herself.*

I pulled back, preparing to withdraw. The mind flexed and the feel of it was almost plaintive now. Without warning I was face to face with the image of Kitta Wren as she had been, spiderwebs glistening. They still looked like shattered gems at first glance and they always would. I concentrated on that thought, sending it toward the image in steady waves. After some timeless interval, new lines appeared in the webs, running like fissures. The mind fought, trying to maintain solidity, but I was right. The cracks crept over her face slowly. I had to strain to keep them going, but they went, dividing her forehead into a myriad of little territories, fragmenting her cheeks, sundering her mouth. The image shuddered, almost held, and then just came apart, every piece sailing away from every other piece. When they were all gone, I withdrew without difficulty.

The first thing I saw after I put my eyes back in was the brain in the canister. The stay-juice looked milky now, a sign of imminent

NEARLY DEPARTED

decay. Without really thinking about it, I leaned forward and shut the maintenance box off.

Nelson Nelson held up an official-looking chip-card. "This is a lawsuit."

I nodded. He put the card down on his desk and picked up another one.

"And *this* is a lawsuit."

I had my own card and I held it up. "And *this* is a countersuit. In case anyone actually has the nerve to go to court."

NN looked tired. "Everything's already being settled out of court. The agency took your side, of course. No one can say I don't back my people, isn't it so?"

It was so. But I could tell by the way that puckered old mouth was twitching that he'd probably thought about filing against me himself for taking it upon myself to shut off the maintenance box. If the morgue laboratory had not come out and said that the composition of the stay-juice had indicated degeneration beyond the point where the mind could be re-entered, I would most likely have been signing my next thirty years of salary over to Nelson Nelson.

"Why'd you do it, Deadpan? What got into you?"

"She was dead. And nothing at all got into me."

"Sabian says the brain couldn't have deteriorated so quickly between the time you went in and the time you came out. Could it?"

I didn't attempt an answer right away. The brain had been a lot deader when I came out than it had been when I'd gone in. I kept thinking in the back of my mind that had something to do with it even though I couldn't have proved it one way or the other. Was there telekinesis after death as well as art? I didn't know and didn't want to know. "Maybe the solution was defective," I said after a bit. "Or hadn't been changed often enough." That was the argument in my countersuit anyway, that Sabian had allowed me to hook into an unstabilized brain which caused me to act in an irresponsible manner by shutting my client off instead of calling for him so he could do it. Sabian was just bitched because it meant he couldn't enter the mind after I was through to do his own little postmortem, figuring he could sell Phylp all the stuff I'd missed. He wasn't gassing me. Nobody filed a lawsuit over a protocol violation.

NN shrugged. "Phylp's charge is more serious."

"Seriouser and seriouser. It'll never hold up. He/she got all the postmortem fragments I could find. I had them all memorized. I did my job. It's not my fault he/she thinks none of them were worth the effort. And he/she can't sue me for the wrongful death of someone already dead."

"It's a little more complicated than that, Allie."

"But that's what it amounts to. He/she's charging that before I broke contact—"

"*Prematurely* broke contact."

"—I dissolved her Self and killed her a second time, compounding that by turning off the box."

"That's the way it looks in the transcript of your report."

"That's the way it was."

I thought Nelson Nelson was going to choke. I sat up, rubbing the small of my back with both hands.

"Just between you and me, NN, yes. That's exactly what I did."

He reached down and fiddled with something on the side of the desk facing him. Of course; he'd been recording. He was always recording. This one would have to be doctored.

"You know how a dead body will twitch when you send a current through it? A dead mind'll do the same. It takes more than current, but it's a good comparison. They had the neurons firing so well, it forgot it was supposed to be dead, and it tried to use me to come back."

"Could it have?"

"I don't know. It didn't work. I killed it."

"But what do you think?"

I sighed. "Possibly I might have ended up incorporating elements of her personality and some of her thoughts and memories. Then you'd have had to have me dry-cleaned to get rid of her."

NN raised his invisible eyebrows. "Now there's an interesting situation."

"Not for me. I wouldn't want any of that woman in me."

"I mean in terms of the legal definition of existence. If such a thing had happened and the agency did have you dry-cleaned, would we, in fact, have been killing her all over again?"

I glared at him. "*No*. She was already dead."

"But if she returned to life in you—well, never mind, Allie. It's just an intellectual exercise at this point." He waved the subject

NEARLY DEPARTED

away. "All this aside, tell me. Did you learn something?"

From a bitter woman who had literally torn herself apart? "I learned she shouldn't have been buying psychoses. She was already fogged in."

"No, now really, Allie. Wasn't there anything in there at all— some insight, or a vision beyond—ah, any final knowledge of any kind?"

I lit a cigarette by way of stalling. How old was Nelson Nelson anyway? And how old was he expecting to get? I wanted to tell him that if there was an answer—or an Answer—it wouldn't have been in a dead mind because you couldn't ask the right questions in there. If you don't know now, you can't know then. Instead, I lay down on the couch again and blew smoke at the ceiling. "Life's a bitch. Then you die."

I could almost hear NN's mouth drop. There was a long, thick moment of silence and then he began to laugh. "That's a good one, Deadpan," he said finally, wiping his eyes. "You almost had me there."

I'd almost been there myself, but I just grinned as though he had caught me out. For his own sake, I hoped he always thought it was funny. Just to be on the safe side, I put myself in for dry-cleaning as soon as the lawsuits were settled. Just to be sure.

A HAND IN
THE MIRROR

Sonia Orin Lyris

"A Hand in the Mirror" was purchased by Gardner Dozois, and appeared in the August 1993 issue of Asimov's, with a cover by Lee MacLeod and an illustration by Ron Chironna. New writer Sonia Orin Lyris is a 1992 graduate of Clarion West who has worked as a software engineer, technical writer (in which capacity she has written several articles on cyberspace), and a sculptor. "A Hand in the Mirror" was her first fiction sale, but she has subsequently made several more sales to Asimov's Science Fiction, as well as sales to Pulphouse and Midnight Zoo. She lives in Tigard, Oregon.

In the compelling story that follows, she explores the razor's edge between fantasy and reality, and between love and betrayal. . . .

The Stanford campus baked under the late summer sun. Lucius Reskin stepped into the cool air of the Computer Science department offices.

He stopped by Judy's desk and pulled out a half-dozen letters from his mail slot.

Computers were supposed to have done away with paper, he thought irritably. He dropped the junk mail into a trash can.

"Morning, Professor Reskin," Judy said amicably. She punched a ringing phone, scrawled something on a scrap of paper and downed half a mug of coffee, all in one motion.

"Your ten o'clock is in," she added.

He nodded and walked down the hall to his office. Maria Lomelli waited in the hall, carrying a large binder of notes.

On time. As usual.

The few truly brilliant students he'd had were never on time, and their notes, if they had any, were scrawled on envelopes, napkins, scraps of newspaper, or even their own hands.

"Good morning, Ms. Lomelli," he said. He unlocked his office door, held it open for her.

Tenure meant he could have his pick of the larger offices, but he preferred to keep this one, where he had been for six years. Even if it was a little crowded. The top of his desk was completely hidden beneath piles of papers, journals, and books. The coffee maker sat atop a stack of books in one corner, and his console sat in the other corner.

"Have a seat," he said to Maria, motioning to one of the two chairs in the room, both of which Lucius made a point of keeping clear.

Maria sat, her binder on her lap, her back straight, her eyes straight ahead. Lucius found his mug, punched the button that set the coffee to brewing, sat down behind his desk.

She was neatly dressed, her frizzy brown hair captured in a knot at her neck.

His desk only looked cluttered; he knew where everything was, but had long ago stopped trying to explain that to anyone else. He moved a few piles to retrieve Maria's thesis proposal.

"So much for the paperless office of the future, eh?" he said.

She smiled briefly, as though she were uncertain if it were a joke.

Lucius skimmed the first page of her proposal, then tossed it on a pile of papers near her side of the desk.

A HAND IN THE MIRROR
21

"I can't make heads or tails of this," he said. "Tell me what it says in English."

Her jaw dropped.

"But—" she exhaled. "Professor Reskin, last month you told me to write up my proposal."

"Yes. And today I'm telling you that this is just technical mumbo-jumbo. All you've done is cite some cyberspace research and a few ancient psychological explanations of human perception. I'm hoping that when you say it out loud, it will sound like something we can use."

She blinked, her mouth still open in surprise. She would doubtless need a few moments. Lucius got up, poured himself some coffee, and tossed in a couple of cream cubes.

Grad student theses usually bored him. Most were just rehashed academic trash. Few students gave a damn about their studies, and of those who did, fewer still were capable of original work. Most were just waiting to get letters after their names.

Maria, for all her faults, was not one of those. Her ideas were rough, but in them lay a kernel of originality.

It was her timing that was flawed. She was years too late.

He sat down again. "Ms. Lomelli?"

She closed her mouth. "All right," she said. "The system I'm proposing is a natural extension of existing cyberspace. We already know how to simulate the physical reality with visual, aural, and olfactory sensory stimulus. We already use standard human inputs: voice, gloves, eyetracking, physiological signs such as pulse, respiration—"

"Ms. Lomelli," Lucius interrupted, "I know the state of the art in cyberspace. I assume that's why I'm your advisor. What's original here?"

"Professor Reskin, this is background I'm building on—"

"Build more succinctly."

She inhaled, held it, exhaled.

"All right," she said. "I think too little research has been done on the *input* side, from the human to the computer. I think we can model not just what the human is *doing* but what the human is *thinking*—"

"Mind-reading computers?" Lucius smiled.

Confusion and annoyance flickered across her face. "If we combine current cyberspace technology, modeling approaches, and some psychological theories about perception, we might be able to design a system that provides collaborative model-building between human and computer, using the cyberspace as a virtual reality."

"We already do that," Lucius said. "Cyberspace *is* a virtual reality."

She shook her head. "But not like what I'm proposing. What we have now is a limited virtual reality, based on simple sensory exchange. It's really just an extension of passive entertainment—like TV and cspace dramas. Sure, there's the human-to-computer input side—voice, eye-movement, gloves—but the computer makes no attempt to model each person's conception of the virtual reality as it's created."

Lucius took a sip of coffee.

"You can't model someone's thought processes just by watching them. Even humans are abysmally bad at that, as you should know from your studies."

Maria nodded, encouraged. "Not by simply watching, no, but by asking the right questions—"

"Ah. I see," Lucius said. "Your system will ask people questions, and then tell them what they're thinking. Very original."

Maria took a deep breath. "There may be other physical ways to pick up input from a person. Perhaps eye-tracking as a map to some sorts of brain activity, or tone of voice. I don't know. But by combing *all* the physical inputs and examining them, while interactively pursuing a *mutual* understanding of basic conceptual classifications, the computer can perhaps begin to build a model of each person and their intent in the cspace."

"Sounds pretty speculative."

"It's *research*, Professor. Of *course* it's speculative."

"Yes, it's research. But there has to be something real to back it up. What would you do with such a system, if you had it? What's it good for?"

She started shuffling through her papers.

"Well, sir, that's not entirely clear yet. I have a paper by Dr. David Samuels at Berkeley. He's trying to use psychological modeling as an aid to treating mentally disturbed patients. Maybe—"

"I know Samuel's work. But I don't think your system's attempt to guess what someone is thinking by watching eye-movement is going to go over well with him. Even psychologists like a little more scientific method in their research."

A HAND IN THE MIRROR

Lucius paused. "I take it," he said, "your cognitive psychology is a little weak."

Her nostrils flared. "Not really," she said tightly. "I have a minor in cognitive psychology, along with my degree in computer science."

"A minor. I see. Very impressive."

Maria clenched her jaw.

Lucius sighed. "Ms. Lomelli," he said, "I know it may seem like I'm trying to sabotage your thesis, but that's not what I'm here for. I have a lot of experience in this area. You don't. That's why grad students have advisors."

She nodded a little.

"In any case, Ms. Lomelli, something like this was tried four years ago at Berkeley. It didn't work. I hope you already knew that."

"Yes," she said, suddenly animated again. "I've looked at Jaeger's research, and I think his approach was too limited; he didn't understand psychological modeling, and his system wasn't interactive enough. I really think I can—"

"I think you're trying too hard, Ms. Lomelli. Are you so desperate for a degree that you'd pursue a thesis built of this kind of flimsy research?" He shook his head. "I know there are professors who believe that the research effort is more important than the results, but I'm not one of them."

She stared at him.

"Ms. Lomelli, you seem to have a great deal of passion about your research. I admire that. Consider pursuing a thesis related to education in cyberspace instead. There is a tremendous amount of interest in this area. I even have some funding for research. I think with your background you would be entirely qualified to pursue this sort of thesis. I'd be happy to help you find a suitable topic if you have any trouble."

"You're saying you won't accept my thesis proposal."

"It isn't a question of my acceptance. There isn't a thesis here."

"But—"

"Ms. Lomelli, are you old enough to remember 'Artificial Intelligence'?"

"Of course."

"We still use the term, but it doesn't mean quite what it did in the eighties. Then it was the magic technology, and everyone was doing it. But in the end it was just computer science and solid engineering mixed together, and there wasn't any need to give it a fancy name just to get some work done."

Her hands lay limp, on top of the binder in her lap.

"But for a while there," Lucius continued, "a lot of people thought that if they could just mix enough computing power with the right kind of software, they'd get intelligent machines."

He smiled.

"And now, Ms. Lomelli, you're saying that if we can just mix enough computing power with *cyberspace*, we'll get a machine that reads minds."

Maria looked down at her hands. Lucius stood, picked her paper off the desk, and offered it to her. She took it, put it carefully on top of her binder, and stood.

For a moment her eyes flickered and she looked as though she might say something more. Lucius waited. She looked down again.

"Think about my offer, Maria. It's a good one."

After a few moments she left.

Evan Ikuta came into the office and grinned.

"Hi. How goes it," he said. He glanced around distractedly, walked to the door, and looked into the hallway.

"Where's the lady?" he asked. "I'm late; she's later."

Lucius rubbed his temples. The interview with Maria had not been reassuring. Time was slipping away from them. He started another pot of coffee.

"Evan. Brew?" he asked.

"Naw. Sara says it disrupts my aura, makes me hyper. I'm restricted." He grinned again.

Lucius couldn't always tell when Evan was serious, but it didn't matter, because Evan got the job done. His thesis work was impressive enough that Lucius had pulled strings to get Evan an assistant professorship the moment Evan graduated. He'd been grateful and then had joined Lucius' three-person team.

"Here she is," Evan said.

Professor Deborah Moreno was a small, slender woman, with short brown hair. She dressed simply and conservatively.

"Sorry I'm late," she said. "Joseph has the flu. I had to take him from daycare to sickcare."

Evan closed the door to the office. Lucius no longer needed to

A HAND IN THE MIRROR

say anything about privacy when they discussed ALICE. They all knew.

"Evan," Lucius said, "the optimizations you made last week work fine. Deborah, can we slow down the feedback response? The focus-loop is a real problem."

Deborah nodded. "I think all we have to do is to introduce more noise as the focus gets tighter if the resource level isn't changing."

Lucius nodded. "Work with Evan on that. See if you can get something ready—is tomorrow too soon, Evan?"

Evan shook his head with a grin. Evan loved pressure—thrived on it, like most really good programmers. Those who hadn't burned out, that was. The best always did, and the better they were, the fewer the years they had to do top-notch work. Lucius took the time to review all of Evan's code. Evan was still in his prime.

"What's the system doing with input, Deborah? Are we seeing patterns yet?"

She sighed. "Lucius, we *have* to have more than just the three of us as test cases. Yes, there are patterns, there are *always* patterns. But neither I nor ALICE can make generalizations until we have more test cases, more sensory output to examine. The meaning of the SQUID brainmagfield map is still largely experimental. We need more test subjects."

Lucius frowned, tapping his pen on a stack of papers. "I don't want it to get out yet. We're too close."

"Hey," Evan said. "We can get more test cases. Just grab some undergrads and hook them up for a few hours. Tell them it's another cspace. You think they'll understand what's going on from an hour in ALICE? Naw. Tell them it's an experiment in subjective visual hallucinations based on random input or something. Tell them they're making it all up."

Lucius frowned.

"Lucius," said Deborah, "we can't generalize without more data."

"First," Lucius said, "I want the three of us to link in to ALICE together. ALICE is supposed to be able to handle more than one person. It's time."

"Uhm," Evan said, looking down. "A lot of stuff that comes out there is—kind of . . . private. You know?"

"I know," Lucius said, "but you can learn to control that. It just takes practice."

26   *Sonia Orin Lyris*

"Yeah, right," Evan said, sounding unconvinced.

"Evan," Deborah said, "we're adults. We aren't going to hold your thoughts against you."

"We're breaking new ground here, Evan," Lucius said, in mock-sternness. "Do you want to be left out?"

"Naw," Evan grinned. "Not me."

"That's better," Lucius said. "The paper's almost done. We can publish in a month, if we push."

Deborah looked away. Lucius knew that look; something was wrong, but she wouldn't volunteer it. She was a brilliant sensory-data analyst, one of the best in the country, but she never argued. If he pushed her, she'd fall silent and stay silent, until he found gentler words. Lucius was used to verbal struggles as a natural part of academia. He couldn't understand how she had gotten through her academic career without a similar capability.

"Deborah?" he prompted gently.

"I can't keep leaving Joseph with my mother every weekend," she said. "I'd like to see him once in a while. I can't go on this way indefinitely."

"I know, Deborah. We're almost there. Stay with us. We need you."

Deborah pressed her lips together, then nodded.

They had reserved three separate cspace lab rooms. Deborah thought the privacy might make Evan more comfortable.

Lucius looked around for a moment, to remember the physical reality he knew best. Then he put the helmet on, adjusted the eye-phones and straps, slipped his hands into the gloves, and lay on the couch.

"Begin," he told ALICE.

Evan was already there, so the landscape was his. Trees, flowers, birds, all together in a lush garden. Now ALICE was responding to Lucius's presence, changing the world to the sparse landscape that Lucius favored. Trees and birds faded.

Lucius tried to stop the change. He wanted Evan comfortable, wanted Evan's landscape stronger than his own. He concentrated on the trees, birds, and flowers, and ALICE responded, trying to please them both, building a landscape that was somewhere in between.

They stood in a small clearing of grass and wildflowers, surrounded by trees. Lucius looked at the flowers, impressed by the

A HAND IN THE MIRROR

detail and variety. Was that from Evan, or was ALICE filling in more effectively?

Evan looked younger. Lucius gave him what he hoped was a reassuring smile. It made Lucius wonder what he looked like in this shared reality. He traced an oval in the air.

"Mirror," he said.

The air shimmered and a mirror appeared. It wasn't quite enough, though, and ALICE knew him well enough to figure out that the mirror was incomplete. He imagined ALICE checking her libraries for something to add. A carved mahogany frame appeared around the mirror.

Lucius looked younger in the mirror, the way he had in grad school. He didn't have a beard, which surprised him. Evan's opinion? He rubbed his chin thoughtfully and turned to Evan.

"Where's Deborah?"

Evan knelt down and began picking flowers.

"Maybe she's watching us?" he said.

"Deborah?" Lucius asked the air.

"I'm here," came her reply, sighing on the meadow breeze.

Deborah appeared beside them. Her hair was long and she was dressed in flowing blue. Lucius and Evan stared in surprise. She shrugged.

"I guess we all see ourselves a little differently than others do."

Silently Evan handed Deborah the flowers he had collected. She smiled, took the flowers, and touched them to her hair, where they clung and grew brighter.

The landscape had changed subtly since Deborah arrived. There was the sound of surf in the distance, sea-salt on the air. Sea gulls flew overhead. But the meadow remained intact.

"This isn't so bad," Evan said.

Lucius nodded. "ALICE merges our landscapes quite smoothly. And it seems that more viewpoints give the Scape more depth of detail."

Lucius inhaled, smelling trees, flowers, sea-air. He heard bees nearby, and the distant surf.

"We've done it," he whispered. Years of struggle and secrecy, coming to this moment.

Deborah's clothes began to fade away, leaving her half-dressed, wearing a lacy black corset, stockings, and red high heels.

She looked down at herself and frowned.

Lucius glanced at Evan, who looked stricken. He vanished.

The landscape changed, becoming a seashore. Deborah's clothes returned.

"Casualty of the medium," Lucius said to her.

She nodded, chuckled. "I just wasn't expecting it."

"We'd better go after him."

She turned to the ocean.

"I like it here, Lucius," she said, sounding relaxed. "It's somehow more—real—with you here."

Lucius wasn't sure he'd ever seen Deborah smile before. He began to understand Evan's fantasy.

Deborah's clothes started to cling, outlining her figure. Lucius shook his head and it stopped. That's what Evan should have done, but it took practice.

"See you in a few minutes," he said. "Stop," he said to the meadow, and he was back in the lab.

He blinked, removed the helmet, and got up from the couch slowly. The Scape could be tiring; the concentration it took to keep images stable was often accompanied by small physical movements. He stretched, left the lab, and found Evan's room.

Evan was sitting on the couch, staring at the floor.

"You're blowing this out of proportion," Lucius said. "It happens. It's not a crime."

Evan shrugged. "Yeah, sure," he said. "I have no control over what I think or feel."

"Oh, come off it, Evan. You just need more practice. You're young."

"I'm not *that* young," Evan snapped.

"Young enough to be thinking about sex with Deborah," Lucius said, smiling into Evan's pain.

Evan couldn't resist the joke. He grinned. "Yeah, yeah." Then he sighed. "Did I ruin our experiment?"

"No. But next time I think you should stay and see how she looks completely naked, after all your trouble."

Evan shook his head, but he was still grinning. "Yeah?"

"Sure. It's a fantasyland, Evan. The rules are different. You know that. Deborah knows it, too."

On cue, Deborah opened the door, and hesitantly walked in. She looked at Evan with concern.

"Black really isn't my color," she said, gently.

A HAND IN THE MIRROR

"Oh God, I'm sorry," he said.

Deborah shook her head. "Don't worry. Really. It's forgotten."

Evan looked away. "Thanks."

Lucius looked at them both for a moment and then stood.

"All right, let's get back to work."

Deborah was sitting in Lucius's other chair. She drooped a little, Lucius thought, like a flower gone too long without water.

They had all been working long hours, for months now. He on the paper, Deborah on the testing, and Evan doing most of the programming.

But now it was all coming together, and Lucius felt invigorated. Not at all tired.

"We have a waiting list of undergrads who want to be test subjects, Lucius," Deborah said.

"Good."

"A long list, Lucius. ALICE is getting very popular. And some of the students are sure we're hiding something. They know the Scape isn't an ordinary cspace. Most of them don't care, they just want their time in ALICE, to play. Now the faculty are asking me questions, too."

"Damn," Lucius said. "I didn't expect it to happen this fast. We'll push. We'll get the paper out by next week. How's the testing going?"

"That's the good news. It looks like there really are some generalizable types who conceptualize in specific ways. It's not as simple as visually-oriented versus verbally-oriented, but it's similar. ALICE can use this information to fine-tune her model of each individual once they're in the Scape."

Lucius picked up a pen, tapped it on a pile of papers.

"Why is ALICE so popular?"

"Computer games," Deborah said. "Most of these kids were raised on them, so they aren't lost in an artificial reality where they don't know the rules." She shrugged. "That's what a lot of games are all about, so most catch on quickly. Then there's the third that quit."

"Why do they quit?"

"I think it's hard work for some of them, creating reality every moment. And then there's the privacy issue; some are so uncomfortable having their thoughts take on form, that they don't stay long enough to learn control."

"I'd like to mention the failure rate in the paper. What's your take on the cause?"

Deborah hesitated. "It would only be a guess."

"Then guess."

"Well," she said, "the ones who do best are those who don't have a constrained view of reality. Those with a strictly ordered world-view get panicky in the Scape, because everything is constantly changing. We can usually identify them by their vital signs."

"Those are probably the ones who'll end up as instructors at Stanford," Lucius said dryly.

Deborah chuckled and shook her head. "They're young, Lucius. Give them time. We were young, once, too."

Lucius looked at her with a barely perceptible smile.

"Well," she said, still smiling, "not you, of course, Professor. You were never young."

He matched her grin and she chuckled again, picking up the papers she'd brought with her, and standing to go. Despite how tired she was, she looked good. Maybe it was the smile.

"Deborah," he said, "one more thing."

"Yes?"

Lucius considered what he had decided to say, rehearsed it once, and then again. It still didn't sound right. A minute passed and Deborah slowly sat down.

Maybe it was just the wrong time, the long hours affecting his judgment. Less palatable was his suspicion that it had been so long that he had lost whatever knack he once had. In any case, he didn't have the time now, not when there was so much else at stake.

"I was thinking," he found himself saying, "that we might have dinner together."

Her frown deepened.

Worse than the wrong time, he realized. He had misjudged their warming friendship, and now she was wondering how to reject his advance. A smooth relationship with Deborah was essential, perhaps now more than ever. What had he been thinking?

"It's all right," he said, giving her an easy smile. "I understand. And you don't need to explain."

"Thanks," she said, nodding. "Dinner. Yes. I'd like that. Tonight?"

A HAND IN THE MIRROR

Lucius had to replay her words to be sure he had heard her correctly. It surprised him a little to discover that it mattered, that it mattered more than a little.

Her eyes were hazel, he noticed for the first time, and there was a small smile on her lips that he was sure he'd never seen before.

Suddenly he was very curious about her.

Deborah walked into Lucius's office. He held up the *Mercury News* science section.

"I saw it this morning," she said, grinning.

Lucius stood up, still holding the newspaper, and walked around the desk to her. He gave her a short, passionate kiss and she stroked his beard.

"Not very technical, though," she said, with a nod at the article.

"We don't want it to be." He picked up the article and scanned it again.

The right kind of attention at the right time—that's what this was about. He'd told the reporter very little of substance about the Scape.

Then he'd posted a brief description of ALICE to world-net's cyberspace newsgroup, giving more tantalizing, vague hints about the Scape. In under a day, his posting had traveled to every net-connected lab in the world.

"I'm getting about fifty e-mail queries a day from the net."

Deborah's eyebrows drew together a bit. "Are you answering them?"

"Absolutely."

"But the paper in the *Cyberspace Journal*—"

Lucius held up a hand. "I'm not giving anything away. No hard facts. Appetizers. I tell them to wait for the paper to come out in the *Journal* next month."

"Then why post at all?"

Lucius poured himself a cup of black coffee and sat down.

"I want them hungry for details, Deborah. And then I want them starving, right about the time the paper is published. The smaller newspapers—the *Metro*, Stanford *Daily*—they'll be coming around soon, too. Probably next week. I'll make sure they have the names of undergrads who have been playing in the Scape. Castles and dragons make for excellent non-technical reading."

Lucius glanced at the red dot on his console; he had received new mail in the last few minutes. Probably more queries.

Deborah looked suspiciously at the half pot of coffee. "Is this fresh?"

"Compared to what?" Lucius replied distractedly.

Lucius hit a few keys to bring up his e-mail. He was getting e-mail queries from research labs everywhere, except Stanford. The Stanford faculty was politely curious, but reserved. The few who knew enough to guess at what ALICE really was had been hounding the department chair to support Lucius's research, to ride the tide of the breakthrough before it passed them by. And yesterday the department chair had phoned him.

"Johnson called me yesterday," Lucius said, scanning screen-fuls of new mail.

"Did he. Why?" Deborah sniffed at the coffee pot and turned away with a wince.

"He wants me to give a small presentation on ALICE to a few faculty members."

"Should I be there?" she asked, picking up the newspaper.

Lucius hit a few keys to send his pre-written reply to the new queries and shook his head. "I'll be fine."

"Lucius, Evan's name isn't in the article at all."

He took a sip of cold coffee. "No. I didn't see any point in mentioning him. Evan's not a particularly good speaker, so it doesn't do us any good to have him talking to the press. And this is a good time for him to take a break, with the brunt of the programming work done."

"Done? But the enhancements we've been planning—"

"There are always enhancements. It's time to concentrate on getting the word out. We've got to freeze the code as it stands."

"Evan knows about this?"

Lucius hit a few more keys on his console, disposing of the rest of his new e-mail, and turned to face Deborah.

"I've been busy. I'll talk to him tomorrow."

Deborah looked doubtful.

"We'll talk about expanding ALICE down the line," he said. "Then we'll need Evan. For now, though, the system is fairly solid, and I know the code almost as well as Evan did. Besides, he's due for a break, don't you think?"

She exhaled and nodded. "I think we're all due for a break. So, what's next?"

A HAND IN THE MIRROR   33

"Next we celebrate. How about dinner?"

"Sorry, Lucius. I promised Joseph I'd be home tonight to play with him."

"All right." Lucius nodded. "We'll take him out with us."

"Lucius . . ."

He stood and stepped close to her.

"And to the Zoo on Saturday," he said, touching two fingertips to her cheek and tracing them over her lips. "How does that sound?"

Deborah smiled.

"Ah. The Z-word," she said. "How can I resist?"

Lucius sat on a couch, looking at the cspace helmet in his hands. Ten years ago the Scape was only a grad student's dream, and now his paper was published in the prestigious *Cyberspace Journal*. The *Journal's* review committee hadn't even bothered to ask him for a rewrite.

It was time to celebrate. He lay down on the couch.

"Begin," he told ALICE.

And he was in the Scape. Green, grassy hills and soft blue sky stretched as far as he could see.

The students who played in the Scape made ALICE into a competitive adventure game. That was what they expected from ALICE, so that was what she gave them. But in time there would be others: engineers, artists, scientists—anyone who wanted to create and design would come to the Scape to do their significant work.

That day was very close now.

But to celebrate—what did he want? He thought of the things he had always wanted. Then he remembered the car, and smiled.

She drove up behind him and passed him with the sound of a deep purr. Then she stopped, revved slightly. Teasingly.

A black, '84 Lamborghini Countache. Not just a machine, but a thing of beauty. Her black shell reflected the Scape with dark clarity, capturing sparkles of sunlight and distant hills. She was waxed to a wet-looking sheen. He reached out and touched her, saw the reflection of his hand grow. His finger left a perfect fingerprint.

The illusion was marvelous. Did ALICE know what this car could do? He almost hoped not. As beautiful as it was, it didn't measure up to the high-performance sports cars of its time.

But here in the Scape it could do anything.

He got in. The seats were plush burgundy, the dashboard polished wood, the wheel leather-wrapped. The engine growled at him. She wanted to go.

He chuckled. Of course she did. He patted the dashboard.

"Let's go, babe," he heard himself say, enjoying the cliché of his own words. What was a fantasy for, after all?

He drove along a road, over hills, up and down the smooth, gentle rises.

The empty road opened up before him, stretching straight into infinity. A deep blue sky stretched above, peppered with soft, fluffy clouds. The car flew onto the road, hungry and growling.

While ALICE could not simulate the effect of movement on his inner ear, the visual and sound effects were convincing enough. This was his dream, come alive.

In the distance, a small figure appeared on the side of the road. As he neared, he saw she was hitchhiking. He pulled the car over to the side of the road and watched her walk to the passenger side in his rear-view mirror. Something about her was familiar. But that made sense; she was his Scape-creation.

She opened the car door and got in.

He frowned. He had barely thought of Maria since his last interview with her. Why would he be thinking of her now?

He chuckled. "What perverted fantasy of mine created you here, Maria?"

"I don't know, professor, what perverted fantasy of yours makes you a megalomaniac?"

Then it was clear; he had not created an image of Maria. It was her.

"Welcome to the Scape, Ms. Lomelli," he said.

"A moment ago it was 'Maria.' " She shook her head. "Can't you decide whether I'm a real person or not, Professor? Gosh, Professor, I'm always sorry to see a man who is so desperate to have his name on an invention that he'd crush anyone in his path."

"See it anyway you like, Maria," he said, pointedly using her first name. "But your thesis proposal *was* weak, and the work *had* been done. Was, in fact, *being* done. Hardly an original idea, and by now that would have been all too clear and you would have been that much further behind."

"You could have told me, you bastard."

A HAND IN THE MIRROR

"Could I? What for? I've been working on this for years, Maria."

"Of course. I'm just a grad student. I couldn't possibly have had anything to add."

"Probably not," he agreed.

Her eyes narrowed. "Then how did I come up with the same idea you did?"

"When the technology reaches a certain level of development, similar ideas rise to the surface."

"I hope you rot in the pits of hell," she said softly.

He held on to his patience. "New technology is competitive, Maria."

"What about the free exchange of knowledge that universities are so famous for?"

"Read my paper."

"Oh, *right*. Now that your goddamned name is on it."

"Yes, now that my goddamned name is on it."

She shot him a furious look.

He was getting tired of this, but he would try one last time.

"You had a good idea, but you didn't have it first, and you didn't have it best. That's the way it goes sometimes. You think I've taken something from you, but I haven't. You never had it. Maybe you should stop blaming me for your past and start thinking about your future."

She shook her head. "That doesn't justify the way you treated me."

"I don't have to justify anything. You're young and you think the world should be handed to you on a silver platter. Grow up."

She spat at him, but the Scape-spit vanished as soon as it landed.

"I think we're done," Lucius said.

The seat was empty.

She'd probably be back. But then, the Scape was the best place for her to vent her frustration at him; anything was possible and everything was safe. It was a poor way to build a future at the university, but he doubted she was thinking about that now.

He pulled back onto the road, pressed the accelerator to the floor and watched the speedometer climb to eighty, one-hundred, one-twenty, then one-forty. Trees went by in a blur.

He grinned as ALICE simulated his car ride in realtime as well as any cscape racing game around.

One-eighty, and the car just wanted to go faster.

Suddenly there was a dark, gray shape on the road before him, stretching from the road to the sky. It was only a Scape-image, but his gut-level fear of tornados had him already braking.

It had to be Maria's creation. He pulled his foot off the brake, floored the accelerator, and drove the car right into the center of the darkness.

The tornado screamed around him as it tried to tear the car apart. He concentrated fiercely, fighting to submerge his fear, to change his conception of the tornado.

It was a tiny dust-devil. A swirling fog. A soft breeze. He had never seen a real tornado, so it had to be a monster. Fantasy. Unreal.

He refused to think of the wind, and thought only of summer breezes, soft flowers, the sound of birds, and the purr of cats.

The transition was abrupt.

He was standing in a large meadow of high grasses, watching a small, lithe grey cat, who was watching a robin on a low branch of a nearby tree. The cat was transfixed, intent, its tail twitching. The robin was oblivious, or acting it; with wings it could afford to. It was timeless drama, repeated here in the Scape in all the simplicity and elegance of real life.

Lucius inhaled meadow scents, listened to the birds, and reinforced the image against Maria's next intrusion.

He could tell the Scape to remove her. But the only way to find out what the Scape could do was to let people use it and see what happened. If they wanted to indulge their fantasies, he would allow it, and if Maria wanted to exact revenge against him, he would allow that, too.

He heard the low, gutteral roar of a big cat. He turned. A large black jaguar stared back at him, its tail twitching furiously. It growled again.

Lucius liked cats, even big ones, but there was something about the voice of a big cat this close that was hard to take lightly.

Not real, he reminded himself.

The cat crouched to spring. He decided to give Maria the first move.

A HAND IN THE MIRROR

"Even the Scape has limitations, Maria," he said, quietly, knowing she would hear him anyway.

The cat sprang at him. He saw sky and the cat's black head at his neck.

There was no sensation, of course, because ALICE could not generate any, but the sound of the cat snapping his Scape-neck and crunching through the cartilage was realistic enough. He could smell the cat. Then he could smell his own blood.

He was probably Scape-dead, but since he didn't believe it, ALICE wouldn't either. He tilted his head up to see better.

He regretted it almost immediately. The cat had a paw on his shoulder and was gnawing on his forearm, tearing strings of flesh away from his bone. Blood soaked the cat's muzzle, the arm, and the tatters of his shirt.

The cat stopped and looked at him a moment, its green eyes bright. Then it tugged on his arm, trying to disconnect it from the rest of his body. There was a pop.

Lucius felt queasy. He was grateful that tactile simulation technology was still prohibitively rudimentary. But what ALICE might lack in ability to generate sensation, she made up for in vivid images, sound, and smell, all of which Lucius was finding surprisingly convincing.

He could stop and leave the Scape anytime. But that would give Maria her victory. No, he would take what she could give. This was his world. He had made it, and he would not run from it.

He could, however, run *with* it. Maria was watching now, of that he was sure. He would give her more.

Maria was wrong, he decided. A cat like this would not settle for an arm when a belly and delicate internal organs were available. He strengthened his conviction. The cat dropped the ruined arm, sniffed at his chest, and moved toward his stomach.

He wasn't sure he wanted to watch this time, so he thought with his eyes closed, listening to the sounds of the cat tearing into flesh. He visualized the liver and other internal organs that a cat might like, while trying to ignore the sounds of his success. He counted on ALICE's libraries to make the images as realistic as possible. He heard the cat rip organs loose, drop them on the ground, and start chewing on them.

"Oh my *God*," Maria cried. "No."

Stay, Lucius thought, encouraging the cat. *Stay and feast.*

He opened his eyes. Maria stood a few yards away, staring at his stomach, which was now in bloody pieces across the grass.

She met his gaze and her eyes widened. Then she turned away and he heard her retch.

She turned back and looked at him again, seeming as fascinated as she was horrified. Lucius nudged the cat again with his mind. The beast stopped chewing and walked over to her, rubbing his head affectionately against her side, leaving blood stains on her hands. She continued to watch him, frozen.

This was, Lucius reflected, as bizarre a confrontation as he had ever had.

"So," he said softly. "You've won, Maria. See? I'm dead. Are you happy now?"

It was ironic that her continued fascination helped keep his image vivid in the Scape. The big cat rubbed against her again. She jerked her hand away with a whimper.

"This isn't real." She looked at the cat.

He laughed. "No, it's not, Maria. Not real. Of course not."

She backed away from him, the cat, the clearing.

"You're doing something to me. What are you doing to me?"

"Sharing the Scape with you. Come on, Maria, you know how this works."

"I didn't do this. This isn't me. It isn't." She shook her head, denying everything.

He snorted. "Believe what you like, Maria. I can always ask ALICE to give me a record of exactly what data she got from you and what she got from me. Then we can see what is and isn't you."

She breathed a sob. Her face, usually careful and rigid, was now all raw, vulnerable fear. Maria vanished from the Scape.

Lucius popped up his umbrella as soon as he got off the rail. He splashed his way through the campus grounds toward his office.

Judy nodded at him and tipped her head toward his office, indicating that he had a visitor. Lucius walked down the hall to his office.

He looked at her for a moment, and she looked away. He unlocked the door and went in, leaving the door open. After a moment she followed.

Lucius peeled off his raincoat, set his umbrella to dripping in a corner, and punched the coffee machine to brew. He sat down.

A HAND IN THE MIRROR

"So, Ms. Lomelli," he said. "What can I do for you?"

Maria stared out the window behind him.

"I want to talk to you about what happened in the Scape last week," she said, still standing, still looking past him. "I want to apologize."

"You mean for attacking me?" Lucius asked.

"Yes."

"I see."

"I was—upset. I know I shouldn't have behaved the way I did." She looked at him briefly and then away. "I didn't mean it to happen the way it did."

"No? How did you mean it to happen, then?"

She opened her mouth, then shut it, and turned away.

"I was upset."

"The Scape does a pretty good job of manifesting intent, Ms. Lomelli. I have to conclude that you meant it to happen exactly the way it did, whether you regret it now or not."

"At the time," she said slowly, "well—yes. But I've had time to think. You were right. About a lot of things."

Lucius waited. "Is there anything else?"

"I—" she said. She sat down in the second chair. "It won't happen again."

Lucius nodded. "So?"

"So, I—want to work in cyberspace research. With you, Professor Reskin. I've read your paper on ALICE. I've been following all the net discussions. What you've done—it's amazing, in some ways so obvious—" she glanced at him quickly, "I mean obvious in the way that some things are once you see them. And you were right, there was more to it than I thought."

She looked at him finally, her expression hopeful. "I want you to continue to be my advisor, Professor. I'll take your advice." She nodded. "Completely. I'll do whatever thesis you think I should."

Lucius considered her. "I appreciate your interest in my work, Ms. Lomelli. And I appreciate your new willingness to take my advice.

"But there's a problem. The Scape is the first truly, objectively shared reality mankind has ever had. It's nearly mind-to-mind contact, which we've wanted for a long time. The way a person sees in the Scape is *active*, and how you think is more important than what you think. Knowing your thoughts well enough to use them instead of having them use you is essential."

She nodded. "I understand that."

"I don't think you have those qualities. I don't think you're well-suited for this kind of research."

She stared at him, her dark eyebrows drawing close together. "I don't understand."

It just wasn't enough that she was sincere and dedicated. Maybe if he had brought her in years ago—but probably not, even then. He hadn't had time then, and he didn't have it now. There were a lot of people who wanted in on the Scape. There wasn't enough room.

"What do you mean?" she asked again. "I made one mistake. Just one." There was an edge to her voice.

"I'm not here to pave the way for you," Lucius said, trying to soften the words. "You don't have a right to do anything you want, you only have the right to try."

Her left hand clutched the chair's arm. Her right hand made a claw and then a fist. She looked past him. "Give me a chance."

"I did," he said simply, regretting the inevitable path this conversation had taken.

"I can change," she said. "I can learn."

"I'm sure you can, and I'm sure you will. But not from me. I don't have the time."

Her right fist opened, tensed into a claw, relaxed, then tensed again. Her eyes were wide.

"Ms. Lomelli," he said.

She looked down at her hand, made a small sound, then put her head in her hands. She began to shake, silently crying. Lucius sighed, wishing he could be somewhere else.

"Maria," he said.

She looked up, her cheeks wet. "What do I do now?" she asked.

"Find another advisor."

"And another school?"

"That's up to you."

She stood.

"Maria," Lucius said. She stopped and turned half away, so he saw only her profile. "A piece of advice. If this defeats you, then maybe research isn't your area. No one held any doors open for

A HAND IN THE MIRROR   41

me, and they won't for you. That's how it is."

"No one helped you, so you don't help anyone else?" She gave a short, bitter laugh. "Is this a university or a jungle?"

"What's the difference?" He shook his head. "If you don't see that, then you aren't cut out for this type of work."

"Only the strong survive?"

"No. Many survive. Only the strong *succeed*."

Her right hand tensed into a fist again.

"Don't you ever have *doubts*, Professor?"

"Doubts? About what?"

She shook her head, opened the door and left.

The rain began again outside, coming down in heavy pats against the window. After a while Lucius got up and poured himself a cup of coffee.

He stopped on his way to his office at Judy's desk, to pick up his paper mail. At the bottom of the small pile of envelopes was a newspaper clipping. A yellow marker had been used to highlight his name and Maria Lomelli's.

Judy looked up from her typing.

"Oh, Professor Reskin, I'm sorry. I'll try to keep a better watch and see who's putting those in with your mail."

"That's okay, Judy. The small papers have as much right to twist facts and invent evidence as the professional rags do. Any other messages?"

"Professor Moreno was by. She said she'd be in the Scape for the performance this morning, that you could find her there."

"Thanks."

"Professor?" Judy looked up at him. "I just wanted to say, we're all very proud of your paper in the *Journal*. No matter what the press says."

"It's a measure of my success, Judy; the press wouldn't bother slamming me if my work wasn't important."

Judy smiled and nodded. "That's the spirit, Professor."

Lucius handed the clipping to Judy, who crumpled it into a ball and dropped it in a trash basket.

Down the hall, on his office door, was another copy of the same newspaper article, this one highlighted in red. He pulled it off, opened the door, and went in.

He checked his e-mail, and then found an empty cspace lab and linked in.

ALICE had created a sunny day for the performance. Across a large, grassy meadow were animals and people dressed in colorful outfits, waiting for the performance to begin.

The air smelled of wine, beer, and—various smokes. Lucius chuckled. Legal and illegal substances abounded, since they existed in the Scape in appearance and odor only. ALICE's original olfactory library did not include some of the scents he recognized now, which meant that Scape participants were mixing and matching, as expected, extending ALICE's library.

Two small children ran through the crowd, both giggling furiously and throwing popcorn at each other. They were probably constructs, since Deborah had decided that children should not yet be allowed into the Scape. Someone must have decided that the day needed children. Lucius agreed, and watched them a moment, lending his attention to them to reinforce their existence.

He looked for Deborah. There were tables with large umbrellas to keep out the Scape-sun. An aproned man stopped at a table where a girl in a blue dress and white pinafore sat, primly drinking from a large tea cup.

Of course. ALICE probably had a full complement of Lewis Carroll's characters in her libraries by now. Lucius looked around and saw animated cards and chess pieces scattered through the crowd, delivering drinks and food. These were doubtless constructs as well. Like the children, they were the supporting cast in a drama where every participant was a star.

At one table a Jabberwock curled around a chair and rested its head on the table top, conversing with a mouse in a small lounge chair. Elsewhere a gryphon and a large, grinning cat sat together eating chocolate sundaes.

He saw Deborah and threaded through the crowd to reach her.

"Hello," he said, sitting down.

"Lucius," she said with a smile.

She was lovely here, and his attention helped; her long Scape-hair shone and her eyes sparkled.

Loud voices distracted him. The mouse had left its chair and was prancing around on the table top, waving a tiny gun threateningly at a large cat who was smiling and hissing back. The man in the apron had stepped up and was waving his hands at both of them.

"Lucius," Deborah said, nodding her head, "over there: they're staring at you."

A HAND IN THE MIRROR 43

Creatures at other tables were looking at him, whispering to each other, and pointing.

"So they are."

Deborah was thoughtful. "Here in the Scape you and I have the freedom to be anyone we want, yet we choose to be ourselves. What do you think that says about us, Lucius?"

"You're the psychologist, Deborah. What does it say about them that they don't?"

Thunder slammed across the sky, stunning everyone into silence. Shots of lightning flashed through the air, leaving yellow and green afterimages. The rumbling sound gradually faded into the distance, followed by a mix of whispers and chimes.

The sky dimmed from daylight to soft dusk. Wisps of clouds, tinted pink and violet, framed the gathering stars. Against the dark sky grew block letters that glowed moon-white. They announced the name of the performance and the artist: "Intimate Responses, a Cyber-Scape performance, by Phyllis Leigh."

Then there was a loud popping sound, and each letter exploded into sparks of white light, falling onto the audience like the trails of fireworks.

There were startled yells. A furry creature stood, swearing and hitting himself to put out the sparks on his fur. A writhing spark fell on the table and erupted into a small white flame. Lucius held his hand out like a gun and squirted water on the flame with his finger until it went out.

"What happened?" Deborah asked.

Lucius looked around. The sparks went out, and as they did, creatures started pointing at Lucius and whispering again.

"The audience has taken over the show," he said.

It was a matter of attention; the audience had been distracted from the sky show by the falling sparks and ALICE had followed their interest. Now the sparks were turning into flames all across the meadow, reinforcing the audience's belief that the sparks would behave this way, the belief feeding back into the flames. When the flames were put out, much of the audience was staring at Lucius.

The sky was lightening. Stars dimmed and vanished. The performance was clearly over.

"Nice idea," Lucius said, standing. "We'll need to work out a few bugs so that Ms. Leigh can get past the credits next time."

Deborah stood. The furry creature stepped up to their table.

"You're Reskin," he said in an accusing, high-pitched tone. He shook a copy of the Stanford *Daily* at Lucius. "We know what you did to Maria Lomelli. You're scum."

"Thanks for sharing your opinion," Lucius said. "Now go away."

A crowd was gathering.

"You should read this, Professor. It says she's going to bring charges against you."

"I doubt it. There aren't grounds for any charges," Lucius said.

A tall, silver-haired woman called out: "Was the Scape really Lomelli's idea first, Professor?"

"This is not a press conference," Lucius shot back.

"Then why did she leave the university, Professor?"

Lucius turned to Deborah. "Amazing, isn't it," he said, in a tone his lecture students would recognize. "They believe everything the media tells them. Their critical faculties have already been crushed into pulp by the same fine journalism that sells breath mints."

"Cute, Professor," the furry creature said, "but that's not an answer."

Lucius looked the crowd over. "When you can ask questions without disguises, I might take you more seriously."

Someone growled, and the crowd muttered.

The furry scowled. "Coward."

Lucius laughed. "I'm not the one hiding behind a mask."

"Yeah? Well, you're the one who—"

A wind suddenly picked up, noisily drowning out the creature's voice, along with all the sounds of the crowd.

"What a shame," Lucius said to Deborah, his voice somehow cutting through the wind. "Our best and brightest." He shook his head.

The furry's mouth moved silently. Frustrated, the furry made a gesture at Lucius with his furry middle finger. Lucius resisted the temptation to return the gesture, which would have terminated the furry's link to the Scape.

Even so, the furry's middle finger was mysteriously growing into a large, furry ball which Lucius was sure must be very heavy. The creature dropped to the ground under the weight, cursing and struggling. Members of the crowd looked on, asking concerned questions and generally reinforcing the creature's unfortunate situation.

A HAND IN THE MIRROR 45

Lucius could continue to use tricks like these, but there was really no point to continuing the struggle.

"Let's go," he said to Deborah. He envisioned the seashore where they had first talked together in the Scape. The crowd around them wavered and then vanished.

The sound of gulls was in his ears and the world was ocean-scented.

"Quite a show," Deborah said.

Lucius was already working on solutions. "ALICE could route half of each participant's resources to the show itself. That would prevent the audience from taking over."

"That's not what I meant."

"Ah." He looked at her. "Some bad press is inevitable."

Deborah looked at the ocean. "How similar was Lomelli's thesis to—" she motioned to take the world, "this?"

"She had ideas similar to those I had years ago."

"And you told her it wouldn't work?"

"I said her research was weak; it was. I said her ideas were unoriginal; they were."

"You discouraged her."

"Yes." He watched Deborah brush her long hair back. "Should I have encouraged her to waste her time? If I'd told her about our work, I'd have risked everything we've done."

Deborah reached down and picked up a sand dollar. She examined it and threw it into the ocean.

"Well?" Lucius asked, beginning to feel frustrated at Deborah's silence. "Should we take her in now, with the best minds in the world begging to get in on the project? Is that what you want?"

Still she did not answer.

"She attacked me in the Scape, Deborah. The newspaper article conveniently fails to mention that. She's emotionally unstable. Would you want to work with someone like that?"

"Lucius," Deborah said, "we're here to teach. Not just to find our own advantage."

"Yes, to teach," Lucius said, "but not to coddle. We teach by doing, not by talking about it. Don't worry about the article, Deborah. We'll get some dirty looks, and a few weeks later the student body will turn its short attention span to some other good cause."

Deborah sat down on the sand and Lucius sat next to her. He started to speak again, then stopped himself. He passed his hand over the ground and a small green plant poked up through the sand. It stretched up and up, spreading itself into leaves and swelling its end into a bud. The bud burst into a large, fragrant red rose.

"It's over, Lucius," Deborah said.

Sunlight dimmed as a cloud passed across the sky.

"Over?"

"I care for you, Lucius, I really do, but—I thought you might care about something besides your own success."

"*My* success? ALICE is *our* success: yours, mine, Evan's."

She pressed her lips together. "Evan, who you wouldn't mention to the press because he might say something inconvenient?"

"You're upset about *that?* He wouldn't have wanted the press hounding him, Deborah. Believe me."

She shook her head. "That's not the point. The point is that Evan was part of the team, but now there's no place for him."

"We're in code freeze, Deborah. It's a temporary situation."

"The people you don't need—just like Maria Lomelli. There wasn't room for her, either."

"It's not at all the same thing, Deborah. Not at all."

Deborah plucked the rose and then pulled the petals off, one by one, discarding them on the sand. A breeze danced by, picked up the petals, and took them away.

"Maybe what you did was reasonable," she said. "It's just not reasonable for me."

"Deborah, you're overreacting. Remember that the newspaper article is slanted against me because that's what *sells*."

"The press came to me, too, Lucius."

"Oh?"

"They wanted to know if I thought it was possible that you deliberately scared Maria Lomelli in the Scape in order to keep her quiet."

Lucius snorted. "That's absurd. If she was scared, she scared herself."

Even in this dimming light, he could see Deborah's hazel eyes clearly. He looked into them. "What did you tell them?"

She looked down. "I told them I couldn't be sure."

The sky was filling with dark clouds.

"I wouldn't do that. She came to me. But—this isn't the place to have this discussion. Let's unlink and talk about it outside."

She stood up. "No. I've said what I have to say."

A HAND IN THE MIRROR

He stepped close to her. "The Scape is reflecting and reinforcing your mood—you know how this works. Don't make any decisions. Not here. Not like this."

It was getting so dark that he could barely see her.

She sighed. "I'm sorry, Lucius. You're just not the kind of man I want to love."

"We've hardly started, Deborah. Give us a chance."

"I'm sorry, Lucius."

"A chance."

"Lucius—"

"Please, just think about it. Will you do that?"

"All right," she said. "But don't expect me to change my mind. Don't hope, Lucius."

And then she was gone.

"Deborah?"

He sat down again.

He could unlink and talk to her outside the Scape, where objects and landscape didn't change with every thought. But he knew how it would go: he would talk and she would listen silently. And then it would be worse because it was the real world, where there was no further appeal to objectivity.

He would do nothing. She would think about it, and then she would come back.

He listened to the hush of the waves, and looked at the dim sparkles of the ocean against a black sky. Now that Deborah was gone, the Scape would change back: the sky would lighten, the sea would turn blue, and gulls would cry overhead.

Lucius stared into the blackness and waited for dawn.

COMPUTER FRIENDLY

Eileen Gunn

*"Computer Friendly" was purchased by Gardner
Dozois, and appeared in the June 1989 issue of
Asimov's, with an illustration by John Barrick.
It was one of a series of eccentric, daring, and wildly
imaginative stories that Gunn has sold to the magazine since her first sale to us in 1988, the cult classic
"Stable Strategies for Middle Management." She is
not a prolific writer, but, like her friend Howard
Waldrop, her stories are well worth waiting for—
she has a twisted perspective on life unlike anyone
else's, and a strange and pungent sense of humor all
her own. She has been a Nebula and Hugo finalist
several times, has also sold stories to markets such as
Amazing, Proteus, Tales by Moonlight, and Alternate
Presidents, and is currently at work on her first novel.
She lives in Seattle, Washington, where she is involved
in the administration of the Clarion West work-
shop.*

*Here she takes us on a tour of the Wonderful
World of the Future, which in her hands becomes a
sort of perverted high-tech Ozzie-and-Harriet Leave-*

*It-to-Beaver suburbia, both funny and chilling at the
same time—and all too likely, I fear.*

Holding her dad's hand, Elizabeth went up the limestone steps to
the testing center. As she climbed, she craned her neck to read the
words carved in pink granite over the top of the door: Francis W.
Parker School. Above them was a banner made of grey cement
that read "Health, Happiness, Success."

"This building is old," said Elizabeth. "It was built before
the war."

"Pay attention to where you're going, punkin," said her dad.
"You almost ran into that lady there."

Inside, the entrance hall was dark and cool. A dim yellow glow
came through the shades on the tall windows.

As Elizabeth walked across the polished floor, her footsteps
echoed lightly down the corridors that led off to either side. She
and her father went down the hallway to the testing room. An old,
beat-up, army-green query box sat on a table outside the door.

"Ratherford, Elizabeth Ratherford," said her father to the box.
"Age seven, computer-friendly, smart as a whip."

"We'll see," said the box with a chuckle. It had a gruff, teasing, grandfatherly voice. "We'll just see about *that*, young lady."
What a jolly interface, thought Elizabeth. She watched as the
classroom door swung open. "You go right along in there, and
we'll see just how smart you are." It chuckled again, then it spoke
to Elizabeth's dad. "You come back for her at three, sir. She'll be
all ready and waiting for you, bright as a little watermelon."

This was going to be fun, thought Elizabeth. Nothing to do all
day except show how smart she was.

Her father knelt in front of her and smoothed her hair back
from her face. "You try real hard on these tests, punkin. You
show them just how talented and clever you really are, okay?"
Elizabeth nodded. "And you be on your best behavior." He gave
her a hug and a pat on the rear.

Inside the testing room were dozens of other seven-year-olds,
sitting in rows of tiny chairs with access boxes in front of them.
Glancing around the room, Elizabeth realized that she had never

COMPUTER FRIENDLY 51

seen so many children together all at once. There were only ten in her weekly socialization class. It was sort of overwhelming.

The monitors called everyone to attention and told them to put on their headsets and ask their boxes for Section One.

Elizabeth followed directions, and she found that all the interfaces were strange—they were friendly enough, but none of them were the programs she worked with at home. The first part of the test was the multiple-choice exam. The problems, at least, were familiar to Elizabeth—she'd practiced for this test all her life, it seemed. There were word games, number games, and games in which she had to rotate little boxes in her head. She knew enough to skip the hardest until she'd worked her way through the whole test. There were only a couple of problems left to do when the system told her to stop and the box went all grey.

The monitors led the whole room full of kids in jumping-jack exercises for five minutes. Then everyone sat down again and a new test came up in the box. This one seemed very easy, but it wasn't one she'd ever done before. It consisted of a series of very detailed pictures; she was supposed to make up a story about each picture. Well, she could do that. The first picture showed a child and a lot of different kinds of animals. "Once upon a time there was a little girl who lived all alone in the forest with her friends the skunk, the wolf, the bear, and the lion. . . ." A beep sounded every so often to tell her to end one story and begin another. Elizabeth really enjoyed telling the stories, and was sorry when that part of the test was over.

But the next exercise was almost as interesting. She was to read a series of short stories and answer questions about them. Not the usual questions about what happened in the story—these were harder. "Is it fair to punish a starving cat for stealing?" "Should people do good deeds for strangers?" "Why is it important for everyone to learn to obey?"

When this part was over, the monitors took the class down the hall to the big cafeteria, where there were lots of other seven-year-olds, who had been taking tests in other rooms.

Elizabeth was amazed at the number and variety of children in the cafeteria. She watched them as she stood in line for her milk and sandwich. Hundreds of kids, all exactly as old as she was. Tall and skinny, little and fat; curly hair, straight hair, and hair that was frizzy or held up with ribbons or cut into strange patterns against the scalp; skin that was light brown like Elizabeth's, chocolate brown, almost black, pale pink, freckled, and all the colors in between. Some of the kids were all dressed up in fancy clothes; others were wearing patched pants and old shirts.

When she got her snack, Elizabeth's first thought was to find someone who looked like herself, and sit next to her. But then a freckled boy with dark, nappy hair smiled at her in a very friendly way. He looked at her feet and nodded. "Nice shoes," he said. She sat down on the empty seat next to him, suddenly aware of her red maryjanes with the embroidered flowers. She was pleased that they had been noticed, and a little embarrassed.

"Let me see *your* shoes," she said, unwrapping her sandwich.

He stuck his feet out. He was wearing pink plastic sneakers with hologram pictures of a missile gantry on the toes. When he moved his feet, they launched a defensive counterattack.

"Oh, neat." Elizabeth nodded appreciatively and took a bite of the sandwich. It was filled with something yellow that tasted okay.

A little tiny girl with long, straight, black hair was sitting on the other side of the table from them. She put one foot up on the table. "I got shoes, too," she said. "Look." Her shoes were black patent, with straps. Elizabeth and the freckled boy both admired them politely. Elizabeth thought that the little girl was very daring to put her shoe right up on the table. It was certainly an interesting way to enter a conversation.

"My name is Sheena and I can spit," said the little girl. "Watch." Sure enough, she could spit really well. The spit hit the beige wall several meters away, just under the mirror, and slid slowly down.

"I can spit, too," said the freckled boy. He demonstrated, hitting the wall a little lower than Sheena had.

"I can *learn* to spit," said Elizabeth.

"All right there, no spitting!" said a monitor firmly. "Now, you take a napkin and clean that up." It pointed to Elizabeth.

"She didn't do it, I did," said Sheena. "I'll clean it up."

"I'll help," said Elizabeth. She didn't want to claim credit for Sheena's spitting ability, but she liked being mistaken for a really good spitter.

The monitor watched as they wiped the wall, then took their thumbprints. "You three settle down now. I don't want any more spitting." It moved away. All three of them were quiet for a few minutes, and munched on their sandwiches.

"What's your name?" said Sheena suddenly. "My name is Sheena."

COMPUTER FRIENDLY   53

"Elizabeth."

"Lizardbreath. That's a funny name," said Sheena.

"My name is Oginga," said the freckled boy.

"That's *really* a funny name," said Sheena.

"You think everybody's name is funny," said Oginga. "Sheena-Teena-Peena."

"I can tap dance, too," said Sheena, who had recognized that it was time to change the subject. "These are my tap shoes." She squirmed around to wave her feet in the air briefly, then swung them back under the table.

She moves more than anyone I've ever seen, thought Elizabeth.

"Wanna see me shuffle off to Buffalo?" asked Sheena.

A bell rang at the front of the room, and the three of them looked up. A monitor was speaking.

"Quiet! Everybody quiet, now! Finish up your lunch quickly, those of you who are still eating, and put your wrappers in the wastebaskets against the wall. Then line up on the west side of the room. The west side. . . ."

The children were taken to the restroom after lunch. It was grander than any bathroom Elizabeth had ever seen, with walls made of polished red granite, lots of little stalls with toilets in them, and a whole row of sinks. The sinks were lower than the sink at home, and so were the toilets. Even the mirrors were just the right height for kids.

It was funny because there were no stoppers in the sinks, so you couldn't wash your hands in a proper sink of water. Sheena said she could make the sink fill up, and Oginga dared her to do it, so she took off her sweater and put it in the sink, and sure enough, it filled up with water and started to overflow, and then she couldn't get the sweater out of it, so she called a monitor over. "This sink is overflowing," she said, as if it were all the sink's fault. A group of children stood around and watched while the monitor fished the sweater from the drain and wrung it out.

"That's mine!" said Sheena, as if she had dropped it by mistake. She grabbed it away from the monitor, shook it, and nodded knowingly to Elizabeth. "It dries real fast." The monitor wanted thumbprints from Sheena and Elizabeth and everyone who watched.

The monitors then took the children to the auditorium, and led the whole group in singing songs and playing games, which

Elizabeth found only moderately interesting. She would have preferred to learn to spit. At one o'clock, a monitor announced it was time to go back to the classrooms, and all the children should line up by the door.

Elizabeth and Sheena and Oginga pushed into the same line together. There were so many kids that there was a long wait while they all lined up and the monitors moved up and down the lines to make them straight.

"Are you going to go to the Asia Center?" asked Sheena. "My mom says I'll probably go to the Asia Center tomorrow, because I'm so fidgety."

Elizabeth didn't know what the Asia Center was, but she didn't want to look stupid. "I don't know. I'll have to ask my dad." She turned to Oginga, who was behind her. "Are you going to the Asia Center?"

"What's the Asia Center?" asked Oginga.

Elizabeth looked back at Sheena, waiting to hear her answer.

"Where we go to sleep," Sheena said. "My mom says it doesn't hurt."

"I got my own room," said Oginga.

"It's not like your room," Sheena explained. "You go there, and you go to sleep, and your parents get to try again."

"What do they try?" asked Elizabeth. "Why do you have to go to sleep?"

"You go to sleep so they have some peace and quiet," said Sheena. "So you're not in their way."

"But what do they try?" repeated Elizabeth.

"I bet they try more of that stuff that they do when they think you're asleep," said Oginga. Sheena snorted and started to giggle, and then Oginga started to giggle and he snorted too, and the more one giggled and snorted, the more the other did. Pretty soon Elizabeth was giggling too, and the three of them were helplessly choking, behind great hiccoughing gulps of noise.

The monitor rolled by then and told them to be quiet and move on to their assigned classrooms. That broke the spell of their giggling, and, subdued, they moved ahead in the line. All the children filed quietly out of the auditorium and walked slowly down the halls. When Elizabeth came to her classroom, she shrugged her shoulders at Oginga and Sheena and jerked her head to one side. "I go in here," she whispered.

"See ya at the Asia Center," said Sheena.

COMPUTER FRIENDLY

The rest of the tests went by quickly, though Elizabeth didn't think they were as much fun as in the morning. The afternoon tests were more physical; she pulled at joysticks and tried to push buttons quickly on command. They tested her hearing and even made her sing to the computer. Elizabeth didn't like to do things fast, and she didn't like to sing.

When it was over, the monitors told the children they could go now, their parents were waiting for them at the front of the school. Elizabeth looked for Oginga and Sheena as she left, but children from the other classrooms were not in the halls. Her dad was waiting for her out front, as he had said he would be.

Elizabeth called to him to get his attention. He had just come off work, and she knew he would be sort of confused. They wiped their secrets out of his brain before he logged off of the system, and sometimes they took a little other stuff with it by mistake, so he might not be too sure about his name, or where he lived.

On the way home, she told him about her new friends. "They don't sound as though they would do very well at their lessons, princess," said her father. "But it does sound as if you had an interesting time at lunch." Elizabeth pulled his hand to guide him onto the right street. He'd be okay in an hour or so—anything important usually came back pretty fast.

When they got home, her dad went into the kitchen to start dinner, and Elizabeth played with her dog, Brownie. Brownie didn't live with them anymore because his brain was being used to help control data traffic in the network. Between rush hours, Elizabeth would call him up on the system and run simulations in which she plotted the trajectory of a ball and he plotted an interception of it.

They ate dinner when her mom logged off work. Elizabeth's parents believed it was very important for the family to all eat together in the evening, and her mom had custom-made connectors that stretched all the way into the dining room. Even though she didn't really eat anymore, her local I/O was always extended to the table at dinnertime.

After dinner, Elizabeth got ready for bed. She could hear her father in his office, asking his mail for the results of her test that day. When he came into her room to tuck her in, she could tell he had good news for her.

"Did you wash behind your ears, punkin?" he asked. Elizabeth figured that this was a ritual question, since she was unaware that washing behind her ears was more useful than washing anywhere else.

She gave the correct response: "Yes, Daddy." She understood that, whether she washed or not, giving the expected answer was an important part of the ritual. Now it was her turn to ask a question. "Did you get the results of my tests, Daddy?"

"We sure did, princess," her father replied. "You did very well on them."

Elizabeth was pleased, but not too surprised. "What about my new friends, Daddy? How did they do?"

"I don't know about that, punkin. They don't send us everybody's scores, just yours."

"I want to be with them when I go to the Asia Center."

Elizabeth could tell by the look on her father's face that she'd said something wrong. "The what? Where did you hear about that?" he asked sharply.

"My friend Sheena told me about it. She said she was going to the Asia Center tomorrow," said Elizabeth.

"Well, *she* might be going there, but that's not anyplace you're going." Her dad sounded very strict. "*You're* going to continue your studies, young lady, and someday you'll be an important executive like your mother. That's clear from your test results. I don't want to hear any talk about you doing anything else. Or about this Sheena."

"What does Mommy do, Daddy?"

"She's a processing center, sweetheart, that talks directly to the CPU. She uses her brain to control important information and tell the rest of the computer what to do. And she gives the whole system common sense." He sat down on the edge of the bed, and Elizabeth could tell that she was going to get what her dad called an "explanatory chat."

"You did so well on your test today that maybe it's time we told you something about what you might be doing when you get a little older." He pulled the blanket up a little bit closer to her chin and turned the sheet down evenly over it.

"It'll be a lot like studying, or like taking that test today," he continued. "Except you'll be hardwired into the network, just like your mom, so you won't have to get up and move around. You'll be able to do anything and go anywhere in your head."

"Will I be able to play with Brownie?"

COMPUTER FRIENDLY

"Of course, sweetheart, you'll be able to call him up just like you did tonight. It's important that you play. It keeps you healthy and alert, and it's good for Brownie, too."

"Will I be able to call you and Mommy?"

"Well, princess, that depends on what kind of job you're doing. You just might be so busy and important that you don't have time to call us."

Like Bobby, she thought. Her parents didn't talk much about her brother Bobby. He had done well on his tests, too. Now he was a milintel cyborg with go-nogo authority. He never called home, and her parents didn't call him, either.

"Being an executive is sort of like playing games all the time," her father added, when Elizabeth didn't say anything. "And the harder you work right now, the better you do on your tests, the more fun you'll have later."

He tucked the covers up around her neck again. "Now you go to sleep, so you can work your best tomorrow, okay, princess?" Elizabeth nodded. Her dad kissed her good night, and poked at the covers again. He got up. "Good night, sweetheart," he said, and he left the room.

Elizabeth lay in bed for a while, trying to get to sleep. The door was open so that the light would come in from the hall, and she could hear her parents talking downstairs.

Her dad, she knew, would be reading the news at his access box, as he did every evening. Her mom would be tidying up noise-damaged data in the household module. She didn't have to do that, but she said it calmed her nerves.

Listening to the rise and fall of their voices, she heard her name. What were they saying? Was it about the test? She got up out of bed, crept to the door of her room. They stopped talking. Could they hear her? She was very quiet. Standing in the doorway, she was only a few feet from the railing at the top of the staircase, and the sounds came up very clearly from the living room below.

"Just the house settling," said her father, after a moment. "She's asleep by now." Ice cubes clinked in a glass.

"Well," said her mother, resuming the conversation, "I don't know what they think they're doing, putting euthanasable children in the testing center with children like Elizabeth." There was a bit of a whine behind her mother's voice. RF interference, perhaps. "Just talking with that Sheena could skew her test results for years. I have half a mind to call the net executive and ask it what it thinks it's doing."

"Now, calm down, honey," said her dad. Elizabeth heard his chair squeak as he turned away from his access box toward the console that housed her mother. "You don't want the exec to think we're questioning its judgment. Maybe this was part of the test."

"Well, you'd think they'd let us know, so we could prepare her for it."

Was Sheena part of the test, wondered Elizabeth. She'd have to ask the system what "euthanasable" meant.

"Look at her scores," said her father. "She did much better than the first two on verbal skills—her programs are on the right track there. And her physical aptitude scores are even lower than Bobby's."

"That's a blessing," said her mother. "It held Christopher back, right from the beginning, being so active." Who's Christopher? wondered Elizabeth.

Her mother continued. "But it was a mistake, putting him in with the euthana—"

"Her socialization scores were okay, but right on the edge," added her dad, talking right over her mother. "Maybe they should reduce her class time to twice a month. Look at how she sat right down with those children at lunch."

"Anyway, she passed," said her mother. "They're moving her up a level instead of taking her now."

"Maybe because she didn't initiate the contact, but she *was* able to handle it when it occurred. Maybe that's what they want for the execs."

Elizabeth shifted her weight, and the floor squeaked again.

Her father called up to her, "Elizabeth, are you up?"

"Just getting a drink of water, Daddy." She walked to the bathroom and drew a glass of water from the tap. She drank a little and poured the rest down the drain.

Then she went back to her room and climbed into bed. Her parents were talking more quietly now, and she could hear only little bits of what they were saying.

" . . . mistake about Christopher. . . ." Her mother's voice.

" . . . putting that other little girl to sleep forever. . . ." Her dad.

" . . . worth it? . . ." Her mother again.

Their voices slowed down and fell away, and Elizabeth dreamed of eerie white things in glass jars, of Brownie, still a dog, all furry

COMPUTER FRIENDLY

and fetching a ball, and of Sheena, wearing a sparkly costume and tapdancing very fast. She fanned her hands out to her sides and turned around in a circle, tapping faster and faster.

Then Sheena began to run down like a wind-up toy. She went limp and dropped to the floor. Brownie sniffed at her, and the white things in the jars watched. Elizabeth was afraid, but she didn't know why. She grabbed Sheena's shoulders and tried to rouse her.

"Don't let me fall asleep," Sheena murmured, but she dozed off even as Elizabeth shook her.

"Wake up! Wake up!" Elizabeth's own words pulled her out of her dream. She sat up in bed. The house was quiet, except for the sound of her father snoring in the other room.

Sheena needed her help, thought Elizabeth, but she wasn't really sure why. Very quietly, she slipped out of bed. On the other side of her room, her terminal was waiting for her, humming faintly.

When she put the headset on, she saw her familiar animal friends: a gorilla, a bird, and a pig. Each was a node that enabled her to communicate with other parts of the system. Elizabeth had given them names.

Facing Sam, the crow, she called her dog. Sam transmitted the signal, and was replaced by Brownie, who was barking. That meant his brain was routing information, and she couldn't get through.

What am I doing, anyway, Elizabeth asked herself. As she thought, a window irised open in the center of her vision, and there appeared the face of a boy of about eleven or twelve. "Hey, Elizabeth, what are you doing up at this hour?" It was the sysop on duty in her sector.

"My dog was crying."

The sysop laughed. "Your dog was crying? That's the first time I've ever heard anybody say something like that." He shook his head at her.

"He was so crying. Even if he wasn't crying out loud, I heard him, and I came over to see what was the matter. Now he's busy and I can't get through."

The sysop stopped laughing. "Sorry. I didn't mean to make fun of you. I had a dog once, before I came here, and they took him for the system, too."

"Do you call him up?"

60   *Eileen Gunn*

"Well, not anymore. I don't have time. I used to, though. He was a golden Lab. . . ." Then the boy shook his head sternly and said, "But you should be in bed."

"Can't I stay until Brownie is free again? Just a few more minutes?"

"Well, maybe a couple minutes more. But then you gotta go to bed for sure. I'll be back to check. Good night, Elizabeth."

"Good night," she said, but the window had already closed.

Wow, thought Elizabeth. That worked. She had never told a really complicated lie before and was surprised that it had gone over so well. It seemed to be mostly a matter of convincing yourself that what you said was true.

But right now, she had an important problem to solve, and she wasn't even exactly sure what it was. If she could get into the files for Sheena and Oginga, maybe she could find out what was going on. Then maybe she could change the results on their tests or move them to her socialization group or something. . . .

If she could just get through to Brownie, she knew he could help her. After a few minutes, the flood of data washed away, and the dog stopped barking. "Here, Brownie!" she called. He wagged his tail and looked happy to see her.

She told Brownie her problem, and he seemed to understand her. "Can you get it, Brownie?"

He gave a little bark, like he did when she plotted curves.

"Okay, go get it."

Brownie ran away real fast, braked to a halt, and seemed to be digging. This wasn't what he was really doing, of course, it was just the way Elizabeth's interface interpreted Brownie's brain waves. In just a few seconds, Brownie came trotting back with the records from yesterday's tests in his mouth.

But when Elizabeth examined them, her heart sank. There were four Sheenas and fifteen Ogingas. But then she looked more carefully, and noticed that most of the identifying information didn't fit her Sheena and Oginga. There was only one of each that was the right height, with the right color hair.

When she read the information, she felt bad again. Oginga had done all right on the test, but they wanted to use him for routine processing right away, kind of like Brownie. Sheena, as Elizabeth's mother had suggested, had failed the personality profile and was scheduled for the euthanasia center the next

COMPUTER FRIENDLY

afternoon at two o'clock. There was that word again: euthanasia. Elizabeth didn't like the sound of it.

"Here, Brownie." Her dog looked up at her with a glint in his eye. "Now listen to me. We're going to play with this stuff just a little, and then I want you to take it and put it back where you got it. Okay, Brownie?"

The window irised open again and the sysop reappeared. "Elizabeth, what do you think you're doing?" he said. "You're not supposed to have access to this data."

Elizabeth thought for a minute. Then she figured she was caught red-handed, so she might as well ask for his advice. So she explained her problem, all about her new friends and how Oginga was going to be put in the system like Brownie, and Sheena was going to be taken away somewhere.

"They said she would go to the euthanasia center, and I'm not real sure what that is," said Elizabeth. "But I don't think it's good."

"Let me look it up," said the sysop. He paused for a second, then he looked worried. "They want my ID before they'll tell me what it means. I don't want to get in trouble. Forget it."

"Well, what can I do to help my friends?" she asked.

"Gee," said the sysop. "It's a tough one. The way you were doing it, they'd catch you for sure, just like I did. It looks like a little kid got at it."

I am a little kid, thought Elizabeth, but she didn't say anything.

I need help, she thought. But who could she go to? She turned to the sysop. "I want to talk to my brother Bobby, in milintel. Can you put me through to him?"

"I don't know," said the sysop, "but I'll ask the mailer demon." He irised shut for a second, then opened again. "The mailer demon says it's no skin off his nose, but he doesn't think you ought to."

"How come?" asked Elizabeth.

"He says it's not your brother anymore. He says you'll be sorry."

"I want to talk to him anyway," said Elizabeth.

The sysop nodded, and his window winked shut just as another irised open. An older boy who looked kind of like Elizabeth herself stared out. His tongue darted rapidly out between his lips, keeping them slightly wet. His pale eyes, unblinking, stared into hers.

"Begin," said the boy. "You have sixty seconds."

"Bobby?" said Elizabeth.

"True. Begin," said the boy.

"Bobby, um, I'm your sister Elizabeth."

The boy just looked at her, the tip of his tongue moving rapidly. She wanted to hide from him, but she couldn't pull her eyes from his. She didn't want to tell him her story, but she could feel words filling her throat. She moved new words forward, before the others could burst out.

"Log off!" she yelled. "Log off!"

She was in her bedroom, drenched in sweat, the sound of her own voice ringing in her ears. Had she actually yelled? The house was quiet, her father still snoring. She probably hadn't made any noise.

She was very scared, but she knew she had to go back in there. She hoped that her brother was gone. She waited a couple of minutes, then logged on.

Whew. Just her animals. She called the sysop, who irised on, looking nervous.

"If you want to do that again, Elizabeth, don't go through me, huh?" He shuddered.

"I'm sorry," she said. "But I can't do this by myself. Do you know anybody that can help?"

"Maybe we ought to ask Norton," said the sysop after a minute.

"Who's Norton?"

"He's this old utility I found that nobody uses much anymore," said the sysop. "He's kind of grotty, but he helps me out." He took a breath. "Hey, Norton!" he yelled, real loud. Of course, it wasn't really yelling, but that's what it seemed like to Elizabeth.

Instantly, another window irised open, and a skinny middle-aged man leaned out of the window so far that Elizabeth thought he was going to fall out, and yelled back, just as loud, "Don't bust your bellows. I can hear you."

He was wearing a striped vest over a dirty undershirt and had a squashed old porkpie hat on his head. This wasn't anyone that Elizabeth had ever seen in the system before.

The man looked at Elizabeth and jerked his head in her direction. "Who's the dwarf?"

The sysop introduced Elizabeth and explained her problem to Norton. Norton didn't look impressed. "What d'ya want me to do about it, kid?"

COMPUTER FRIENDLY 63

"Come on, Norton," said the sysop. "You can figure it out. Give us a hand."

"Jeez, kid, it's practically four o'clock in the morning. I gotta get my beauty rest, y'know. Plus, now you've got milintel involved, it's a real mess. They'll be back, sure as houses."

The sysop just looked at him. Elizabeth looked at Norton, too. She tried to look patient and helpless, because that always helped with her dad, but she really didn't know if that would work on this weird old program.

"Y'know, there ain't much that you or me can do in the system that they won't find out about, kids," said Norton.

"Isn't there somebody who can help?" asked Elizabeth.

"Well, there's the Chickenheart. There's not much that it can't do, when it wants to. We could go see the Chickenheart."

"Who's the Chickenheart?" asked Elizabeth.

"The Chickenheart's where the system began." Of course Elizabeth knew that story—about the networks of nerve fibers organically woven into great convoluted mats, a mammoth supercortex that had stored the original programs, before processing was distributed to satellite brains. Her own system told her the tale sometimes before her nap.

"You mean the original core is still there?" said the sysop, surprised. "You never told me that, Norton."

"Lot of things I ain't told you, kid." Norton scratched his chest under his shirt. "Listen. If we go see the Chickenheart, and *if* it wants to help, it can figure out what to do for your friends. But you gotta know that this is a big fucking deal. The Chickenheart's a busy guy, and this ain't one-hunnert-percent safe."

"Are you sure you want to do it, Elizabeth?" asked the sysop. "I wouldn't."

"How come it's not safe?" asked Elizabeth. "Is he mean?"

"Nah," said Norton. "A little strange, maybe, not mean. But di'n't I tell you the Chickenheart's been around for a while? You know what that means? It means you got yer intermittents, you got yer problems with feedback, runaway processes, what have you. It means the Chickenheart's got a lot of frayed connections, if you get what I mean. Sometimes the old C.H. just goes chaotic on you." Norton smiled, showing yellow teeth. "Plus you got the chance there's someone listening in. The netexec, for instance. Now there's someone I wouldn't want to catch me up to no mischief. Nossir. Not if I was you."

"Why not?" asked Elizabeth.

"Because that's sure curtains for you, kid. The netexec don't ask no questions, he don't check to see if you maybe could be repaired. You go bye-bye and you don't come back."

Like Sheena, thought Elizabeth. "Does he listen in often?" she asked.

"Never has," said Norton. "Not yet. Don't even know the Chickenheart's there, far as I can tell. Always a first time, though."

"I want to talk to the Chickenheart," said Elizabeth, although she wasn't sure she wanted anything of the kind, after her last experience.

"You got it," said Norton. "This'll just take a second."

Suddenly all the friendly animals disappeared, and Elizabeth felt herself falling very hard and fast along a slippery blue line in the dark. The line glowed neon blue at first, then changed to fuchsia, then sulfur yellow. She knew that Norton was falling with her, but she couldn't see him. Against the dark background, his shadow moved with hers, black, and opalescent as an oilslick.

They arrived somewhere moist and warm. The Chickenheart pulsated next to them, nutrients swishing through its external tubing. It was huge, and wetly organic. Elizabeth felt slightly sick.

"Oh, turn it off, for Chrissake," said Norton, with exasperation. "It's just me and a kid."

The monstrous creature vanished, and a cartoon rabbit with impossibly tall ears and big dewy brown eyes appeared in its place. It looked at Norton, raised an eyebrow, cocked an ear in his direction, and took a huge, noisy bite out of the carrot it was holding.

"Gimme a break," said Norton.

The bunny was replaced by a tall, overweight man in his sixties wearing a rumpled white linen suit. He held a small, paddle-shaped fan, which he slowly moved back and forth. "Ah, Mr. Norton," he said. "Hot enough for you, sir?"

"We got us a problem here, Chick," said Norton. He looked over at Elizabeth and nodded. "You tell him about it, kid."

First she told him about her brother. "Non-trivial, young lady," said the Chickenheart. "Non-trivial, but easy enough to fix. Let me take care of it right now." He went rigid and quiet for a few seconds, as though frozen in time. Then he was back. "Now, then, young lady," he said. "We'll talk if you like."

COMPUTER FRIENDLY 65

So Elizabeth told the Chickenheart about Sheena and Oginga, about the testing center and the wet sweater and the monitor telling her to clean up the spit. Even though she didn't have to say a word, she told him everything, and she was sure that if he wanted to come up with a solution, he could do it.

The Chickenheart seemed surprised to hear about the euthanasia center, and especially surprised that Sheena was going to be sent there. He addressed Norton. "I know I've been out of touch, but I find this hard to believe. Mr. Norton, have you any conception of how difficult it can be to obtain components like this? Let me investigate the situation." His face went quiet for a second, then came back. "By gad, sir, it's true," he said to Norton. "They say they're optimizing for predictability. It's a mistake, sir, let me tell you. Things are too predictable here already. Same old ideas churning around and around. A few more components like that Sheena, things might get interesting again.

"I want to look at their records." He paused for a moment, then continued talking.

"Ah, yes, yes, I want that Sheena right away, sir," he said to Norton. "An amazing character. Oginga, too—not as gonzo as the girl, but he has a brand of aggressive curiosity we can put to use, sir. And there are forty-six others with similar personality profiles scheduled for euthanasia today at two." His face went quiet again.

"What is he doing?" Elizabeth asked Norton.

"Old Chickenheart's got his hooks into everythin'," Norton replied. "He just reaches along those pathways, faster'n you can think, and does what he wants. The altered data will look like it's been there all along, and ain't nobody can prove anythin' different."

"Done and done, Mr. Norton." The Chickenheart was back.

"Thank you, Mr. Chickenheart," said Elizabeth, remembering her manners. "What's going to happen to Sheena and Oginga now?"

"Well, young lady, we're going to bring your friends right into the system, sort of like the sysop, but without, shall we say, official recognition. We'll have Mr. Norton here keep an eye on them. They'll be our little surprises, eh? Timebombs that we've planted. They can explore the system, learn what's what, what they can get away with and what they can't. Rather like I do."

"What will they do?" asked Elizabeth.

"That's a good question, my dear," said the Chickenheart. "They'll have to figure it out for themselves. Maybe they'll put together a few new solutions to some old problems, or create a few new problems to keep us on our toes. One way or the other, I'm sure they'll liven up the old homestead."

"But what about me?" asked Elizabeth.

"Well, Miss Elizabeth, what about you? Doesn't look to me as though you have any cause to worry. You passed your tests yesterday with flying colors. You can just go right on being a little girl, and some day you'll have a nice, safe job as an executive. Maybe you'll even become netexec, who knows? I wiped just a tiny bit of your brother's brain and removed all records of your call. I'll wipe your memory of this, and you'll do just fine, yes indeed."

"But my friends are in here," said Elizabeth, and she started to feel sorry for herself. "My dog, too."

"Well, then, what do you want me to do?"

"Can't you fix my tests?"

The Chickenheart looked at Elizabeth with surprise.

"What's this, my dear? Do you think you're a timebomb, too?"

"I can *learn* to be a timebomb," said Elizabeth with conviction. And she knew she could, whatever a timebomb was.

"I don't know," said the Chickenheart, "that anyone can learn that sort of thing. You've either got it or you don't, Miss Elizabeth."

"Call me Lizardbreath. That's my *real* name. And I can get what I want. I got away from my brother, didn't I? And I got here."

The Chickenheart raised his thin, black eyebrows. "You have a point there, my dear. Perhaps you could be a timebomb, after all."

"But not today," said Lizardbreath. "Today I'm gonna learn to spit."

CHIP RUNNER

Robert Silverberg

"Chip Runner" was purchased by Gardner Dozois, and appeared in the November 1989 issue of Asimov's *with an illustration by Anthony Bari. It was one of a long series of distinguished pieces by Silverberg, including three Hugo Award winners, that have appeared in the magazine since its inception, under four different editors.*

In the story that follows, he takes us on an unusual and suspenseful journey into the realms of the ultra-small—and even deeper into the heart of obsession.

Robert Silverberg is one of the most famous SF writers of modern times, with dozens of novels, anthologies, and collections to his credit. Silverberg has won five Nebula Awards and four Hugo Awards. His novels include Dying Inside, Lord Valentine's Castle, The Book of Skulls, Downward to the Earth, Tower of Glass, The World Inside, Born With the Dead, Shadrack in the Furnace, Tom O' Bedlam, Star of Gypsies, *and* At Winter's End. *His collections include* Unfamiliar Territory, Capricorn Games, Majipoor Chronicles, The Best of Robert Silverberg,

At the Conglomeroid Cocktail Party, *and* Beyond the Safe Zone. *His most recent books are* Nightfall *and* Child of Time, *two novel-length expansions of famous Isaac Asimov stories, the novel* The Face of the Waters, *and a massive retrospective collection* The Collected Stories of Robert Silverberg, Volume One: Secret Sharers. *For many years he edited the prestigious anthology series* New Dimensions, *and has recently, along with his wife, writer Karen Haber, taken over the editing of the* Universe *anthology series. He lives in Oakland, California.*

He was fifteen, and looked about ninety, and a frail ninety at that. I knew his mother and his father, separately—they were Silicon Valley people, divorced, very important in their respective companies—and separately they had asked me to try to work with him. His skin was blue-gray and tight, drawn cruelly close over the jutting bones of his face. His eyes were gray too, and huge, and they lay deep within their sockets. His arms were like sticks. His thin lips were set in an angry grimace.

The chart before me on my desk told me that he was five feet eight inches tall and weighed seventy-one pounds. He was in his third year at one of the best private schools in the Palo Alto district. His I.Q. was 161. He crackled with intelligence and intensity. That was a novelty for me right at the outset. Most of my patients are depressed, withdrawn, uncertain of themselves, elusive, shy: virtual zombies. He wasn't anything like that. There would be other surprises ahead.

"So you're planning to go into the hardware end of the computer industry, your parents tell me," I began. The usual let's-build-a-relationship procedure.

He blew it away instantly with a single sour glare. "Is that your standard opening? 'Tell me all about your favorite hobby, my boy'? If you don't mind I'd rather skip all the bullshit, doctor, and then we can both get out of here faster. You're supposed to ask me about my eating habits."

CHIP RUNNER

It amazed me to see him taking control of the session this way within the first thirty seconds. I marveled at how different he was from most of the others, the poor sad wispy creatures who forced me to fish for every word.

"Actually I do enjoy talking about the latest developments in the world of computers, too," I said, still working hard at being genial.

"But my guess is you don't talk about them very often, or you wouldn't call it 'the hardware end.' Or 'the computer industry.' We don't use mundo phrases like those any more." His high thin voice sizzled with barely suppressed rage. "Come on, doctor. Let's get right down to it. You think I'm anorexic, don't you?"

"Well—"

"I know about anorexia. It's a mental disease of girls, a vanity thing. They starve themselves because they want to look beautiful and they can't bring themselves to realize that they're not too fat. Vanity isn't the issue for me. And I'm not a girl, doctor. Even you ought to be able to see that right away."

"Timothy—"

"I want to let you know right out front that I don't have an eating disorder and I don't belong in a shrink's office. I know exactly what I'm doing all the time. The only reason I came today is to get my mother off my back, because she's taken it into her head that I'm trying to starve myself to death. She said I had to come here and see you. So I'm here. All right?"

"All right," I said, and stood up. I am a tall man, deep-chested, very broad through the shoulders. I can loom when necessary. A flicker of fear crossed Timothy's face, which was the effect I wanted to produce. When it's appropriate for the therapist to assert authority, simpleminded methods are often the most effective. "Let's talk about eating, Timothy. What did you have for lunch today?"

He shrugged. "A piece of bread. Some lettuce."

"That's all?"

"A glass of water."

"And for breakfast?"

"I don't eat breakfast."

"But you'll have a substantial dinner, won't you?"

"Maybe some fish. Maybe not. I think food is pretty gross."

I nodded. "Could you operate your computer with the power turned off, Timothy?"

70 *Robert Silverberg*

"Isn't that a pretty condescending sort of question, doctor?"

"I suppose it is. Okay, I'll be more direct. Do you think you can run your body without giving it any fuel?"

"My body runs just fine," he said, with a defiant edge.

"Does it? What sports do you play?"

"Sports?" It might have been a Martian word.

"You know, the normal weight for someone of your age and height ought to be—"

"There's nothing normal about me, doctor. Why should my weight be any more normal than the rest of me?"

"It was until last year, apparently. Then you stopped eating. Your family is worried about you, you know."

"I'll be okay," he said sullenly.

"You want to stay healthy, don't you?"

He stared at me for a long chilly moment. There was something close to hatred in his eyes, or so I imagined.

"What I want is to disappear," he said.

That night I dreamed I was disappearing. I stood naked and alone on a slab of gray metal in the middle of a vast empty plain under a sinister coppery sky and I began steadily to shrink. There is often some carryover from the office to a therapist's own unconscious life: we call it counter-transference. I grew smaller and smaller. Pores appeared on the surface of the metal slab and widened into jagged craters, and then into great crevices and gullies. A cloud of luminous dust shimmered about my head. Grains of sand, specks, mere motes, now took on the aspect of immense boulders. Down I drifted, gliding into the darkness of a fathomless chasm. Creatures I had not noticed before hovered about me, astonishing monsters, hairy, many-legged. They made menacing gestures, but I slipped away, downward, downward, and they were gone. The air was alive now with vibrating particles, inanimate, furious, that danced in frantic zigzag patterns, veering wildly past me, now and again crashing into me, knocking my breath from me, sending me ricocheting for what seemed like miles. I was floating, spinning, tumbling with no control. Pulsating waves of blinding light pounded me. I was falling into the infinitely small, and there was no halting my descent. I would shrink and shrink and shrink until I slipped through the realm of matter entirely and was lost. A mob of contemptuous glowing things—electrons and protons, maybe, but how could I tell?—crowded close around me, emitting

CHIP RUNNER 71

fizzy sparks that seemed to me like jeers and laughter. They told me to keep moving along, to get myself out of their kingdom, or I would meet a terrible death. "To see a world in a grain of sand," Blake wrote. Yes. And Eliot wrote, "I will show you fear in a handful of dust." I went on downward, and downward still. And then I awoke gasping, drenched in sweat, terrified, alone.

Normally the patient is uncommunicative. You interview parents, siblings, teachers, friends, anyone who might provide a clue or an opening wedge. Anorexia is a life-threatening matter. The patients—girls, almost always, or young women in their twenties—have lost all sense of normal body-image and feel none of the food-deprivation prompts that a normal body gives its owner. Food is the enemy. Food must be resisted. They eat only when forced to, and then as little as possible. They are unaware that they are frighteningly gaunt. Strip them and put them in front of a mirror and they will pinch their sagging empty skin to show you imaginary fatty bulges. Sometimes the process of self-skeletonization is impossible to halt, even by therapy. When it reaches a certain point the degree of organic damage becomes irreversible and the death-spiral begins.

"He was always tremendously bright," Timothy's mother said. She was fifty, a striking woman, trim, elegant, almost radiant, vice president for finance at one of the biggest Valley companies. I knew her in that familiarly involuted California way: her present husband used to be married to my first wife. "A genius, his teachers all said. But strange, you know? Moody. Dreamy. I used to think he was on drugs, though of course none of the kids do that any more." Timothy was her only child by her first marriage. "It scares me to death to watch him wasting away like that. When I see him I want to take him and shake him and force ice cream down his throat, pasta, milkshakes, anything. And then I want to hold him, and I want to cry."

"You'd think he'd be starting to shave by now," his father said. Technical man, working on nanoengineering projects at the Stanford AI lab. We often played racquetball together. "I was. You too, probably. I got a look at him in the shower, three or four months ago. Hasn't even reached puberty yet. Fifteen and not a hair on him. It's the starvation, isn't it? It's retarding his physical development, right?"

"I keep trying to get him to like eat something, anything," his stepbrother Mick said. "He lives with us, you know, on the weekends, and most of the time he's downstairs playing with his computers, but sometimes I can get him to go out with us, and we buy like a chili dog for him, you know, a burrito, and he goes, Thank you, thank you, and pretends to eat it, but then he throws it away when he thinks we're not looking. He is *so* weird, you know? And scary. You look at him with those ribs and all and he's like something out of a horror movie."

"What I want is to disappear," Timothy said.

He came every Tuesday and Thursday for one-hour sessions. There was at the beginning an undertone of hostility and suspicion to everything he said. I asked him, in my layman way, a few things about the latest developments in computers, and he answered me in monosyllables at first, not at all bothering to hide his disdain for my ignorance and my innocence. But now and again some question of mine would catch his interest and he would forget to be irritated, and reply at length, going on and on into realms I could not even pretend to understand. Trying to find things of that sort to ask him seemed my best avenue of approach. But of course I knew I was unlikely to achieve anything of therapeutic value if we simply talked about computers for the whole hour.

He was very guarded, as was only to be expected, when I would bring the conversation around to the topic of eating. He made it clear that his eating habits were his own business and he would rather not discuss them with me, or anyone. Yet there was an aggressive glow on his face whenever we spoke of the way he ate that called Kafka's hunger artist to my mind: he seemed proud of his achievements in starvation, even eager to be admired for his skill at shunning food.

Too much directness in the early stages of therapy is generally counterproductive where anorexia is the problem. The patient *loves* her syndrome and resists any therapeutic approach that might deprive her of it. Timothy and I talked mainly of his studies, his classmates, his stepbrothers. Progress was slow, circuitous, agonizing. What was most agonizing was my realization that I didn't have much time. According to the report from his school physician he was already running at dangerously low levels, bones weakening, muscles degenerating, electrolyte balance

CHIP RUNNER

cockeyed, hormonal systems in disarray. The necessary treatment before long would be hospitalization, not psychotherapy, and it might almost be too late even for that.

He was aware that he was wasting away and in danger. He didn't seem to care.

I let him see that I wasn't going to force anything on him. So far as I was concerned, I told him, he was basically free to starve himself to death if that was what he was really after. But as a psychologist whose role it is to help people, I said, I had some scientific interest in finding out what made him tick—not particularly for his sake, but for the sake of other patients who might be more interested in being helped. He could relate to that. His facial expressions changed. He became less hostile. It was the fifth session now, and I sensed that his armor might be ready to crack. He was starting to think of me not as a member of the enemy but as a neutral observer, a dispassionate investigator. The next step was to make him see me as an ally. You and me, Timothy, standing together against *them*. I told him a few things about myself, my childhood, my troubled adolescence: little nuggets of confidence, offered by way of trade.

"When you disappear," I said finally, "where is it that you want to go?"

The moment was ripe and the breakthrough went beyond my highest expectations.

"You know what a microchip is?" he asked.

"Sure."

"I go down into them."

Not I *want* to go down into them. But I *do* go down into them.

"Tell me about that," I said.

"The only way you can understand the nature of reality," he said, "is to take a close look at it. To really and truly take a look, you know? Here we have these fantastic chips, a whole processing unit smaller than your little toenail with fifty times the data-handling capacity of the old mainframes. What goes on inside them? I mean, what *really* goes on? I go into them and I look. It's like a trance, you know? You sharpen your concentration and you sharpen it and sharpen it and then you're moving downward, inward, deeper and deeper." He laughed harshly. "You think this is all mystical ka-ka, don't you? Half of you thinks I'm just a

74 *Robert Silverberg*

crazy kid mouthing off, and the other half thinks here's a kid who's smart as hell, feeding you a line of malarkey to keep you away from the real topic. Right, doctor? Right?"

"I had a dream a couple of weeks ago about shrinking down into the infinitely small," I said. "A nightmare, really. But a fascinating one. Fascinating and frightening both. I went all the way down to the molecular level, past grains of sand, past bacteria, down to electrons and protons, or what I suppose were electrons and protons."

"What was the light like, where you were?"

"Blinding. It came in pulsing waves."

"What color?"

"Every color all at once," I said.

He stared at me. "No shit!"

"Is that the way it looks for you?"

"Yes. No." He shifted uneasily. "How can I tell if you saw what I saw? But it's a stream of colors, yes. Pulsing. And—all the colors at once, yes, that's how you could describe it—"

"Tell me more."

"More what?"

"When you go downward—tell me what it's like, Timothy."

He gave me his lofty look, his pedagogic look. "You know how small a chip is? A MOSFET, say?"

"MOSFET?"

"Metal-oxide-silicon field-effect-transistor," he said. "The newest ones have a minimum feature size of about a micrometer. Ten to the minus sixth meters. That's a millionth of a meter, all right? Small. It isn't down there on the molecular level, no. You could fit two hundred amoebas into a MOSFET channel one micrometer long. Okay? Okay? Or a whole army of viruses. But it's still plenty small. That's where I go. And run, down the corridors of the chips, with electrons whizzing by me all the time. Of course I can't see them. Even a lot smaller, you can't see electrons, you can only compute the probabilities of their paths. But you can feel them. *I* can feel them. And I run among them, everywhere, through the corridors, through the channels, past the gates, past the open spaces in the lattice. Getting to know the territory. Feeling at home in it."

"What's an electron like, when you feel it?"

"You dreamed it, you said. You tell me."

"Sparks," I said. "Something fizzy, going by in a blur."

CHIP RUNNER

"You read about that somewhere, in one of your journals?"

"It's what I saw," I said. "What I felt, when I had that dream."

"But that's it! That's it exactly!" He was perspiring. His face was flushed. His hands were trembling. His whole body was ablaze with a metabolic fervor I had not previously seen in him. He looked like a skeleton who had just trotted off a basketball court after a hard game. He leaned toward me and said, looking suddenly vulnerable in a way that he had never allowed himself to seem with me before, "Are you sure it was only a dream? Or do you go there too?"

Kafka had the right idea. What the anorexic wants is to demonstrate a supreme ability. "Look," she says. "I am a special person. I have an extraordinary gift. I am capable of exerting total control over my body. By refusing food I take command of my destiny. I display supreme force of will. Can you achieve that sort of discipline? Can you even begin to understand it? Of course you can't. But I can." The issue isn't really one of worrying about being too fat. That's just a superficial problem. The real issue is one of exhibiting strength of purpose, of proving that you can accomplish something remarkable, of showing the world what a superior person you really are. So what we're dealing with isn't merely a perversely extreme form of dieting. The deeper issue is one of gaining control—over your body, over your life, even over the physical world itself.

He began to look healthier. There was some color in his cheeks now, and he seemed more relaxed, less twitchy. I had the feeling that he was putting on a little weight, although the medical reports I was getting from his school physician didn't confirm that in any significant way—some weeks he'd be up a pound or two, some weeks down, and there was never any net gain. His mother reported that he went through periods when he appeared to be showing a little interest in food, but these were usually followed by periods of rigorous fasting or at best his typical sort of reluctant nibbling. There was nothing in any of this that I could find tremendously encouraging, but I had the definite feeling that I was starting to reach him, that I was beginning to win him back from the brink.

Timothy said, "I have to be weightless in order to get there. I mean, literally weightless. Where I am now, it's only a beginning. I need to lose all the rest."

"Only a beginning," I said, appalled, and jotted a few quick notes.

"I've attained takeoff capability. But I can never get far enough. I run into a barrier on the way down, just as I'm entering the truly structural regions of the chip."

"Yet you do get right into the interior of the chip."

"Into it, yes. But I don't attain the real understanding that I'm after. Perhaps the problem's in the chip itself, not in me. Maybe if I tried a quantum-well chip instead of a MOSFET I'd get where I want to go, but they aren't ready yet, or if they are I don't have any way of getting my hands on one. I want to ride the probability waves, do you see? I want to be small enough to grab hold of an electron and stay with it as it zooms through the lattice." His eyes were blazing. "Try talking about this stuff with my brother. Or anyone. The ones who don't understand think I'm crazy. So do the ones who do."

"You can talk here, Timothy."

"The chip, the integrated circuit—what we're really talking about is transistors, microscopic ones, maybe a billion of them arranged side by side. Silicon or germanium, doped with impurities like boron, arsenic, sometimes other things. On one side are the N-type charge carriers, and the P-type ones are on the other, with an insulating layer between; and when the voltage comes through the gate, the electrons migrate to the P-type side, because it's positively charged, and the holes, the zones of positive charge, go to the N-type side. So your basic logic circuit—" He paused. "You following this?"

"More or less. Tell me about what you feel as you start to go downward into a chip."

It begins, he said, with a rush, an upward surge of almost ecstatic force: he is not descending but floating. The floor falls away beneath him as he dwindles. Then comes the intensifying of perception, dust-motes quivering and twinkling in what had a moment before seemed nothing but empty air, and the light taking on strange new refractions and shimmerings. The solid world begins to alter. Familiar shapes—the table, a chair, the computer before him—vanish as he comes closer to their essence. What he sees now is detailed structure, the intricacy of surfaces: no longer a forest, only trees. Everything is texture and there is no solidity. Wood and metal become strands and webs and mazes.

CHIP RUNNER

Canyons yawn. Abysses open. He goes inward, drifting, tossed like a feather on the molecular breeze.

It is no simple journey. The world grows grainy. He fights his way through a dust-storm of swirling granules of oxygen and nitrogen, an invisible blizzard battering him at every step. Ahead lies the chip he seeks, a magnificent thing, a gleaming radiant Valhalla. He begins to run toward it, heedless of obstacles. Giant rainbows sweep the sky: dizzying floods of pure color, hammering down with a force capable of deflecting the wandering atoms. And then—then—

The chip stands before him like some temple of Zeus rising on the Athenian plain. Giant glowing columns—yawning gateways—dark beckoning corridors—hidden sanctuaries, beyond access, beyond comprehension. It glimmers with light of many colors. A strange swelling music fills the air. He feels like an explorer taking the first stumbling steps into a lost world. And he is still shrinking. The intricacies of the chip swell, surging like metal fungi filling with water after a rain: they spring higher and higher, darkening the sky, concealing it entirely. Another level downward and he is barely large enough to manage the passage across the threshold, but he does, and enters. Here he can move freely. He is in a strange canyon whose silvery walls, riven with vast fissures, rise farther than he can see. He runs. He runs. He has infinite energy; his legs move like springs. Behind him the gates open, close, open, close. Rivers of torrential current surge through, lifting him, carrying him along. He senses, does not see, the vibrating of the atoms of silicon or boron; he senses, does not see, the electrons and the not-electrons flooding past, streaming toward the sides, positive or negative, to which they are inexorably drawn.

But there is more. He runs on and on and on. There is infinitely more, a world within this world, a world that lies at his feet and mocks him with its inaccessibility. It swirls before him, a whirlpool, a maelstrom. He would throw himself into it if he could, but some invisible barrier keeps him from it. This is as far as he can go. This is as much as he can achieve. He yearns to reach out as an electron goes careening past, and pluck it from its path, and stare into its heart. He wants to step inside the atoms and breathe the mysterious air within their boundaries. He longs to look upon their hidden nuclei. He hungers for the sight of mesons, quarks, neutrinos. There is more, always more, an unending series of worlds within worlds, and he is huge, he is impossibly clumsy, he is a lurching reeling mountainous titan, incapable of penetrating beyond this point—

So far, and no farther—

No farther—

He looked up at me from the far side of the desk. Sweat was streaming down his face and his light shirt was clinging to his skin. That sallow cadaverous look was gone from him entirely. He looked transfigured, aflame, throbbing with life: more alive than anyone I had ever seen, or so it seemed to me in that moment. There was a Faustian fire in his look, a world-swallowing urgency. Magellan must have looked that way sometimes, or Newton, or Galileo. And then in a moment more it was gone, and all I saw before me was a miserable scrawny boy, shrunken, feeble, pitifully frail.

I went to talk to a physicist I knew, a friend of Timothy's father who did advanced research at the university. I said nothing about Timothy to him.

"What's a quantum well?" I asked him.

He looked puzzled. "Where'd you hear of those?"

"Someone I know. But I couldn't follow much of what he was saying."

"Extremely small switching device," he said. "Experimental, maybe five, ten years away. Less if we're very lucky. The idea is that you use two different semiconductive materials in a single crystal lattice, a superlattice, something like a three-dimensional checkerboard. Electrons tunneling between squares could be made to perform digital operations at tremendous speeds."

"And how small would this thing be, compared with the sort of transistors they have on chips now?"

"It would be down in the nanometer range," he told me. "That's a billionth of a meter. Smaller than a virus. Getting right down there close to the theoretical limits for semiconductivity. Any smaller and you'll be measuring things in angstroms."

"Angstroms?"

"One ten-billionth of a meter. We measure the diameter of atoms in angstrom units."

"Ah," I said. "All right. Can I ask you something else?"

He looked amused, patient, tolerant.

"Does anyone know much about what an electron looks like?"

CHIP RUNNER

"*Looks* like?"

"Its physical appearance. I mean, has any sort of work been done on examining them, maybe even photographing them—"

"You know about the Uncertainty Principle?" he asked.

"Well—not much, really—"

"Electrons are very damned tiny. They've got a mass of—ah—about nine times ten to the minus twenty-eighth grams. We need light in order to see, in any sense of the word. We see by receiving light radiated by an object, or by hitting it with light and getting a reflection. The smallest unit of light we can use, which is the photon, has such a long wavelength that it would completely hide an electron from view, so to speak. And we can't use radiation of shorter wavelength—gammas, let's say, or x-rays—for making our measurements, either, because the shorter the wavelength the greater the energy, and so a gamma ray would simply kick any electron we were going to inspect to hell and gone. So we can't 'see' electrons. The very act of determining their position imparts new velocity to them, which alters their position. The best we can do by way of examining electrons is make an enlightened guess, a probabilistic determination, of where they are and how fast they're moving. In a very rough way that's what we mean by the Uncertainty Principle."

"You mean, in order to look an electron in the eye, you'd virtually have to be the size of an electron yourself? Or even smaller?"

He gave me a strange look. "I suppose that question makes sense," he said. "And I suppose I could answer yes to it. But what the hell are we talking about, now?"

I dreamed again that night: a feverish, disjointed dream of gigantic grotesque creatures shining with a fluorescent glow against a sky blacker than any night. They had claws, tentacles, eyes by the dozens. Their swollen asymmetrical bodies were bristling with thick red hairs. Some were clad in thick armor, others were equipped with ugly shining spikes that jutted in rows of ten or twenty from their quivering skins. They were pursuing me through the airless void. Wherever I ran there were more of them, crowding close. Behind them I saw the walls of the cosmos beginning to shiver and flow. The sky itself was dancing. Color was breaking through the blackness: eddying bands of every hue at once, interwoven like great chains. I ran, and I ran, and I ran, but there were monsters on every side, and no escape.

Timothy missed an appointment. For some days now he had been growing more distant, often simply sitting silently, staring at me for the whole hour out of some hermetic sphere of unapproachability. That struck me as nothing more than predictable passive-aggressive resistance, but when he failed to show up at all I was startled: such blatant rebellion wasn't his expectable mode. Some new therapeutic strategies seemed in order: more direct intervention, with me playing the role of a gruff, loving older brother, or perhaps family therapy, or some meetings with his teachers and even classmates. Despite his recent aloofness I still felt I could get to him in time. But this business of skipping appointments was unacceptable. I phoned his mother the next day, only to learn that he was in the hospital; and after my last patient of the morning I drove across town to see him. The attending physician, a chunky-faced resident, turned frosty when I told him that I was Timothy's therapist, that I had been treating him for anorexia. I didn't need to be telepathic to know that he was thinking, *You didn't do much of a job with him, did you?* "His parents are with him now," he told me. "Let me find out if they want you to go in. It looks pretty bad."

Actually they were all there, parents, step-parents, the various children by the various second marriages. Timothy seemed to be no more than a waxen doll. They had brought him books, tapes, even a lap-top computer, but everything was pushed to the corners of the bed. The shrunken figure in the middle barely raised the level of the coverlet a few inches. They had him on an IV unit and a whole webwork of other lines and cables ran to him from the array of medical machines surrounding him. His eyes were open, but he seemed to be staring into some other world, perhaps that same world of rampaging bacteria and quivering molecules that had haunted my sleep a few nights before. He seemed perhaps to be smiling.

"He collapsed at school," his mother whispered.

"In the computer lab, no less," said his father, with a nervous ratcheting laugh. "He was last conscious about two hours ago, but he wasn't talking coherently."

"He wants to go inside his computer," one of the little boys said. "That's crazy, isn't it?" He might have been seven.

"Timothy's going to die, Timothy's going to die," chanted somebody's daughter, about seven.

CHIP RUNNER 81

"Christopher! Bree! Shhh, both of you!" said about three of the various parents, all at once.

I said, "Has he started to respond to the IV?"

"They don't think so. It's not at all good," his mother said. "He's right on the edge. He lost three pounds this week. We thought he was eating, but he must have been sliding the food into his pocket, or something like that." She shook her head. "You can't be a policeman."

Her eyes were cold. So were her husband's, and even those of the step-parents. Telling me, *This is your fault, we counted on you to make him stop starving himself.* What could I say? You can only heal the ones you can reach. Timothy had been determined to keep himself beyond my grasp. Still, I felt the keenness of their reproachful anger, and it hurt.

"I've seen worse cases than this come back under medical treatment," I told them. "They'll build up his strength until he's capable of talking with me again. And then I'm certain I'll be able to lick this thing. I was just beginning to break through his defenses when—when he—"

Sure. It costs no more to give them a little optimism. I gave them what I could: experience with other cases of food deprivation, positive results following a severe crisis of this nature, et cetera, et cetera, the man of science dipping into his reservoir of experience. They all began to brighten as I spoke. They even managed to convince themselves that a little color was coming into Timothy's cheeks, that he was stirring, that he might soon be regaining consciousness as the machinery surrounding him pumped the nutrients into him that he had so conscientiously forbidden himself to have.

"Look," this one said, or that one. "Look how he's moving his hands! Look how he's breathing. It's better, isn't it!"

I actually began to believe it myself.

But then I heard his dry thin voice echoing in the caverns of my mind. *I can never get far enough. I have to be weightless in order to get there. Where I am now, it's only a beginning. I need to lose all the rest.*

I want to disappear.

That night, a third dream, vivid, precise, concrete. I was falling and running at the same time, my legs pistoning like those of a marathon runner in the twenty-sixth mile, while simultaneously I dropped in free fall through airless dark toward the silver-black surface of some distant world. And fell and fell, in utter weightlessness, and hit the surface easily and kept on running, moving not forward but downward, the atoms of the ground parting for me as I ran. I became smaller as I descended, and smaller yet, and even smaller, until I was a mere phantom, a running ghost, the bodiless idea of myself. And still I went downward toward the dazzling heart of things, shorn now of all impediments of the flesh.

I phoned the hospital the next morning. Timothy had died a little after dawn.

Did I fail with him? Well, then, I failed. But I think no one could possibly have succeeded. He went where he wanted to go; and so great was the force of his will that any attempts at impeding him must have seemed to him like the mere buzzings of insects, meaningless, insignificant.

So now his purpose is achieved. He has shed his useless husk. He has gone on, floating, running, descending: downward, inward, toward the core, where knowledge is absolute and uncertainty is unknown. He is running amongst the shining electrons, now. He is down there among the angstrom units at last.

A CONEY ISLAND
OF THE MIND

Maureen F. McHugh

*"A Coney Island of the Mind" was purchased by
Gardner Dozois, and appeared in the February 1993
issue of* Asimov's, *with an illustration by Laurie
Harden. Another new writer who has made a powerful
impression on the SF world of the early 1990s with a
relatively small body of work, McHugh was born in
Ohio, but spent some years living in Shijiazhuang in
the People's Republic of China, an experience that has
been one of the major shaping forces on her fiction to
date. Upon returning to the United States, she made
her first sale in 1989, to* Asimov's, *and soon became
a frequent contributor to the magazine, as well as selling to* The Magazine of Fantasy and Science Fiction,
Alternate Warriors, Aladdin, *and other markets. In
1992, she published one of the year's most widely
acclaimed and most talked about first novels,* China
Mountain Zhang. *Coming up is a new novel, tentatively entitled* Half the Day Is Night. *Recently married, she lives, appropriately enough, in Loveland,
Ohio.*

In the sly little story that follows, she takes us on

84   *Maureen F. McHugh*

> *a kinky and unforgettable stroll through some of the*
> *shadier neighborhoods of cyberspace. . . .*

Reality Parlor.

He pays his money and goes back to the cubicle with the treadmill and pulls on the waldos, puts on the heavy eyeless, earless helmet. He grabs for the handlebars suspended before him, blind in the helmet that smells intimately of someone else's hair.

Now he can see. Not the handlebars hung from the ceiling on a tapewrapped cable, not the treadmill. He is the cat with future feet. He sees a schematic of a room; all the lines of the room are in pink neon on velvet black, and in his ears instead of the seasound of the helmet he hears the sound of open space. A room sounds different than a helmet even when there's nothing to hear.

A keyboard appears, or rather a line drawing of a keyboard with all the letters on the keys in glowing neon blue. Over it in neon blue letters is the message, "Please type in your user ID."

"Cobalt," he types, letting go of the handlebars. The waldos give him the sensation of hitting keys, give him feedback. His password is nagasaki.

A neon pink door draws itself in the velvet wall in front of him. The keyboard disappears and the handlebars appear in pink neon schematic until he grabs them. Then they disappear from sight, but he can still feel them, safe in his gloved hands. He starts forward [the treadmill lurches a bit under his blind feet but it always does that at first so he is accustomed to it, doesn't really think about it, just kind of expects it and forgets about it] through the door which opens up ahead of him, pulling apart like elevator doors into the party.

The party isn't a schematic, the party looks real. The party is a big space full of people dressed all ways—boys with big hair and girls with latex skulls and NPC in evening gowns and tuxes—and as he comes out of the elevator he looks to the right, to the mirrors, and sees himself, sees Cobalt, sees a Tom Sawyer in the twenty-first century, a flagboy in a bluesilk jacket and thigh high boots with a knotwork of burgundy cords at the hips.

A CONEY ISLAND OF THE MIND

All angles in the face, smooth face like a razor, a face he had custom configured in hours of bought-time at the reality parlor, not playing the reality streets, not even looking, just working on his own look. Cobalt eyes like lasers, and blue-steel braids for hair.

Edgelook, whatta-look, hot damn.

Not what he looks like at all in the mundane world of Cincinnati, Ohio, but he isn't in Cincinnati, ho, flagboy, he's not in Kansas anymore, he is at *the party*. Here he is, a serious dog, a democratic dog, but he doesn't think he'll spend a lot of time at the party today, looking around he doesn't see anyone he knows. Not that that means they aren't there, because anybody can look like anything, but if they don't have a handle he recognizes and they don't go calling out to Cobalt then they don't want to be the people he knows, right? And anyway, this afternoon the partyroom is full of off-the-racks, look-like-your-favorite-movie-star or take-a-basic-template-what-color-are-your-eyes-your-hair-look-like-a mannequin which he can't abide because he's looking for people with style so he angles over toward the far wall [his real feet, his mundane feet in their grass-stained sneakers that he wears when he mows the lawn just keep heading straight ahead on the treadmill, if he angles he'll step off the treadmill, but he turns the handlebars to the left and he's done it so long that he doesn't get confused by his feet saying one direction and the handlebars telling him another] to the far wall, full of blank doorways, and he stops to read the menu.

It's better now that he's turned eighteen, more choices. Games and Adventures, Simulations, Tanks and Airplanes and Spaceships—but he's not really interested in a lot of that because he's on a treadmill, not sitting down, so back to Games and Adventures, Places to Go and Things to Do, where he is likely to find some people he knows, someone to hang out with; Quixote and Bushman and Taipei.

"Any messages?" he asks out loud.

Soft chime that can be heard over the whole room of the party (except that no one else does). No messages. Nobody in the swim? Then he'll look for a place where maybe he'll meet serious dogs. He almost selects Chinatown but changes his mind and [left hand lets go of the handlebars and reaches out] pushes the button for Coney Island.

[Feedback through the waldo, it feels like pushing something.]

A line of electricity forms at the top of the door, a forcefield, an edge of static that rolls down like a window shade only draws down an opening on a place.

Black night on the boardwalk with the ferris wheel and the parachute drop all decked out in colored lights off in the distance. Cobalt steps through the door and his feet thump the hollow wood of the boardwalk. The booths spill bright white and yellow light onto the boards. He can hear the ocean. A guy is selling hotdogs. Coney fucking Island.

So he walks down the boardwalk, checking out the crowd, checking out how much is just program—the sailor and his girl at the Toss The Ring who are always at the Toss The Ring every time he comes—and how much is real people. It's a quiet night on the boardwalk.

Maybe he should go back to the party, check out Chinatown. Hey, he's here, maybe he'll just dogtrot on down the boardwalk, out toward the rides, see if there's someone. Then he'll go back to Chinatown.

Moving along the boardwalk, past the cotton candy, past the tattoo parlor, past the place where the counter is a two-tone Cadillac, dog gone, dog going, into a dog eat dog world.

And the queens (who are mostly black and tall and female and camp, that being the current fashion in queens) are calling "Hey sweetcakes," "Hey, be my blueboy," "Are you hotwired, babyface?" "Are you wired for sound?" Which he's not because he rents time in a fucking public reality parlor (no pun intended) where they aren't going to supply equipment to wire your crotch.

But it's all just noise, white noise, background hiss, the sound of Coney Island and not what he's looking for anyway although who's to say what he'd be looking for if he had the option? But he doesn't, so he isn't, he's looking for his mates, his team, his dogpack. He's checking under the boardwalk behind the Chinese food place, and watching the Mustangs crawl up the street because Quixote likes simulations, likes to drive fast cars in crazy places. Watching for spies because Taipei likes adventure games where he fights off attackers, watches for gang members because they all like to play Warriors and Coney Island is where it starts, where they catch the subway to the cemetery in the Bronx.

A CONEY ISLAND OF THE MIND 87

But the streets are all full of programming, of nonplayer characters, and kids without style, which is to say that this night Coney Island is empty.

So he's thinking that he'll check one more place, maybe take in a movie, or call up the airlock and go on to Chinatown, and he stops where he can see the ocean and looks for a moment, the stone dark ocean rolling and making that sound, hypnotizing him and he likes it because there isn't much ocean in Cincinnati, hell, there isn't even much sin in Cincinnati.

She leans next to him with a star hanging off her ear, one lone star in the smoke nebula of her hair, no off-the-rack handle but a costume full of style, like himself, like the dogpack, this woman has taken some time. "Hey blueboy," she says.

"Hey yourself," he says and imagines she smells like perfume, smells like ash. She has full breasts and brown skin in the yellow light. She has yellow snake eyes, not like dice, like rattlesnakes, and hair that doesn't act like real hair at all but fills some indefinite space, swallows light, absorbs light, no reflections. Soft looking. Nice touch, that. She's a chimera, she's not content to take a strictly human template, she's diddled the programming.

He's a lucky dog.

They make noise in the night, what's your name, Cobalt what's yours? (Rattlesnake, he wonders, or cobra, coral snake, black racer, asp, gila monster, his mind all in a rush before she answers—)

Lamia.

Which isn't what he expects at all and doesn't mean a thing except it sounds liquid. He wishes he had more access, he wishes he had preprogrammed something, an ashen rose maybe, to pull out of the air and give to her, but all he has are things that are useful in adventure games; a smoke bomb, a rope, a bottle that can be broken and used like a knife.

"That's pretty," he says.

She reaches out and takes his hand. And sighs happily.

The ocean rolls in.

"Squeeze," she says in a throaty whisper.

For a moment he doesn't understand but then he squeezes her hand and she half-closes her eyes. "Flagboy," she says, "I think I like you."

"Want to walk on the beach?" he asks.

She shrugs and kneads his fingers, he can feel her hand, all the bones of it and her long fingers, and she can feel his because of the waldos. He pulls her toward the steps and she gives a throaty, gaspy laugh.

She's wearing high heels, spikes with toes like cloven hooves—except that her feet don't look human. Her smoky hair has horns, then it's a halo, a madonna veil, all smoke. She follows him in a clatter across the hollow boards and down the steps into the sand. Their footsteps become silent [it never feels any different, because his feet are still on the treadmill, and his right hand is still on the handlebars, but his left holds the air and the waldos mimic the pressure of her hand.]

"Not so tight," she says and he loosens his grip on her hand.

Eyes and hands, eyes and ears and hands. How real is real?

The light from the star in her hair falls on her bare shoulders, on her collarbones. Her clothing has no reason to stay covering her breasts but it does. She wouldn't feel it if he touched her breasts, not unless she's wearing a hotsuit. Could she be wearing a hotsuit, have her whole body wired for touch? Does she have a place at home, a treadmill, the whole bit? Spoiled Fifth Avenue girl? LA girl? Maybe she's forty years old, he doesn't know. Maybe she's ugly.

Interesting thought, that. He looks at her smoky hair and her skin and the hollow leading into her heart shaped top and squeezes her hand and she sighs. Huuuhhh.

And he sighs, too. Maybe she's ugly, or fat, or old. Maybe she is blind, or deformed. Maybe she is married. Wild thought that this beautiful girl can be anything.

His heart is pounding. She stops and they are facing each other, holding hands. If they kissed, there would be nothing but air. Strange to feel her through his palm and fingers, the waldos giving him all the feelings of her hand, of the weight of her body behind the hand, and knowing that he could pass his arm through her. She is nothing but light. If he thinks about it he can feel the weight of the helmet on his head.

And her hand. All the bones and tendons and ligaments, the elastic play of her muscle. He finds her fingers, presses them one-by-one. She is watching him with slit pupiled snake eyes gone from amber to green, although he can't remember when

A CONEY ISLAND OF THE MIND 89

that happened. The ocean roars behind them.

He laces his fingers through hers. "Where are you?" he asks, although it's rude to ask people that.

"On the boardwalk," she says, her voice coming out in a breath. She is watching him, lazily intent, and he is playing with her hand. She closes her eyes and catches her lip in her teeth. Her face is so strange.

"Don't stop," she whispers and he doesn't know what she is talking about and then he realizes it is her hand, her hand in his blue gloved one. Her face is almost empty of expression, but small things seem to be happening in it independent of anything that is in his face.

"Squeeze," she says again.

Confused, he does, and feels her squeezing rhythmically back, pulsing little squeezes, and he realizes in horror just—

[She's hotwired her hand.]

—as she comes. Eyes shut, her smoky hair rising in horns, she gasps a little. He jerks his hand away, but she is standing there oblivious, and it's too late anyway.

[You take a hotsuit and re-wire the crotch so the system thinks it's a hand, then anytime someone touches your hand . . .]

He is embarrassed, angry, shocked. He doesn't know if he should just go or not.

[His fingers squeezing her and he didn't know.]

"Blueboy," she says, and sits down on the sand. "Oh Christ, blueboy."

He will go and he does [turning the handlebars; feet, as always, straight on the treadmill] and starts back for the steps.

"Come on," she says, "what's so awful about it?"

"You didn't tell me," he says, all indignation.

"Prissy little virgin," she says, and laughs behind him.

"Airlock," he says, which is a system command, a gateway back to the party. The line of static starts at the height of a door, and the forcefield rolls down like a window shade.

"Huff on out of here," she says. "Righteous little bitch. Are you a girl?"

"What!?" he says

Which makes her laugh. "Well, I guess not, sweetcakes, but for a moment I sure thought you were."

Sweetcakes. [Somewhere in Cincinnati his cheeks are burning.]

"I'm glad," she says, "because I'm not into girls. I just like wearing girl bodies because I like you righteous boys, you sweet straight boys."

He starts to step into the party and stops. "What?" he says.

"Draws you all like moths to a flame," she said. Or he said, or it said.

His first swift thought is that he'll have to change his look, never look like this again, abandon Cobalt, be something else.

She laughs that ashen laugh. "Go on home, blueboy."

And he does, steps back into the party, leaves Coney Island behind. The party, neutral ground, where he shakes his head, dog shaking water off his coat. He blinks in the lights of the party. Thinks of going home, going back to Cincinnati, to thinking about Ohio State in the fall.

Trying not to think about feet like hooves, high heels.

What a frigging nut case!

Bad luck, Quixote is waving across the space. Cobalt doesn't know, just wants to go home.

"Where you been," Quixote says, "you're looking democratic."

Shrugs. What's he going to say, I met this girl—I met this girl and her hand . . . he starts to smile, what a dog story. Quixote is going to be green.

"You won't believe what happened to me in Coney Island," Cobalt says.

He doesn't have to tell everything.

"No way!" Quixote says.

It's a dog eat dog world, sometimes.

DREAMWOOD

Cherry Wilder

"Dreamwood" was purchased by Gardner Dozois, and appeared in the December 1986 issue of Asimov's, *with an illustration by Laura Lakey. Wilder has sold only a handful of stories to the magazine, but they've all been worth waiting for, and we hope to coax more out of her in the future. Born in New Zealand, Cherry Wilder has also lived for long stretches of time in Australia and Germany. She made her first sale in 1974 to the British anthology* New Writings in SF 24, *and since then, in addition to a number of sales to* Asimov's, *has sold to markets such as* Interzone, Universe, Strange Plasma, *and elsewhere. Her many books include* The Luck of Brin's Five, The Nearest Fire, The Tapestry Warriors, Second Nature, A Princess of the Chamein, Yorath of the Wolf, The Summer's King, *and* Cruel Designs.*

In the powerful and somberly evocative story that follows, she takes us to the inner regions of the mind, and deep into the hidden corners of the human heart.

In the green heart of the wood, he comes to a grove of birch trees with trunks of black and silver and loose light-green foliage, beautiful as young girls. He is young, strong, free . . . the old men are vanquished. He can manage the wood far better than the others who dispute his tenure. By God, he is straightened out at last, and he has done it with love, with caring, without violence. He takes great joy in the leaves under his feet, the declinations of the path, the way the light falls upon the trunks of the birch trees. Beyond them he can see the forest, full of strange dark conifers. He sends forth his creative power: the cedar tree waits for him. He is carrying pine planks under his arm. There is Laurel, best and brightest, Apollo's bride; she comes to him, smiling, takes his hand, he can feel her hand in his. " . . . dearest of all . . ." she says at last, but it might be "clearest of all . . ."

She lets his hand fall; shrugs free, still smiling, when he puts his arm around her shoulders. Then, raising a hand in greeting, she walks off to join the two other men who have come through the dark fir trees. She turns back to him as if she felt his distress and calls: "It is the search theme! Register all this!"

He is alone again, still heading for the cedar tree. He sees a child, a little kid of about seven in a blue padded jacket with a hood, playing in a patch of sunlight. He knows this is not the child they are searching for . . .

The widow, Anna Hay Gordon, did not return to the New England house for more than a year. She drove up alone in the fall, turning abruptly into their overgrown access road, hearing the long grass slap against the sides of the new station wagon. She came up to the metal gate that Wallace had had put in before he died; her heart missed a beat, she trod on the brake, and felt the car slide a fraction. A tall man in a gray-and-blue checkered shirt was inside the gate, fumbling with the mailbox. He was tall, gray-haired, loose-limbed, and the shirt, surely the *shirt* . . . yet he was no ghost. He ran off awkwardly into the autumn trees beside the drive as she heaved the big wagon up to the gate. He was not Wallace, he was nothing like him. This man was ungainly, almost lame.

Anna unclamped her hands from the wheel and peered up the drive. A strange man at the house? She saw a red car parked

DREAMWOOD 93

beyond the tank stand, and the mystery was solved. Sam, her stepson, had people at the house. It was tactless, but Sam Gordon *was* tactless. He had brought up odd visitors in the old days. Very odd, some of them. The rock group, the two much-wanted Weatherpersons, the draft-dodging boys en route to Canada . . . Now Sam was harboring some old guy who had run off through the trees wearing—she was sure of it—one of Wallace's shirts.

Anna dragged herself out of the driver's seat. Sam's voice creaked through the intercom on the gatepost.

"Anna? Anna?"

"Let me in, Sam!"

The gate swung open with difficulty; damn them, why didn't these freaks ever cut the grass! She went barreling down the drive, and passed the man in the shirt taking the path to the back door, through the Japanese maples. Sam was standing ankle-deep in leaves before the house. He was full of ill-controlled excitement, swinging his long arms like a gorilla.

Anna switched off her engine and watched him. Sam was growing older, if not precisely growing up. What would he be now? Thirty-five? Soon his gangling good looks would fade, would harden into an untidy middle age. Already he looked like a lecturer, not a student. She saw a girl come down the steps of the house, saw how neat she was, a chestnut-haired girl in a green divided skirt and some kind of a white jacket.

"Hey, you gave us a scare!" said Sam.

He turned to the girl. "It *is* Anna!" he said. "No sweat."

His tone was placatory. He made a quick introduction without looking away from the girl, whose name was Laurel Weiss. Anna could not smile, and neither could the girl, Laurel. She said: "We have a security problem, Ms. Gordon. We're hiding from the press. Did you stop in Rexford?"

"Nope!" said Anna. "But I damn near turned around and drove back there and got the police. I saw a strange man at my mailbox, wearing one of my late husband's shirts."

"For Christ's sake, Anna," said Sam, waving his arms. "He *needed* the shirt. . . ."

A third visitor came down off the porch. He was about forty-five years old, and heavily built. His nose had been broken at some time; he wore a turtle-neck sweater and tracksuit pants. He nodded politely to Anna and murmured to the girl, Laurel.

"How many people do you have in my house, Sam?" demanded Anna. "What kind of a circus are you putting on this time?"

"You don't understand . . ." Sam and Laurel spoke together.

The big man, the security guard, smiled pleasantly; Anna realized that he liked the look of her. It was a lonely assignment up here in the autumn woods. He grinned and slapped Sam on the back and came to open the car door.

"Mayhew," he said. "I'm Chet Mayhew, Ms. Gordon. We should go inside. Hey . . . let me get that bag. You'll see . . ."

There was something very sane and comforting about Mayhew.

"Come on in," Mayhew said. "Come on in and meet our friend Mr. Brown."

Anna followed him in a dream. They all trooped up the steps, across the porch and into the big living room. A fire was burning; there was a pleasant whiff of coffee and bacon, but the place had been well-aired. The vases were filled with leaves and pods; the slip covers were on the chairs and the couch. All that she had planned to do and dreaded doing a little in this poor house had already been done.

The man in Wallace's shirt sat at the table, turning the pages of a Sears Catalogue. Anna remembered another dream, clear and cruel, in which Wallace came back from the dead subtly changed, easier to love. The man at the table had a long fair face, the beginnings of a beard. His large hands were unsteady. She had never expected to see him again. He was one of their oldest friends; he had come from the ends of the earth. He was Oleg Anton Kirrilow. Poet. Translator. Dissident. He stared at her, opening his blue eyes very wide; his lips moved soundlessly.

"Oleg!"

As she went to him, the girl Laurel said in a warning voice: "He is under treatment. . . ."

"My dear friends," whispered Oleg. "My dear friends Wallace Gordon and . . . and . . ."

"Anna," she said.

She sat down beside him and took one of his large moist hands.

"Anna!" he said triumphantly. "Yes! Anna, the new wife. Anna!"

"You got out," she said. "They let you go."

"They insisted upon it!" he said. "It's wonderful to see you. I

DREAMWOOD
95

was expecting you every minute. Where is Wallace?"

She did not bother to look at Sam and the others. She took it upon herself to protect Oleg from the shock.

"He's very sick," she said, "but I know he'd be so glad . . . so happy to see you in this house at last. Remember how we spoke of this place when we met in Zagreb?"

"The New England house," said Oleg, "the house in Maine, deep in the woods. We sang that old song . . . you . . . was it you, Anna, who sang that old student song to me?"

"Yes!" cried Anna.

And they burst out singing together, two friends, two lost unhappy creatures, two birds in the wilderness:

"Riding down from Bangor, on an eastern train,
After weeks of hunting in the woods of Maine . . ."

The others laughed and applauded. Oleg drew breath and shook his head from side to side.

"Forgive me," Oleg said. "Forgive me, Anna. I think . . ."

"What is it?"

"Wallace is dead?"

"Yes," she said in a low voice. "It's been more than a year now. But what I said is true. He *would* be so pleased to see you here. Our house is yours."

"It went very quickly," Oleg said. "I was flown from Zürich, from a clinic in Zürich. At the plane I was received by the doctor and by Sam . . . I met Sam at last."

Sam came to lay a hand on Oleg Kirrilow's shoulder. Anna managed to smile. She caught the eye of Laurel Weiss. She was a little ashamed . . . she had taken the girl for a nurse or social worker, one of Sam's girls, helping out.

"Dr. Weiss?" she said.

"Yes, Ms. Gordon?"

"Could we all do with some coffee?"

"Chet!" ordered the doctor crisply. "How about some coffee for Ms. Gordon? She has come a long way, driving from Mexico."

"Stay where you are, Mr. Mayhew," said Anna.

She sprang up and went into the kitchen—her own contrary holiday kitchen with the rubble drain that had to be cossetted and the battered electric stove that had cooked so many turkey dinners. My God, she thought, Oleg is here to stay, we can keep

Thanksgiving here, maybe, and Christmas. She had never thought to do that any more; she had thought of the house in the woods as a dead place, dead along with Wallace. She stood at the sink bench, gazing out into the woods, and Sam came to stand beside her, whistling a little old popular song that she could not place. The coffee had begun to percolate, banging against the lid of the pot.

"What does the government think of all this?" she asked.

"They de-briefed him already," said Sam. "He spent a day with them in New York. Oh, there's no personal interest in Oleg . . . they just wanted the names of other dissidents at the fancy political booby-hatch he was in. He has to report to them now and then. And not talk to the press."

"You mean to say Mayhew is *not* a government man?"

"Retired," said Sam. "He's a security guard at Latimer, in the Clinic. Laurel figured we needed him."

The name of the College where Sam worked had been taboo in the house for so long that Anna almost turned her head to make sure they were alone. Wallace had despised Latimer. Once triggered off he would vituperate against its faculty, its Medical Research Clinic, its publications, to the point of madness. Now the angry voice was still forever. Anna said shakily, "Laurel works at the clinic?"

"Sure," said Sam. "They do fantastic things. Oleg is responding to the treatment."

"I hope so," said Anna. "Sam, what about your own work? I'm sorry I haven't been keeping up. Do you have tenure?"

"Yes, of course," he said. "You don't have to worry. This counts. I'll write an article on this work with Oleg. I'm working on . . . oh, a whole heap of things . . ."

She laughed.

"How's Frances?" asked Sam. "How are the kids?"

Sam loved Frances, his half-sister, Anna's own child. As a difficult boy of thirteen he had been "straightened out," not for the last time, by her birth; he had watched devotedly over her childhood. Anna was swept away suddenly by memories of the good times they had had here, right here in this house in the woods. When Wallace was working well on one of the history projects; when Sam was in school; when Fran was a little kid in a pink down parka, feeding the birds . . .

DREAMWOOD 97

"They are all fine," she said. "They send love to you. I hear nothing but Uncle Sam, Uncle Sam down in Mexico. Very patriotic."

"Hey, I *saw* her!" cried Sam. "I must tell Laurel. I saw Fran in the wood. It could be a personal construct, one of the images we've been waiting for!"

"What are you talking about? You saw *Fran*?"

"In my dream," he said patiently. "I saw her as a kid, playing out there in the woods in her blue anorak . . ."

"Pink," said Anna. "It was pink. I was just thinking . . ."

But Sam had gone striding off into the living room to tell pretty Dr. Weiss his dream. Good heavens, thought Anna, is she his *analyst*? There was a burst of excited laughter from the other room, she heard the bass note of Oleg Kirrilow joining in: group therapy of some kind. She remembered the name of the old song Sam had been whistling; it was called "My Dreams Are Getting Better All The Time."

When she went in with the coffee they all fell silent, but their faces, turned towards her, were so cheerful that she could have wept with relief. Surely this was better than her planned retreat in the cold house, going about with gritted teeth sorting Wallace's things.

"Sit here, Ms. Gordon," said Laurel Weiss.

She sat between Oleg and the doctor. Oleg filled the old brown armchair comfortably, but seemed to find it difficult to relax. He talked well, trying to catch up with the last eight years since they had all met in Zagreb. His manner was halting; she found herself listening hard, prompting, giving him a few forgotten names and topics. When he asked questions, she took care to be precise and clear and not to take too long with her answers. She knew instinctively that he must not be over-burdened "with new material," as Wallace would have said. Just as instinctively, she lied about Wallace, about the tirades and the anxieties of his last years, but she did this with some hope. Eventually, if Oleg were to stay and to get better, she might bring out a truer picture. He was one of the few persons in the world who might understand the historian's defeat, the nightmare of ill-health.

"I could bring no papers out," said Oleg. "Not a scrap. There was so much that might have been useful for the biography."

"Not to worry," said Anna. "We will take some notes together."

She pressed his hand again. "Ah, to have you here . . ."

"Sam," he said, "Sam wants to write it . . ."

"Well," she temporized, "it is something to think about."

Anna realized that Sam and Mayhew had melted away. Only the doctor remained, quiet as a mouse. When Oleg excused himself to go to the bathroom, Laurel Weiss reached out smoothly towards a brown box that lurked on the coffee table, not really hidden by a bowl of leaves. She grinned at Anna.

"You can speak off the record at any time," she said. "This sliding contact is best."

"I hate being recorded," said Anna. "I hate it even more in my own house when I am talking to an old friend."

"We know the situation," said Laurel. "Believe me, Ms. Gordon, our only interest in Kirrilow is clinical, as a man suffering from loss of memory, partially drug induced. The whole program here is directed towards his rehabilitation, using a particular spectrum of new techniques. You are providing the things we cannot give: memories, peer contact, partnering . . ."

"Things you can't give?" asked Anna.

"We know that you and Kirrilow were lovers," said Laurel Weiss. "He would benefit from . . ."

Anna burst out laughing. "I wonder how you know *that*?"

"Please don't be embarrassed . . ."

"Some people *are* going to be embarrassed," said Anna. "Some people are going to be hurt, Dr. Weiss. How can gossip and family . . . arrangements help Oleg? You are barking up too many wrong trees!"

"Hey, what a great image!" said the girl, smiling more winningly than ever. "We *do* know, Ms. Gordon . . . Anna . . . We know it from the dreams, from Kirrilow's own dreams. He has immense creative power . . . he has helped us create the dreamwood."

"You're studying dreams?" Anna asked lamely.

She remembered a report on "dream therapy" that Sam had been unwise enough to show Wallace. No, he had showed him an article he had published, and this report on dream work at the university clinic had been on a neighboring page. It had received a blistering criticism, along with the article. Wallace raged and sneered ever afterwards; dreams and dreaming were black-listed, like so many other topics, and like the names of so many men and women. Anna thought of the interviews with literary reporters

DREAMWOOD

and student editors, of the poor guys from Archive Films who lost days of work when the interviewer insisted on slipping in the question about Marcuse.

"We are *sharing* our dreams, Anna," said Oleg Kirrilow from the doorway.

He advanced into the room with a more certain gait, his eyes shining. He spoke in Russian; she thought he was quoting from a poem. Laurel Weiss smiled again, pressed Anna's arm with a glance at the recorder, and slipped away.

"I don't have enough Russian," said Anna. "I am not the Russian expert."

He grinned and returned to his chair.

"Anna," he said. "The *new* wife, Anna."

"What is this dream-stuff?"

"What I said. It is a game, I think, not much more, but a fascinating one. The little doctor believes it helps my memory, along with her health program."

"She puts you to sleep? Gives you dream stimulants? Puts one of those metal caps with wires on your head?"

"How disapproving you sound, Anna. Yes, we do some of those things. It is a team sport . . . SRD, Shared Recreational Dreaming. We pooled our images in a preliminary session. Now we meet in the dreamwood."

"Sam and the girl and you . . ."

"Even the guard, Mayhew."

"Is it safe? Are you sure it's safe?"

"What have I got to lose?" said Oleg, with a touch of his old world-weariness. He had been very cynical, she remembered; moody, passionate, full of sly humor.

"Wallace was very much against dream research," she said. "You know how he could be . . . against things."

But Kirrilow, after their brisk talk about dreaming, had leaned back and shut his eyes. When he opened them again he said: "Nanuschka!"

"No," she said softly. "*Anna . . .*"

"Come into our dreamwood. It is a kind of paradise."

"No," she said. "I am still too sad. This conversation reminds me of the Palm Lounge of the Hotel Esplanade."

"Tell me," he said. "I have completely forgotten. I have forgotten my poems. I have forgotten my childhood. I have forgotten my women."

"Perhaps you have telescoped some of your experiences," she said, teasing.

He lay back in the chair, relaxed and smiling, and went to sleep. Anna walked to the window and saw Laurel and Sam raking the leaves together for a bonfire. She went quietly into the hallway, then looked back into the room at Kirrilow. He sighed in his sleep and groaned.

Mothering trees, tree-mothers, rocking me in their branches . . . I wrote that in fifty-two. No, where? Nowhere. They are giving me plenty of rope, all I need is the right branch. I will elude you, comrades, after all, I will fly by your nets. I am the dada and the sun . . . Zürich my kind old mattress . . . Zürich has a lot to answer for. My images are being despoiled hourly by fools, by non-poets, dolts from east and west. Nanuschka, you seized my tower, you robbed me cruelly of my seed, you were a ball-biting clock puncher. Galina, you were an unspeakable disappointment. I was robbed of all my children. They were aborted, or kidnapped to the west in utero. What a swathe I might have cut as a young man in the holy wood, in hollywood, peopled the green breast of the new world with my ikons. Girls, you have let me down, you birch trees, you shaggy tree mothers. I will tread you, set my foot on your faces . . . as I do upon these mushrooms beside the path. Sweet needle carpet. Magic carpet carrying me deeper and deeper into the dreamwood. My wood, my world, my word. In the beginning was the word and the word was odd. One of Wallace's jokes. Old friend, you have gone off and left me in this dark wood with only your stale mates. Who is that long boy, that unwise child who is threatening to despoil my wood with a watchtower? I cannot permit it. Certainly I will take Anna, even if she is sullen, even if she laughed at me in the Hotel Esplanade. She was not there in our heyday, in the days of the commune. I must remain alert in my wood . . . from the watchtowers in the grounds of the clinic one could be picked off through the trees. See there, what did I tell you, my soul, there is the palm court I made here in the wood for Anna, and that pig Mayhew is truffling about in it. I have drawn him into the wood with the aid of the little tree-doctor and her wonder drugs. He may not escape. I hide among my trees and watch him. Ah, by sleeping, only by sleeping and dreaming, to wreak revenge upon the whole world! Annihilating all that's made . . . could I die thus? Is it like lying

DREAMWOOD 101

down in the snow? To cease upon the midnight with no pain. I cannot see what flowers are at my feet or what soft incense hangs about the boughs. Incense is the opium of the people. Tee-hee. I am falling into my anecdotage. I will wake, I suppose. I will wake at least once more . . .

Anna was going about examining the sleeping arrangements. Someone who lived out of a gray kit-bag was quartered in her workroom beside the kitchen; Mayhew of course, with a view of the drive and of the front gate.

Upstairs, everyone slept alone. Kirrilow had the big double bedroom, Dr. Weiss the study. She went a little way up the ladder and stuck her head into the kids' roomy attic. Sam was using his old bed and his old patchwork quilt. Anna worked out that she had been placed in the guest room.

She went in and almost screamed. Chet Mayhew lay face down on the blue-chintz bed cover, one hand trailing; he lay where he had fallen, as if he had been sapped. He had set her bags down neatly beside the bed . . . then he seemed to have fallen asleep. An exposition of sleep had come upon him, like Bottom among the fairies. When she shook him the big man simply curled up and made himself more comfortable.

Anna went to the window and called for Dr. Weiss.

"What is it?" shouted Sam.

Anna shouted back, straight-faced: "Someone is sleeping in my bed!"

She stood watching Mayhew while Sam and Laurel came thundering up the stairs and burst in at the door. The noise did not reach the sleeper at all.

"God damn it, Anna, couldn't you keep him from falling asleep!" cried Sam.

"What are you talking about?"

"*Oleg!*"

"This is good old Chet cluttering up my room," she said. "Oleg is in his chair downstairs. What kind of a crazy house . . . ?"

Laurel Weiss quietened Sam with a glance.

"Mayhew is over-sensitive to the inductors," Laurel said. "It's a rare side effect."

She rolled up Mayhew's sleeve and gave him a shot with a disposable needle. Anna felt sick. A gust of wind hit the spruce tree outside the window and rustled its branches violently. It was Wallace turning in his grave.

"Oleg Kirrilow has a powerful empathetic personality," continued Laurel. "When he sleeps he can draw Chet back into the image matrix."

Chet Mayhew woke up. He was wide awake, his eyes straining open, his muscles tense.

"Sorry!" he panted. "Sorry, Ms. Gordon . . . it is the darnedest thing. . . ."

"You were in the wood?" asked Laurel smoothly. "You were in the wood and you saw Kirrilow . . . ?"

"No," he said. "I knew he was there, but I didn't set eyes on him. It was a part of the wood I hadn't been in before, more like a tropical rainforest. The palm trees were very tall, some had black trunks like tree ferns, and I was walking across a bridge to some kind of picnic area with white wrought-iron furniture. There was music playing . . . kind of like gypsy violins. There was still a touch of the old search-party then . . . I knew we were strung out through the wood looking for the lost child. I think this comes from me a little, I told you about the search parties I was in. Anyhow, I went on down towards the music, hoping to find the band leader, or someone to get a drink from. I looked off to the left, through the palm trees, and saw a girl I knew sitting at a table, tall girl with black hair, very smooth black hair . . . a girl I haven't thought of for years, name of Scott, Nan Scott. It was a composite, not the real Nan Scott but a dream version of her, wearing a dress of shiny blue cotton."

"Chintz," put in Anna softly.

"Uh-huh," said Laurel, "Chintz, like the bedspread. Go on, Chet . . ."

"I went towards the girl, feeling pleased, and then the needle took effect. I woke up."

"Okay," said Laurel. "Not a lot of Kirrilow in the dream that we can see at present. Perhaps you are blocking his experience, Chet, trying to control the images yourself. Let's break it up."

Laurel helped Mayhew up and urged him out of the room. As Sam went to follow, Anna detained him.

"I must talk to you," she said.

He wagged his head about in the old sulky way, as if to say "Here comes the bawling out!"

"Please, Sam . . ."

DREAMWOOD

She led the way across the passage and round a corner into the study. It was the room she dreaded most. There were the books, there was the desk with its photographs in a set of cherrywood frames, the gift of a Japanese graduate student. They sat side by side on the big studio couch, which had been made up as a bed for Doctor Weiss, and stared at the relics of Wallace Gordon: historian, critic, political theorist, biographer, teacher, lover, family man, bellyacher, boss.

"I know what you're going to say," said Sam. "The Old Man hated this kind of therapy. It made him foam at the mouth, okay? But he is dead, Anna. This is *your* house. It was *always* your house, that is why it was always such a great place for me. It is my winter home, just as the house in La Jolla is my summer place. The Old Man wasn't the only influence in my childhood . . . I had *two* mothers, Mom and Anna, and they were both swell, both broad-minded, both caring. Please, Anna, don't let me down. Don't make me pass up this opportunity to help Oleg and to help Laurel with her research."

"You're a sophist," said Anna. "You argue unfairly. Sam, I am afraid of this damned dreamwood, this dream world of yours, and of your smooth-tongued little doctor who knows nothing about Oleg or about this family. More than anything, I am afraid of the 'inductors'—group hallucinogens, of course, and highly illegal."

"Nope!" said Sam. "This is a properly controlled medical experiment performed by a doctor. And it *is* helping Oleg Kirrilow . . . when he first arrived he was *much* worse, truly, Anna. You can check with old Brodski in New York . . . we took him there for a back-up medical opinion."

It was a sensible thing to do, she had to admit.

"What did Abe Brodski have to say?"

"A lot of head shaking. He recommended rest and the company of friends. He played chess with Oleg. He said did we have another Master or Class I player to keep Oleg amused . . ."

Sam's voice shook. They looked at the desk: there were two photographs of Fay Gordon, Sam's mother, Wallace's first wife, who had died in an automobile accident five years past. A slim fair woman. The larger photograph showed her winning a women's regional championship. She was the only chess player in the family; Wallace had been very proud of her chess—she had never let him win. Anna had never liked nor understood Wallace's first wife, but the two women had done their best. *They* had never exchanged a cross word. Yet some of Fay's gambits were puzzling.

"She was a great player, Sam," and Anna. "Did she ever tell you about the Russian tour, when they first met Kirrilow?"

"She had all her games published," said Sam.

"No," said Anna patiently. "Did you hear about the very first trip they made after the war? London, Moscow, Zürich . . . they saw a lot of Kirrilow. He turned up wherever they went. He was with them in Zürich for three months, recovering from a bout of pneumonia. Did Fay ever speak of that time?"

"I always wanted to go along!" said Sam.

"Sam, you weren't even *born*!"

"I was sick of hearing about Europe," he said. "Hey—something I remember! They brought back all kinds of crazy wooden toys and a nutcracker. A nutcracker shaped like a soldier in a blue uniform with a pointy helmet and a gray beard made of rabbit fur. I used to think this Oleg they were always talking about must look like the nutcracker. I must tell him that. The nutcracker from the Nutcracker Suite!"

He was flinging about the small room in his old restless fashion.

"Must get back!" he said. "Chet and Laurel will be dishing up lunch."

"About Kirrilow," she said faintly, losing heart. "About Kirrilow . . . have they woken him up? Does he keep dropping off and returning to this dream place?"

"Of course not. That was probably just a side-effect from meeting you. Just like the business with Chet is a side-effect. Who would have thought that poor old Chet was so sensitive to the inductors? Normally he doesn't take part in the sessions. He stays on watch."

Well, that makes two of us, thought Anna.

"Go on down," she said. "I'll freshen up."

"And you won't upset the experiment?"

"No," she said. "No. But don't expect too many good vibes from old Anna."

"Kirrilow loves you," he said suddenly, with a cheeky, foolish grin that showed he had understood nothing at all. "That old guy is still carrying a torch!"

He ducked out of the room cheerily, as if she might throw a cushion at him. Anna sat in silence and despair. What shall

DREAMWOOD 105

I do? she asked. *Wallace ... Fay ... what shall I do?* In her mind, Wallace gave his usual answer. In his last years he had been consumed by a rabid impatience, hardly able to speak a civil word to anyone, least of all to his wife. *"To hell with you, you're a fool, get away from me, not another word ... !"* And Fay, looking up from some eternal chess game, did not understand the question.

Anna hurried out of the room, cursing the pair of them. She changed out of her creased denim jacket and trousers and went down to eat tough stew; Mayhew and the doctor had failed to get the hang of the old stove. Oleg was subdued at lunch but more lucid than ever. All might yet be well.

In the afternoon, she went for a walk in the woods with Mayhew and Oleg, both very gallant, helping her to step over the roots of trees. Mayhew had a professional bonhomie that she associated with male nurses or even bodyguards. He kept saying "There you go ..." They walked along an easy track, and saw the remains of Sam's old tree house in a mighty cedar. Oleg made some remark in Russian and when she turned to him he was distressed, pale and gasping. He backed against a tree trunk and would not speak English any more. When she came closer he shouted at her, harsh words, invective. Mayhew, whose Russian was good, drew her aside.

"Take it easy," he said. "He's talking to someone else. Maybe to his wife."

Kirrilow was wide-eyed. She guessed he was telling someone to go, get away, leave him alone. He stood propped against the tree in Wallace's check shirt and abused his young wife, Galina, who had left him more than twenty years ago and settled down with a film-maker.

"I don't like what he's saying," muttered Chet Mayhew.

"What is it?"

"Oh, the Doc said there was no risk," he said, "but I always hate it. He talks of death. Of dying ... you know, ending it all."

Anna lost her temper. She went up to Kirrilow and shouted, "Oleg, you bastard, I'm up to here with this shit! I took too goddamn much of it from Wallace! Snap out of it and let us help you!"

Kirrilow blinked and said crossly, "No need to shout!"

"What was bothering you?" she demanded.

"Nothing. I don't remember," he said, sulking. "It was that . . . that platform in the tree. Reminded me of a guard's tower in the grounds of the asylum."

She went closer to him and gripped his big, soft hands. She said firmly, "You are safe here. You're in Maine, U.S.A., in Wallace's house. No one is threatening you. You want to live . . . to start a new life!"

He looked at her keenly and replied in the same manner, angry but straightforward, "I'm not at all sure about that."

He walked between her and Mayhew, blundering along the track back towards the house. They followed him in silence. Anna was determined to press her advantage, if she had one. She sat Kirrilow down in the living room, poured him a vodka and asked, "Why did they give you such a bad time, Oleg?"

"They didn't," he said. "I wasn't important to them. As a young man I was one of the performers, you know? I was an artist, permitted to travel about in Europe. Helsinki, West Berlin, Zürich, even Paris. I never took advantage, never abused my privileges. How else could I have kept up a real friendship with Wallace and Fay and yourself? Perhaps I was cowardly in my choice of themes and books to translate. At any rate, I led a charmed life. I was poor, of course, but relatively honest. Then, just as my poems and the translations of English classical authors began to do a little better, my publisher got into trouble over another matter. We fell together. I had no influential friends. So the bad time began at last."

"Oleg, why did they let you go?"

"I put in many applications."

He downed a second drink.

"I am old and mad," he said. "They were afraid."

The light was fading; tree shadows had spread into the room. Anna felt that this was Kirrilow as she remembered him: sad, self-centered. She was filled with compassion.

"Please, Oleg," she said, "please take care. Please take heart. Surely you have much to live for . . ."

He took another drink and fixed her with his glittering eye. "Come into the dreamwood, Anna."

"No," she said, "no, I'm damned if I will. But I will be here when you wake. I was thinking of Christmas, here in this house in the woods. With Sam and Laurel, if she is his girl, and Frances, my own daughter, you've never met her, and her husband Dick,

DREAMWOOD

and her two sons, Wally and Gray. A real Christmas, with turkey and a tree . . . it has been so long . . ."

"Simple pleasures!" he said loftily. "And that great booby Sam was babbling away at lunch about the Nutcracker Suite. To think that I once longed with all my heart . . ."

"Leave Sam alone. He knows nothing."

"You're telling me!" said Oleg.

She could not help laughing, although she called him a brute. This was how they had talked in the Hotel Esplanade. If she turned her head the woman she would see reflected in the window's dark mirror would be a younger version of herself, with a smooth fall of dark hair. Laurel Weiss came in, wagged her finger at them, and took away the vodka bottle. Anna turned on a lamp and Kirrilow built up the fire. There was a coming and going of automobiles before the house: Sam came in with pizzas, french fries, thick shakes. It turned out that Mayhew had gone to spend the night in a motel.

"Just a precaution," murmured Laurel.

"Hey, Oleg," said Sam, "I must give you a copy of Mom's book, with all her games."

"He is a thoughtful boy, Anna," said Kirrilow, "to give me a book of his mother's games."

Anna could not meet his eyes, but the heavy irony did not register on Sam or on the doctor. They sat comfortably together in the firelight, and Laurel said, "We must do the preparation."

"Stay with us, Anna," said Oleg Kirrilow softly. "Doctor . . . tell Anna every step so that she is no longer afraid."

"I can't go along," she said.

"Hush . . ." said Oleg. "We will just show you."

"You might change your mind," said Sam. "All we do is meditate a little. We think of the wood, the dreamwood."

He reached out and took her hand on one side, as Oleg did on the other. Laurel, on a leather hassock, completed the circle. Anna thought of the woods near the house; she thought of the northern forests and birch groves of Russia, Kirrilow's homeland. Laurel came in like a voice-over in a documentary film: "We have all taken our first induction capsules . . . they keep working with time-regulated dosage. To return to the shared image pattern, we need only put on the sleep helmets upstairs, which help create a particular sleep rhythm. Anna, you can take part in the experiment even if you don't take the inductor capsule.

I believe that our combined image strength can draw you into
the dreamwood even in natural sleep. Certainly it would do so
if you took the capsule . . . you wouldn't need the sleep helmet
with a first dosage. So whatever you decide to do, think of the
dreamwood, help us establish the pattern again and meet there
together as we have done for three nights now . . ."

"Is it like a dream?" asked Anna. "Like a *real* dream, with
changes of atmosphere, changes of shape . . . is it truly dreamlike,
or more like an hallucination?"

"Better than a dream," said Sam. "The action is clearer, more
controlled. You can speak to each other, communicate . . ."

"Make love," said Laurel. "Eat and drink. Take notes and recall
them afterwards."

"*In the forest of the dream*
The poet makes and unmakes his bracken bed."

Kirrilow was quoting his favorite author in his own trans-
lation.

"*Memories fall thick as leaves . . .*"

Anna said, "So that is where you found the dreamwood!"

He smiled and pressed her hand. She wished she could remember the next lines of the poem. Was it called "Elegy"? Soon
afterwards, Laurel was satisfied with the preparation. The three
dreamers bade Anna goodnight and went upstairs, leaving her
with only a large capsule of an exquisite violet blue. She rolled
it around on the coffee table, hunting for yet another literary
reference . . . there was a violet capsule and it hadn't worked.

Free association brought nothing except a feeling that the
author was unpopular in this house, on Wallace's black list.
She settled down to an uncomfortable evening; it was barely
eight o'clock. She was weary, but she dared not sleep . . . if she
did manage to drop off naturally, she would wake again at twelve
or at two.

Anna threw out food containers, then washed the dishes remaining from lunch. It was too late to drink coffee, too early for a
night-cap. She considered calling Abe Brodski in New York, or
her good friend Nell in the shabby atelier in New Jersey where
they did industrial photography. She considered shrieking with
frustration and anxiety. She searched for a volume entitled *Soviet
Nature Poets* from the Freedom Press, and realized it was probably
in the study upstairs where Laurel was dreaming. She found, as one
always did, a book she had wanted to re-read . . . the biography of

DREAMWOOD

a woman writer. So the hours passed; she made a cup of tea; and read on and on.

She finished her book between two and three, and crept warily to bed, as if the upper floors might be full of trees and forest creatures. She was unpleasantly tired, but her nerves still jangled. She placed the blue inductor capsule in a bowl on the dressing table of the guest room and took two of her own sleeping pills. She slept deeply and did not dream at all.

II

The sun came into the guest room and blazed at her from the mirror and the vase of maple leaves. Anna was cold; there was not much warmth in the autumn sun. She lay wide-awake after her dreamless sleep and heard the absolute forbidding silence of the house. Her watch was lying somewhere about, maybe in the bathroom, but it must be getting on for ten o'clock. The dreamers slept late. She pulled up a down quilt and still shivered.

This was an old nightmare of hers: to be awake in the morning while the whole world slept in. Everyone had done this to her, first her parents, then Wallace. Wallace and Sam and even Fran, they were all late sleepers. She got up now with the silence of the upper floor weighing upon her spirit, and dressed. She scuffled into her track suit so as. to be the one in the house who was dressed, ready to answer the phone or deal with callers.

In the kitchen, she continued a long double take over the time of day. Her watch lay on the bench; it had stopped shortly after midnight, ten after twelve. She put on the coffee and went into the living room. When she drew the curtains the sunlight streamed in; she went to sweep out the grate and saw the digital clock on the mantelpiece. Twelve after twelve. Hey . . . she had slept for eight, nine hours! She heard the coffee plunking, the birds singing, the wind in the trees. Her heart thumped painfully. The dreamers had slept for *fifteen hours*.

She sat anxiously at the kitchen table, drinking her coffee. This was how it would be, she cursed, the whole deal was programmed. She was alone with them, not knowing whether to wake them. Surely it was unhealthy, wrong for them to sleep so long. She *must* look . . . must look and somehow not recall how she had run up those stairs once before, and looked, and found Wallace dead in his sleep in the room where Kirrilow now slept.

She went to Sam first of all. He looked terrible, comically awful, sprawled all over his too-small bed like Frankenstein's monster, in a plastic headband and a pair of thermo trousers. His face was pale, he breathed noisily through his mouth. Anna gritted her teeth, ready to cope with his displeasure; she slipped off the plastic headband and tried to wake him. She worked on him for a quarter of an hour, beginning with timid pats and whispers, quickly followed by shaking, *violent* shaking, shouts and cries. Sam moved only once, jack-knifing into a foetal position; his face did not move. He groaned faintly when she pulled his hair and tweaked his nose, but his eyes remained tightly shut and she did not try to pry them open. What came after sleep? Was he stuporous? In a coma? Were these states blurred now because of the inductor drug and the sleep headband? She covered him with the patchwork quilt, climbed down from the attic and stormed into the study.

Laurel Weiss slept neatly, and reacted a little more than Sam had done. Anna boldly removed the headband and turned back the bed clothes. Maybe if she was colder, the girl would wake. She understood the use of the thermo trousers . . . necessary equipment for wanderers in the dreamwood: they had a waste system. Was this a sign that the dreamers expected to sleep very deeply and for a long time?

She went to the bookcase and took down *Soviet Nature Poets*, then drifted around to the main bedroom. She stood in the doorway, stilling the beating of her heart, and watched Oleg Kirrilow. He lay propped up on his pillows, smiling faintly, with his arms stretched out on top of the bedclothes. She turned to the poem he had quoted and found that it was called "Threnody":

In the forest of the dream
The poet makes and unmakes his bracken bed.
Memories fall thick as leaves
But he brushes them aside . . . treads down
all his former loves,
The old cruel systems, the lost children,
(Only a child reared is a child worth loving)
So he returns at last to his wood, his world,
The shade of his mothering trees,
Where he can roam untrammeled, singing
a last song,
Passing through nature to a wished oblivion . . .

DREAMWOOD

There was more of it, but Anna did not turn the page. As she stood staring at the sleeping poet, angrily wishing him to wake, the electric buzzer from the front gate rang downstairs and continued ringing in staccato bursts. She went flying down to answer it.

" . . . Highway Patrol, Ma'am." She had not caught the officer's name. "Is that Ms. Gordon?"

"Yes," she said. "I'm just on my way to the gate to fetch the mail. I'll speak to you there, okay?"

She jogged down the drive. Hold the fort. Keep away the press and the police. Two academics and a refugee poet comatose in her house.

Sergeant Schmidt smiled warily; he had his cap off, revealing thick fair hair. They got younger every year.

"Trouble at your turn-off, Ma'am," he said. "Driver of a Ford Fiesta, light gray. Ran into a tree."

He rattled off the license number; Anna was gripping the top of the metal gate.

"Recognize the car, Ms. Gordon?" The sergeant nodded at his colleague, sitting at the wheel of the patrol car. "We had an idea he was coming to the Professor's house. Charles Edward Mayhew . . . address on the campus of John Latimer University College."

"We know him," said Anna. "He was coming to visit us. He's an associate of my son, Sam Gordon. Is he . . . ?"

"Doesn't look good," said the sergeant. "I guess he has a skull fracture. Does your son know his folks?"

"I don't think so," she said. "Where is he now?"

"On the way to the hospital in Bingham," said the sergeant.

"This is a terrible thing . . ."

The young man looked at her with professional sympathy and shook his head.

"I'll tell Sam," she said. She almost added "Is there anything we can do?" but then drew back. If the sergeant asked to talk to Sam, she would say he was out walking in the woods.

"You okay, Ms. Gordon?"

"Yes," she said. "Yes, thank you. I'll tell Sam what happened. We'll call the hospital."

"Don't forget your mail, Ms. Gordon."

"Sergeant . . . how did it happen? Was there a collision?"

"No," he said. "Looked as though he just collapsed at the wheel."

Anna jogged back up the drive through the uncut grass, clutching a wine brochure and a catalogue of rare books; Wallace had always received high class junk mail. Wake! she shouted in her mind as she came up to the house. Inside she found her voice and shouted and roared at the sleepers.

"Wake up! Wake up! Mayhew is hurt! You have nearly killed him with your dreaming!"

The silence flowed back when she stopped yelling; the house creaked a little, was scraped by tree branches; the pipes sighed. She was filled with a sick, paralyzing anxiety for Sam. She had been the only one left to look after him, and she had failed, had delivered him into the power of mad Kirrilow and the little doctor. She must wake the doctor first . . .

Laurel went on tip toe over the soft grass of the clearing and began to dance, raising her hands above her head. The old man was watching her from the larch trees, Sam was still asleep in the tree house. As she danced, naked, she was able to recapitulate. There was a distinct sense of time-lapse here, she noted. Kirrilow had led her on a merry chase at first, hiding, running, raising up thickets and ancient tracts of forest where the leaf mold was knee-deep and the mossed trunks of fallen trees, soaked by the melting snows, formed a morass. All his doing. She tried to add nothing, but it was nearly impossible. For instance, she must soften the grass for her dancing floor. Of course, she had managed an interview with the old man in the course of the session. When he'd come back, black-browed, clutching a sporting gun, over-excited about the tree house, which he took for a watchtower; the same excitement Chet had reported from the afternoon walk. She had calmed him in the usual way, with her smile, her wise/girlish look, the touch of her hands. She moved her hands now, beckoning and fluttering. The morning wind made her shiver. Kirrilow had been in a strange mood. He had enthroned himself on a tree stump and begun drinking vodka from a silver flask. Spoke jeeringly of women, saying they were all whores. When Sam had come to join them the old man was abusive, calling him a son-of-a-bitch. Then the old man had smiled and seemed to relent—called them his poor lost children, his babes in the wood, spoke of them all being covered with leaves while he sang a last song. Time-lapse. There was the

DREAMWOOD

place! Laurel ran across to where she had left her clothes; she slipped into her old blue joggers, which did not seem to have too much warmth in them.

There was a loud shout from the larch trees beside the swift-flowing brook. She ran across and saw Chet Mayhew lying upon the farther bank. He was hurt, blood ran down his face, he groaned and mouthed horribly.

"Whose image is this?" cried Laurel. "Who put *you* here? . . . you're not here, Chet!"

"Laurie, wake up!" panted Chet. "The old devil has smashed me!"

Kirrilow, in his hunting gear—a kind of Norfolk jacket and cap—came out of the trees beside the injured man. He carried a blood-stained tomahawk. My God, would this make a paper for the journal! Dream killing! Blood! Complete submergence in the dream matrix!

"Why did you do that?" she called. "Oleg? You made an image of Chet Mayhew and killed him. He isn't in the wood. He's miles away."

"Alas, yes," said Oleg Kirrilow. "Too far away now. I am no friend of secret policemen."

He flung aside the hatchet and stood near the body of Mayhew, which wavered and faded. It turned into a heap of leaves. Kirrilow sat down, smiling, and lit a pipe.

"I have immortal longings in me," he said. "Sleep some more, child."

She sat down cross-legged on the grass and grew a small birch tree, a berioska, to lean against. She was sleepy; time spun out.

"Anna didn't show after all," she said dreamily. "Are you sad, Oleg, because your Nanuschka stood you up?"

"Stupid child," said Kirrilow. "Anna is the *new* wife. She is *not* the Nanuschka whose name I called."

"That's interesting," said Laurel, sitting up eagerly. "I must make a note . . ."

As she stood up, a whole section of the bank gave way and she plunged into the icy waters of the brook.

Anna stood back grimly, holding the bucket of ice-water. The girl sat up, gasping and shrieking. Her eyes, wide open, focussed on Anna at last.

"Are you c-crazy . . . ?"

"Wake up!" said Anna. "Wake up quickly, Doctor. Chet Mayhew is badly hurt. He crashed his car."

She handed Laurel Weiss a towel. The girl reacted as quickly as she could have wished.

"What time is it?" she demanded.

"One o'clock, thirteen hours?" said Anna. "Sam is still sleeping. Kirrilow is a madman."

Laurel Weiss sprang from the soaked couch and went into the bathroom. She came out in seconds, wearing an old bathrobe, checked Kirrilow first, then climbed the ladder and checked Sam. Anna stood in the passageway and shouted information. Laurel came down from the attic and flung past her, going down the stairs. Anna went after her, shouting angrily: "Wake him up! Wake Sam! Give him a shot!"

"Sam is fine!" said the girl. "Ms. Gordon, Anna, you're freaking out . . . do you know that? Calm down. Let me have some coffee."

"Do you want me to call the John Latimer Clinic?" said Anna. "Do you want me to call the police, and an ambulance?"

"The phone is out," said Laurel. "It's disconnected."

She poured two fresh beakers of coffee and sat down at the kitchen table in a patch of sunlight. Anna saw that she was shivering a little with shock and cold. She sat down herself.

"You think *he* did that?" Laurel whispered. "You think Oleg kept us in the dreamwood until Chet drove back . . . then drew him in, made him fall asleep at the wheel . . . ?"

"Yes!" said Anna. "He is suicidal. And dangerous. He is full of hatred. He does not mean to wake."

"He wouldn't harm Sam. He couldn't. The son of his old friends . . ."

"*His own son*," said Anna. "His lost child. He still half believes it. But he's not satisfied with Sam. Neither was Wallace."

"What are you talking about?"

"I was never Kirrilow's lover," said Anna. "It was Fay Gordon, Sam's mother, the chess player. The three of them, Fay, Wallace, and Oleg, were a *menage à trois*, in Zürich, wherever they met. Oleg was convinced that *he* was the father of Fay's child. I never knew what Fay herself thought. They all remained friends . . . argued, suffered, agonized about the child."

"Blood tests?"

"Inconclusive," said Anna. "In Zagreb, years later, Kirrilow

DREAMWOOD

suggested that Fay and Wallace had falsified the tests."

"Crazy," said Laurel. "And they said nothing to Sam! *You* knew . . . *you* said nothing."

"Sam was a difficult enough child without laying *this* on him," said Anna. "Wallace was very demanding. He was also a hard act to follow. Sam would have run away for good if there had been the slightest suggestion that Wallace was not his father."

"You're to blame as much as anyone," said Laurel. "This is a big study in parental incompetence."

"Wake Sam," said Anna, "or this will be a big study in malpraxis. Drug misuse. A gift for those East-Bloc alienists who sent Kirrilow away so that he could commit suicide in the west."

"I don't accept this notion that Oleg is suicidal!"

"Oleg spoke of 'ending it all' . . . he spoke of it in Russian, and Chet Mayhew warned you of these death threats!"

"He can't offer violence to anyone in the dreamwood . . ."

"Consciously or unconsciously, he managed to harm *Mayhew*," said Anna. "How did Kirrilow behave? What did he say?"

Laurel sipped her coffee. "He called us both his children," she said. "Yes . . . I hate to do this piecemeal. It makes me botch the total recall of the notes. He called Sam and me his poor lost children . . . he said we should all be covered with leaves while he sang a last song . . ."

"I beg you . . . get Sam away from that crazy old man!"

"Yes," said Laurel Weiss slowly. "Okay. But take it easy. You must help me. I'm going to have to obtain certain equipment. I'll also call the hospital . . . see how Chet is doing."

"Equipment?" said Anna in a choked voice.

"I want them both on a drip. I don't want to try a jolt on Sam, certainly not on Kirrilow."

"For God's sake . . ."

"Will you listen, Anna? I want you to go into the dreamwood to help me. You're the only one who can do it."

Anna gave a gusty sigh. She heard the sounds of the house and of the trees outside the house stretching away to the mountains and to the sea.

"I slept a long time last night," she said. "I may have trouble dropping off. . . ."

Anna wakes after a short confused dream of Wallace and the children. She is fully dressed, even to her boots; she flings aside the quilt and goes to the window. Yes, she must go into the wood. And with that thought she is *in* the wood, standing by the old cedar. She takes in the exquisite new reality of the dreamwood, feels the bark of the cedar, speaks aloud and hears herself speak. It is so beautiful: the old cedar tree stands on a small hill in the midst of a springtime birch forest. The trunks of the trees are black in shadow, silvery when the light strikes them. Through the feathery green of the underbrush she glimpses the still waters of a lake.

"*Anna?*"

She starts at the sound of the voice, then watches calmly as Sam comes down the ladder from the tree house.

"Hey, what a great session," he says. "I can tell you're not just an image. You really did it!"

His voice is strange, a voice half in her mind.

"Where is Oleg?" she asks awkwardly.

"He was here a while back."

He touches her arm and leads the way down the hill. She follows eagerly, looking at the path, a rough ordinary track through the bracken.

"Wait, Sam! Do we see the same wood? Do we see this same path?"

"Sure," he says. "We alter the wood unconsciously all the time, and we accept the changes that others make."

Before them lies a clearing among the birch trees, and what she took to be a lake is a little rushing stream with fir trees and blue spruce and other gaunt, dark conifers growing thick and wild upon the further bank. The wood itself and the dream state intoxicate her; she looks up to the sky and twirls around like a child, watching the tops of the trees. She looks down giddily and watches bluebells, crocuses, and daffodils growing in the soft grass at the base of the birch trees. Kirrilow is there. She can sense him. She looks about for him, but sees only a movement among the branches across the stream.

"Sam . . ."

She must run, leaping over a few fallen branches, to catch up to him, far across the clearing.

"Sam . . . listen to me!"

"What?"

"Laurel wants you to end the session. To wake as soon as you can."

"Aw, come on now . . ."

He is unbelieving, balky, childish. She feels a rush of irritation; she shakes his arm. This was how it used to be, a continual pushing and pulling, daylong, yearlong. The raising of Sam: stubborn, moody, ornery from sun up, when he would not wake, to sundown, when he began the long fight against going to bed.

"Okay," says Anna. "You're all grown up, Sam. But that is the message."

"Laurie wouldn't leave the group!" he says angrily.

"She is awake. I swear it. *Please* end the session."

Sam stretches his arms high above his head, and leaps up to touch a certain branch. It is an expression of his freedom and well-being. He shouts out loud, "Hey, Oleg! Oleg Kirrilow! Look who's here!"

Anna gestures to him—even cries out "No! No!"—but he grins and dances away like a schoolboy, crying out again.

"Here's Anna Hay, Anna Hay . . . come to spoil our fun . . ."

A bear-like shape parts the branches of two ragged trees; Kirrilow stands upon the far bank of the river, wearing a long officer's greatcoat slung over his hunting dress. Anna perceives that he is young, younger than she has ever seen him. He has all his hair again, thick and golden-brown, carelessly cropped at the level of his strong jaw. His voice is powerful; he speaks in Russian, very slow and clear, for her to understand.

"*Send away the whore's son!*"

"Be damned to you!" says Anna. "Speak English. Send him away yourself!"

Kirrilow spreads his arms and lifts his noble head. He utters a long sad cry, full of passion, full of pain.

"*I was a poet!*" he says, before the echoes have died away. "*I strove all my life . . .*"

"You were and *are* a mean, egotistical pain in the ass!" replies Anna. "You're also a coward. You tried to murder Chet Mayhew!"

Sam is deeply affronted; he dances about, seizes Anna by the arm.

"Are you out of your mind? You can't talk to Oleg that way!" He calls to Kirrilow, "Don't take any notice of her . . . she's crazy. It's only old Anna Hay . . ."

"My dear boy," says Kirrilow nastily.

He seats himself upon a convenient stump and takes from the

pocket of his greatcoat a pipe that seems to be permanently alight. When he puffs, polluting the dreamwood, Anna can smell nothing.

"Anna, the *new* wife . . ." he muses. "Have we come so far, my dear, that you abuse me? Why have you come so late to the forest of dreams? I think it is a put-up job from the little doctor. You're trying to rile me, to provoke me so that I will wake. I am proof against your polemic, Anna Hay."

"Is that what you're doing, trying to make him mad?" asks Sam. "*Is* Laurel awake? Did she leave us?"

"Yes!" cries Anna. "Sam . . . wake up!"

Kirrilow roars with laughter.

"What a fool! What a booby! And *that* should be my own son? *That* should be the son of Wallace Gordon? I think Nanuschka, our blonde fairy-fay, betrayed *both* her lovers, and chose a moron to sire her child."

"Like I said," Anna hears her voice tremble. "A cruel and cowardly old man."

She turns towards Sam and watches him very closely. His dreamwood face is a composite of his real face, like the eerie composite photograph of Lombroso's "criminal type." In his wavering features at that moment Anna can discern both his putative fathers, as well as the unworldly look of his mother as a young woman. He staggers, puts out a long arm to steady himself against a tree, and stands firm. He looks at last exactly like Sam, thirty-five years old; he takes in the information so long withheld and does not protest or fidget. She sees that he has grown up after all. It is so great a relief that she begins to weep. She feels hot tears welling out of her eyes and coursing down her cheeks.

"Don't cry," says Sam. "After all this time, it's not important what they did."

She shakes her head, trying to smile at him.

"What's with Mayhew?" he asks.

"He collapsed over the wheel of his car down at the end of our road. He's in the hospital."

"Come on, now!" says Sam. "That's his heart, or maybe the inductors . . . not Oleg. What time of day is it?"

"I entered the wood at fourteen hours."

"I'll wake. Anna, come with me. Leave him here."

"Stay!" roars Kirrilow. "This is my country. Stay with me! *You cannot leave the dreamwood . . .*"

DREAMWOOD

Sam runs off into the wood, putting his hands over his ears. Anna feels faint with the effort of imparting so much information. Straight talk is not the language of the dreamwood. She sinks down on the soft grass and leans against a convenient birch tree.

"I read your poem," she says. " 'Threnody.' "

"A free rendering," says Kirrilow. "It is always better in Russian."

The euphoria of the place is taking hold of her again; she floats and soars. Kirrilow is intoning his verses softly in his own language. At last she says, "Oleg, you've stayed too long in the dreamwood. You should wake."

"I will never leave my little kingdom," he says. "I am healed! I am young again! I have total recall . . . well, very nearly. I can summon up remembrance of things past."

As he speaks, a young woman in gray trousers and a short fur coat comes slowly out of the trees on his side of the stream. It is Fay Gordon. Anna watches with a soft detachment which is another property of the dreamwood state. She perceives that Fay has no independent life, not even the waywardness of a ghost. Oleg has summoned up this image, but he cannot talk to his old love, or take her hand.

"Oh, come on now!" calls Anna, echoing Sam. "You can remember better than *that*. Wake up! Start living again!"

Oleg is enraged. He turns away from the image of young Fay and it fades at once. He throws up his arms as he comes to the bank of the stream and a bridge of logs is ready for him to cross. He rushes down upon Anna, but she is too fast for him. She is not quite brave enough to sit still and see if he can touch her.

"Run then, you foolish woman!" he cries. "Go far and wide! *You will never come out of the forest of the dream!*"

Anna turns to face him, marveling still at the trees, the grass, the foliage taking on the autumn colors of the wood around the house.

"Oleg," she says, pleading. "Why should we quarrel? I came to help you. I'm your friend."

"Never!" he says, shaking his handsome head. "You are a meddler, a person of no understanding. Wallace had your measure, oh yes! How he bewailed your incompetence, your triviality, your second class mind! See . . . *that* hurts you, Anna Plurabella. That was what Wallace said in Zagreb, while we enjoyed in turn the little Intourist girl, the fat one. How he laughed at your prudishness in the Palm Court, your pathetic loyalty!"

Anna feels sick, punch-drunk. She tries to crack back at him, but has no words left, either soothing or angry. She blunders off into the wood to hide her shame and embarrassment. Oleg Anton Kirrilow. Always their friend. One name never black-listed in their house. I had to meddle, she tells herself, leaning against a sturdy oak, I had to give it a try. She feels sure that Sam is awake now, he is safe. She leans against the oak, eyes closed, thinking "I will wake soon."

The first person that she sees when she opens her eyes is Sam. Laurel Weiss stands at the foot of her bed, neat and unruffled.

"Very good!" she says briskly.

"Sam," says Anna, "are you okay?"

"Fine . . . just fine . . ."

His voice seems to come from a long way off. Anna lets sweet relief wash over her for a few seconds, than croaks guiltily, "How is Oleg? How is poor Mayhew?"

"Responding to treatment," says Laurel Weiss.

Anna turns her head on the pillow, but she cannot see Sam any more. She sees the chest of drawers with its vase of red maple leaves. More than that, a whole maple tree, right there in her room. She begins to be afraid. She stares at the doctor. Laurel Weiss lifts her arms above her head, smiling. Her limbs and trunk are defined first; as the change sweeps over her the girl's face becomes lost in a shower of bright green leaves. She turns into a birch tree.

Anna, sick with disappointment, is back in the wood again.

She is completely lost now, with nothing to guide her. She wanders desolately, uphill and down dale. She feels Kirrilow's presence like a dark cloud, piling up above the wood. She hears a murmur of voices. Beside the path in a patch of sunlight a boy and girl are playing. Sam is showing little Fran how to build a wigwam. He has three broomsticks tied at the top and an old striped blanket that they call "the Indian blanket." She watches with sad delight. The wood is full of life and movement; she sees a pair of chickadees on a branch overhead. She passes a patch of brambles and eats ripe blackberries. She should pick some and take them back to make a pie. It is not so far to the house now,

DREAMWOOD

she can almost see it through the trees. Going home.

A man in a checkered shirt, blue and gray, comes out of the trees and walks ahead of her down the path. He turns and waits for her: it is not Kirrilow, it is Wallace. It is Wallace as he lived, a compromise between the thin, stiffly-erect old man he became and the jauntier, smiling scholar she married.

"Don't dawdle!" he says. "We must get you home!"

"Will walking do it?" asks Anna wearily.

"Yes. Keep going," Wallace orders.

"Oleg is here somewhere . . ."

"I know. I know everything that you know," Wallace says. "If you think back . . . which I wouldn't really enjoin you to do . . . you'll see that Kirrilow's outburst, which upset you so much, was an ingenious—a poetical—arrangement of half-truths. And the bit about the poor Russian girl was complete nonsense."

"You're just saying that," she grumbles. "You're just a figment of my imagination."

"You're right for once!"

He smiles and lifts an eyebrow in a way that she once found charming.

"Remember this," he says, "you stuck it out the longest."

"Do you mean that I knew you best?"

"Possibly," says Wallace.

He runs up a steep bank and comes to the cedar tree.

"Wives always think that they know a fellow best," Wallace continues. "What was it that the poor Welshman's wife said in a preface . . . 'An intensive handful of meetings, at divided intervals, do not do justice to the circumference of the subject.' I haven't got it quite right but it sums up the relationship I had with Oleg Kirrilow."

"You weren't a poet," she says irrelevantly.

"Thank your lucky stars!" says Wallace.

He reaches up with a youthful spring, catches a branch of the cedar tree and swings on it for a second. Anna recognizes a kind of physical restlessness, a young man's trait that Wallace had almost grown out of by the time she met him . . . a trait that she swears Kirrilow has never possessed. Yet Sam shows it very strongly.

"Hurry!" says Wallace. "We have no more to say to each other. This vile drug-induced forest-of-the-dream is no place for a reconciliation."

He strides on down the path towards the house. A wind follows him, tossing the branches of the trees and tearing down leaves in handfuls. Anna watches him go through a changing season, fall into winter; clouds rush across the sky in time-lapse vortices. She is unutterably tired of being in the dreamwood. She turns to the north and sees the Fimbul winter hastening down upon her from the Canadian wild. The snow is dry and gritty, drifting upon the steps of the tree house. Oleg comes wearily out of the low door; he is no longer young.

"Let's go back to the house," says Anna.

"You are a brilliant image-maker," he sighs. "Wallace . . . very life-like. Let me take my walk, Anna. You wake if you can."

He goes off through the thick snow, leaving a deep track into the pines. He is not dressed for winter, she reflects; perhaps he will lie down in the snow and fall asleep. She considers following him, saving him some way, sending a bear after him. She decides not to meddle. She is too tired. She drags herself up the steps of the tree house; inside it is lined with fur and feathers, a cozy nest. She curls up and sleeps, and after an unknown passage of time, dreamwood time or other time, she half wakes to a wisp of down which brushes her cheek, then her chin.

She thrust it away, trying to sleep, to burrow into her nest, but the stroking of her face went on more firmly. She ungummed her eyelids. Sam was wiping her face with a wet washcloth.

"Anna?" he asked fearfully. "Anna, are you awake?"

She groaned aloud.

"I hope so," she said. "*Am* I awake, Sam?"

It was dark outside. Sam was pale and subdued. She jumped when a tree struck the window, but it kept its distance. She was awake. She flexed her limbs, remembering the feel of her dreamwood body, how it imitated life.

"What's the time?" she demanded. "How long have I slept?" And then, remembering, "How is Chet Mayhew?"

"He was lucky. He has a bad concussion, but he'll pull through."

"How is Oleg? Is he awake?"

"He'll be fine," said Sam. "He's just coming round. Laurel is with him and a male nurse from the Latimer Clinic. You want to look in on him?"

"No," said Anna.

DREAMWOOD

"You want to get up? There's coffee and toast . . ."

"What time did you say it was?"

"Around eleven. Twenty-three hours."

They went down and sat by the fire and held no post mortem on the dreamwood session. Presently, Laurel Weiss came down to join them. Anna saw how very neat she was, trim and clean and controlled. She came to Anna, smiling, and tried to shake her hand.

"We're getting some amazing stuff from the session," she said. "You are a marvelous subject, Anna. Oleg is full of admiration."

"Did you have trouble waking him?" asked Anna.

"A little. He has explained it . . . his reluctance to leave the dreamwood."

"Dr. Weiss," said Anna, "how is Kirrilow's general health? Are you quite sure of the strength of his heart?"

"Yes," said the little doctor. "He has to take things easy, but he is quite sound."

"Great," said Anna. "Then you can move him to the clinic tomorrow morning early. You can use the new station wagon if you prefer it."

They stared at her, appalled. Sam began to wave his arms; he mouthed, but no sound came.

"Your old friend!" said Laurel Weiss. "In his present state . . ."

"That's impossible!" shouted Sam. "Anna, how can you be so goddamned cruel to the poor old guy. . . ."

"Will you tell him, Ms. Gordon?" said Laurel. "Will you please speak with Kirrilow?"

"No," said Anna. "No, not any more. Nor with you, Dr. Weiss. Sam is the only person welcome in this house. I'll just make myself comfortable in this room until you have all gone."

She settled by the fire and found herself books, even a piece of knitting. It had started out as a sweater for Wallace, now she decided it would do for herself. She felt as if she would never need to sleep again. She walked out on to the verandah and looked at the stars and the sleeping woods, stretching far into the north, home of the winter. Christmas alone, why not? Or with Nell, or even in Mexico.

At seven o'clock, when it was getting light, she heard them escort Kirrilow down the stairs. Sam came into the living room and said, "Anna, this is some crazy *reaction* of yours. Oleg has nowhere else to go. He might . . . hell, he might even be . . ."

"He isn't your father," she said. "I decided that he isn't. And I bet you recall Fay telling you one thing . . . that Wallace *was* your father. Because it was true."

"Yes," he said. "Maybe she did. But all the same . . . Oleg . . ."

She turned her head away. She sat in the armchair that Kirrilow had used the day before and listened to them trying to start their cold engines. My God, she thought, what a mean woman you are. What a terrible thing to do to that poor old man. She smiled. She could not help smiling. A procession of automobiles roared away down the drive; the silence was broken only by the creaking of the house, the cry of a bird, the wind in the trees. I will write it all down, she thought. She even had a special book to write it in. Her grandson Wally, Fran's eldest boy, had given her a fat travel diary with the words *My Trip* embossed in gold.

Anna finished another row of knitting and took a sip of cold coffee. Her fault. Her foolishness. Pandering to Sam and his girl, to Oleg and his fantasies, to Wallace and the narrowing vision of an old, sick man. She had played along with all of them for too long. Had the dreamwood taught her that? Was there any value in the dreamwood experience, in Shared Recreational Dreaming? She must do a little reading on altered states. The words sent a shiver down her spine; she shut her eyes and saw the birch trees, heard the rushing stream. *I am in an altered state of consciousness,* she thought.

At last. At last.

REALM OF THE SENSES

Geoffrey A. Landis

"Realm of the Senses" was purchased by Gardner Dozois, and appeared in the Mid-December 1990 issue of Asimov's, with an illustration by Pat Morrissey. A physicist engaged in doing solar cell research, Geoffrey A. Landis is also a frequent contributor to Asimov's Science Fiction and Analog, as well as having sold to Interzone, Amazing, and Pulphouse. His story "Ripples in the Dirac Sea," an Asimov's story, won him a Nebula Award in 1989, and his story "A Walk in the Sun," another Asimov's story, won a Hugo Award in 1992. His first collection, Myths, Legends, and True History, was also published in 1992. He lives in Brook Park, Ohio.

Here he gives us a harrowing look at an all-too-plausible future amusement. . . .

Disorientation and transformation: a maelstrom of lights and sound and color. She screamed.

Reb Shenkel would really rather have had a son, but he loved his daughter no less for his disappointment. The family had no abundance, but there was always enough, and Rachel grew up enfolded in an atmosphere of unspoken love.

When Rachel reached thirteen she was betrothed, and for the first time met the boy she was to marry. He was tall and awkward, two years older than she, from the next village down the river, where she would go to live when she was married. His name was Isaac. He had dark liquid eyes, and she dreamed of him for weeks. He would come over on the Sabbath for dinner, tongue-tied, but unable to keep his eyes off her. Between them there passed a secret understanding. Later, still a year from the wedding, she gave herself to him, completely, unreservedly. He was shy and awkward there, too, and she had to show him what to do (she, who surely could have had no more experience than he!), but the next time was better, and the time after that better yet. She didn't love him, no, but she had a deep affection for him, and for the moment that was enough. Love, her parents would say contentedly, comes later, after years of marriage. She lived in a world of contentment.

Her world was a circumscribed one, isolated far from the tumult and discord of the world at large. From time to time a traveler would come from outside, and the elders would cluck their tongues at the news from the world, marveling at the folly of man, and light-heartedly speculating that such tidings of disaster surely must mean that the end of all things could not be far away. But the distant news did not much affect their village, save only that itinerant peddlers came less frequently, and on occasion they could see on the horizon the haze of distant smoke. Then one day faint booming sounds could be heard from the distance, and all that day and the next they continued, gradually growing louder. Artillery, said Elder Heilman, the most learned man in the village, who had once traveled as far as distant Krakow before he settled down. The noise went away, but it left behind a feeling of uneasiness in the village, some unspecified dread that no one would speak of directly.

And then the soldiers came, barking out peremptory commands in a guttural language that she could barely understand. They herded all the villagers together in the fields. A few of them

REALM OF THE SENSES

resisted, dragging out ancient rifles from God alone knows what hiding places. Among them was Isaac. He was torn apart by the German machine guns and left to lie in the dust, his eyes registering nothing but surprise, his mouth open as if he had just one more word to say, a truth of great importance, that now no one would ever know. The remaining villagers were crowded into wooden wagons drawn by oxen. The village livestock was slaughtered, and the carcasses loaded onto other ox-drawn wagons. As they left, she could see the flames of the burning village behind her.

In the confusion she had somehow become separated from her parents. They had been loaded on a different wagon, and though she searched for them while the villagers were huddled together with a thousand others at the railway station, she never saw them again.

At the camp, she found true love, in a thin, dark-haired girl named Drusilla. Her ear lobes had been shredded where gold earrings had been ripped out by the soldiers. She was thin and dark with long black hair where Rachel was large and peasantish. She was Romany, and spoke Rachel's language slowly and hesitantly, with peculiar syntax and occasional struggling for words. Nevertheless they would chatter endlessly, at every chance they could. They shared what little food they got, bread and thin soup and the occasional insect they could catch, and combed one another's hair.

It was there that Rachel discovered that Isaac had left her a present, as her belly began to round out even as the rest of her wasted away. She and Drusilla would wonder what sort of world the child would be born to, but that, she knew, was entirely in the hands of God.

Many of the younger girls would offer themselves to the guards, in a futile hope to earn themselves special treatment, but Drusilla and Rachel both vowed never to do such a thing. At night, as they lay crowded together on their narrow shelf, Drusilla would gently stroke Rachel's hair and speak to her softly in her own language, while Rachel would rub her belly, staring into space and thinking of nothing at all.

They could tell that the war was not going well for their captors. The incinerators ran day and night, and replacement guards were ever fewer and ever younger boys. Eventually there was no more bread, and as one week without food went on to another, Rachel knew that her child would never be born alive. She sorrowed for the memory of poor Isaac, whose son would now never walk in his father's footsteps.

Once again there were distant booms to be heard on the horizon. Work at the camp stepped up to a frantic pace.

When at last they were stripped and led into the chambers, Drusilla and Rachel held hands. As the gas began to hiss, while others held their hands over their mouths or tried to hold their breath, they began to softly sing.

Unimaginably far away in both space and time, she returned home.

"Don't you agree," they asked (although not in words; words were far too clumsy and awkward), "that was an experience like no other?"

"Staggering," she said. "Such intensity! And the best part, the most important, was the overwhelming sense of *finite*ness. Whatever happened, it would last only a little while. Such a feeling of," she paused, struggling for the right concept, "*poignancy!*"

"And I loved the way that your memory was removed right at the beginning," said another, "so you could experience it without preconceptions. That was half of what made it so intense!"

"*Pain*," she said, struggling over the concept. "That was another thing. Such an incredible concept. I've never felt anything like it."

"There's a waiting line of almost fifty years," said another. "Let's go again! I hear the next show is going to be even better than the one we just did!"

"Indeed? Let's! What is this one called?"

"I think they call the next show 'Nuclear Holocaust.'"

"I can hardly wait!" she said.

NIGHT WIN

Nancy Kress

"Night Win" was purchased by Shawna McCarthy, and appeared in the September 1983 issue of Asimov's, with an illustration by Bob Walters. It was one of a long sequence of elegant and incisive stories by Kress that have appeared in Asimov's under four different editors over the last decade, since her first Asimov's sale to George Scithers in 1979—stories that have made her one of the most popular of all the magazine's writers.

Here she takes us along to a dangerous and unexplored territory, the inside of the human mind—a hostile and mysterious battlefield upon which a woman must wage a fight she can't win, but can't afford to lose. . . .

Born in Buffalo, New York, Nancy Kress now lives with her family in Brockport, New York. Her books include the novels The Prince of Morning Bells, The Golden Grove, The White Pipes, An Alien Light, *and* Brain Rose, *and the collection* Trinity and Other Stories. *She won both the Hugo and the Nebula Award in 1992 for her novella "Beggars in Spain," an* Asimov's *story; the novel version,* Beggars in Spain, *appeared the following year. Her most recent book is a new collection. She also won a Nebula Award for her story "Out of All Them Bright Stars."*

The river dissolved. One minute it tore through high, dim banks booming with the rapids around the bend; the next it lifted and spread, flooding the air with gray particles that turned from water to smoke to grainy nothingness behind Rachel's eyelids, nothingness spreading in an even wash like blindness like sleep like entropy like stillness like——

"Rachel! Rachel!"

——nothingness——

"Rachel!"

Her ear muffs were yanked off so quickly that the flexible metal band snapped against her temple. She put up one hand to rub the temple, at first unaware that she did so, eyes focusing more slowly than hand. Always the eyes more slowly; the hand remembered first, not deceived. Instinct? It must be instinct. Over her chair, Don's thin body leaned urgently. Her ear muffs dangled from his left hand. Even through the wispy nothingness she could feel the tautness in his body, gone sharp as a bowstring. If she touched him she would bleed.

"Rachel?"

The hospital room sprang into focus: metal bed, tightly woven blue blanket, blue-flowered drapes drawn against the night, miniature plants in a green ceramic pot, a gift from somebody. Dracaena, jade plant, philodendron, schefflera. The schefflera was wilting; probably over-watered. Under the blue blanket Rachel could see Mrs. Angstrom lying still, worn out with not dying.

"Are you all *right*?"

"I——lost it," Rachel said. She closed her eyes, then forced them open again. Sounds, always the last to focus, came leaking in from the corridor: a linen cart rolling by, an elevator door opening with a soft whoosh of air. At the nurse's station around the corner and down the hall someone chuckled. A second later a

NIGHT WIN

different voice murmured, the words indecipherable as a foreign language. Somewhere a phone rang.

"Rachel——can you get back In?"

"Can you?"

"Yes. But now. It has to be now."

Sweat beaded on his upper lip. One hand, Rachel saw, was shaking. Always the hands—even for Don, who had so much control she sometimes hated him.

"It wasn't like the last time," Rachel said slowly. "This was—— nothingness. Just nothingness. I lost it to nothingness." Her big body shuddered.

"There's no *time*. It has to be *now!*"

In the bed Mrs. Angstrom groaned and turned over.

"All right," Rachel said. "All *right*. I'm ready."

Don took her hand. She pulled it away, but then forced herself to leave it in his. He was right; she needed the extra contact, even at the price of the tactile distraction. His fingers were spindly and cold. With her free hand Rachel pulled the ear muffs over her head, leaned back, and closed her eyes.

She slipped In.

The raft had drifted farther towards the rapids—how had it gotten so far downstream? Don was splashing towards it, only his bony, naked shoulders and bobbing head showing above the slimy black water. Another ten yards and he would reach the raft, but the water flowed faster here and his splashing was not narrowing the distance. On the raft Mrs. Angstrom screamed, but Rachel heard no sound; the woman's mouth was a silent black O. Rachel tried to move towards Don, but the water pressed in, stinging like needles. Cold——it was so cold. She tried to raise the temperature, but the water would not warm. Don must need it this cold; she couldn't affect it at all.

Ahead of her Don reached the raft and grasped it with both hands at one corner. For a second Rachel could feel the wood, water-logged and spongy, bucking under his hands. *Hands—— not now! Don't think of hands now!* Don braced himself against an underwater rock, leaning backwards until his weight balanced the forward drag of the current against the raft, and called back over his shoulder for Rachel to help pull.

Her body, so big and ponderous on land, felt light in the water. Her breasts, blue-veined and fatty, floated in front of her. But the stinging was growing even worse; the water was so cold it burned. Rachel struggled to make herself take a step, to move through the black water over the unseen sand underneath. Just as she succeeded in lifting her naked foot and shoving it forward, a fish swam by her legs.

Startled, she stopped moving. A *fish?* There couldn't be a fish, not here, not in this river. And it was beautiful——tapering slim shape and crimson dark scales, streaking across the dark water. But how could a fish have been——

"Rachel!"

"I'm coming!"

She splashed forward, flailing her arms. The raft had swung sidewise under Don's backward pull. One corner pointed directly down the river, like a prow. Mrs. Angstrom was still screaming, and now Rachel could hear her over the rapids, a shrill scream with a scraping flutter in it, doubling and redoubling in echoes off the bluffs that crowded the river on both sides. Around her the slimy water moved faster, singing darkly.

Don's skin felt clammy with gooseflesh. Rachel forced her hands around his waist and threw her weight backward. He staggered, but then caught her rhythm and stepped back with her over the jagged rocks. (Jagged rocks? It had been sand when she started. Rocks, cold——why did he make everything as goddamn *hard* as possible?) The muscles in the back of Don's neck knotted with each step. Slowly the raft eased backward, moving upstream, against the current.

Mrs. Angstrom went on screaming.

They were almost back to where Rachel stood before, angling in towards a rock shelf at the foot of the bluff, when a fish swam by again. Suddenly there were two of them, slashing the coldness with bright streaks of warm color. She tried to yell to Don to look at the fish, but he didn't turn his head. Wood chips from the raft, smelling of rot and slime, hung in his hair.

How quick the fish were! How alive and yet not alive, glowing with passionate flashes of red, more intense than any color she had ever seen. More intense than any being she had ever seen——pure, whole, free, and with a passion glimpsed only in night dreams. Passionately red. Streaking across the night blackness, burning deeper and deeper, the searing crimson flaring out like a nova until the water itself was warmed. How could she have thought it was cold? It was only cold until you were used to it, then warm and bright with the glow, the yearning, the

NIGHT WIN

flowing between your legs like black velvet. Red fins and slim tapering bodies leading you down into the sweet silent water, the longed-for, half-remembered temperature, salty and thick, warm as blood.

She let go of Don and slipped in a slow sliding curve under the blood-warm water.

"MorMedic Campbell. Come on, now, wake up. This is Nurse Ferrier. Wake up, now."

The young voice trying to be old went on and on, patiently. Rachel turned over and tried to pull the blanket over her head.

"None of that. Come on, MorMedic——Rachel. Wake up, now. Please wake up."

A hand began slapping her hesitantly on the cheeks, first the left one, then the right. When Rachel reached up to bat the hand away it caught her wrist and pulled a little.

"Rachel, come on. You're supposed to wake up now."

"I'm awake."

"Then open your eyes. Please open your eyes."

The face was leaning over her, blocking the window. Chubby cheeks, blond curls, oily skin: Rachel recognized her as the latest of the young nurses who followed Don around, smiling wistfully. Sarah, Sandy——Susan. Susan something. The nurse moved her head and Rachel was assaulted by sunlight, then memory. Abruptly she sat up.

"Mrs. Angstrom——"

"Alive. The fever broke. She's over the worst."

"She'll make it?"

"The prognosis is hopeful," the nurse said primly. The corners of her young mouth turned down. Rachel saw the grimace for what it was: the involuntary distrust of the technician of the body for the technician of the mind, of the concrete for the shadowy, of the dutifully licensed for the hired outsider. Probably Nurse Ferrier didn't even notice what her mouth was doing; that didn't help.

Why the hell were they like that? It seemed to Rachel that nearly all of them, all the hospital personnel and the academic researchers and even the next-of-kin who paid for the services of a Mortality Medical Team, spent most of their living energies in willful, edgy misunderstanding of what that team did.

Not that there was much about metaphorical healing that was concrete enough *to* understand. So many unknowns: how did MorMedics ease themselves into synchronous trance? How did they wordlessly choose and construct a metaphor for death, and then ensnare the minds of the dying into becoming passive participants in the metaphor? How did they pull the dying back from the idea of death, and why should the body often follow the idea? Often, so often, but not always. Why not always? Why at all? Why this, why that, why was this stupid girl standing here blushing at her, why, why——

Why did I let go of the raft?

"Of course," Susan Ferrier said awkwardly, "I know I don't understand any of it. I didn't mean to imply——I know that Don——MorMedic Bareis—he does wonderful work. So many people have said they——not that there's any way of knowing it wasn't just the basic medical care that wasn't really the cause for—but he really does give it everything he's got. He really tries. And you, too, of course," she added hastily.

"Of course," Rachel said sourly, and swung her heavy legs over the side of the bed.

"Let me help you. Do you feel all right?"

"*You* couldn't do anything about it if I didn't," Rachel said, and waited for the girl to take offense. But instead she smiled, a smile so patient and open that it changed her whole face, making even the bad skin a shiny reflection for the sunlight that filled the room, a meek acceptance of whatever was offered. Rachel felt dimly ashamed; she scowled and looked away.

Don lay in an empty bed parked in an unused alcove by the linen room. He was still asleep. Lying on his left side, his legs drawn up, he looked even smaller than usual. Where did it come from, all that power in that delicate, balding skull with the last sideburns in Boston? His right shoulder hunched up toward his chin; Rachel could see where the collarbone, chicken-skinny, met the shoulder. Such delicate shoulders; so much unseen, over-regulated power.

Holding those shoulders in her arms had never been able to excite her. She had tried——God knows she had tried, wanting to make their obligatory intercourse something more than the required playing through of common sexual metaphors. Her metaphors, violent and restless, had repelled him; his metaphors, stately and secretive, had bored her. Or maybe his had never really surfaced at all, never really broken through all that awesome

NIGHT WIN

control. Always that control, that careful consideration of ends rather than means. Not that she didn't admire it professionally, of course. But in all six months that they had lived together, she had never had an orgasm. She had come to know Don through and through, and nowhere had she found that abandonment, that complexity, that passionate struggle that might have made her respond to him. She had lain next to him, holding him as she gazed out his window at the night clouds whipping over Boston Bay, and it had been like holding a child in her arms.

But, free of sexual metaphors, they had made such ideal working partners! His the initiation and control, hers the passion and energy. They were the best team on the East Coast, really; once they had worked at an operation on a former president of United Europe. But that had been years ago; she had never lost the metaphor then, never given in to——what?

Leaning against the wall of the linen room, Rachel felt the sour little bubbles rise in her stomach, and scowled. She hated, above all else, the rare times she felt afraid.

Don was awake. He lay looking at her, his light gray eyes compassionate.

"I'm sorry, Don. I lost it. I was with you and then I just . . . lost it."

"Rachel——"

"No. Don't. I know."

He looked away from her, into the linen room. Crumpled sheets lay in a pile on the floor. His small, delicate-veined hand clenched at his side, and she spoke quickly, anything, before he could speak.

"How did you get the raft to shore?"

"I didn't."

"Then——"

"It happened to snag on a rock, so I left it to pull you out. The rock wasn't mine. Yours?"

"You know better than that."

"Then it must have been hers. Latent ability, maybe, I don't know——it was just sheer luck. The one-in-a-thousand chance. Not something I could count on again. Rachel——"

"Was I hard to get out?"

"No. You had already swallowed enough water by the time I could grab you."

"Did Mrs. Angstrom try at all to——"

"Rachel. Stop it."

"Don't tell me what I can ask or not ask about a——"

"I can't work with you any more."

She looked at him. Somewhere, down the hall, around a corner where she couldn't see, a patient coughed.

"Don't look at me like that, Rachel. Rachel——"

Why were people always doing that, always starting their speeches to her with the name? Nobody else was addressed so much by name. Did they think it gained them something: time, her attention, her favor? Fools. She hated her name. "Rachel, weeping for her children, because they are no more . . ." She fought, not wept. It was the wrong metaphor.

"Rachel, at least listen to me. To start with, you need some time off, a few weeks to rest. Tiredness——"

"If you knew I was tired, why did you use the river? You know I have trouble with all the water constructs, we've been over this a hundred times, yet you go right ahead and use it anyway, you don't seem to——"

"Don't attack, Rachel. Attacking won't help."

" 'Attack'. God, you even *talk* in metaphors."

He passed a hand over his eyes, but he wasn't deterred. They had worked together for fourteen years, had been mortal friends for twelve.

"A rest would do you——"

"No, it wouldn't. I'd go crazy. I need to work, you know that!"

"You could do some of your gardening, take a trip. Visit your sister in Detroit."

"I can't stand my sister in Detroit. I need to work."

"So take a job at an algae factory!" Don snapped, and despite the panic in her stomach, Rachel grinned. It still had the power to surprise her, this unexpected exasperation that could break the surface of his bland, slow patience. Impulsively she reached out and put a hand on his shoulder.

"No, Rachel. I mean it. Mrs. Angstrom, and last week the brain surgery. Shapiro."

"They both pulled through!"

"You deserted me in the middle. Shapiro wasn't water, either."

It had been night, the oldest metaphor of all. Don and she had crouched on a vast plain, plying enormous bellows, pumping toward a tiny spark of fire on a pile of messy ashes. They

NIGHT WIN

was the whole damn *point*——whatever it took, she didn't have it. She was only the raw energy, the lightning without a ship's mast, the flooding river, rampaging lost beyond its banks.

"Rachel, see the psychiatrist."

Under his even tone she heard the jaggedness that might have been pain, but when she turned his face was still controlled, closed as a fortress. Beyond him Susan Ferrier had not moved, her hand still to her mouth in the dusty sunshine. They were both such small people, such controlled, bodiless, sunlit people, so content with what they had . . . Rachel pushed past them, shoving Susan out of the way with one hand.

"I need you, Rachel," Don said. He had climbed out of bed and stood naked on the tile floor; the top of his head reached her chin. He looked defenseless, vulnerable——deliberately vulnerable? On the floor his bony toes splayed outward.

"I need you."

"I'd take you Under first!"

He shook his head, but whether to deny her words or just to deflect them, Rachel didn't see. She kept on pushing down the hall, not looking back, the sunlight white and placid behind her.

She began to remember her dreams. That had never happened when she was working; it had been years since dreams had made the crossing to her conscious mind. In the night she would sit up and cry out, waking herself, sweat clammy under her nightgown. Her hands would be clenching the metal bed frame so hard that welts would stay on her palms for hours. Yet the dreams themselves were calm, ordinary: she was picking a bouquet of early asters in the garden, she was stirring the rice in its enameled pot on the stove, she was painting a window frame in her tiny Commonwealth Avenue apartment. Sunshine washed through the window and over the wet paint, making moving shadows where her hand swished back and forth. The paint smelled clean and permanent, like glue. When the frame was painted, she cleaned her brush in warm water, slapping the bristles back and forth, each separate bristle distinct and pleasantly tingling against her hands.

Hands——always hands. But she woke screaming.

During the day Rachel worked in the garden. She had chosen the shabby, cramped apartment on Commonwealth Avenue for its fenced garden, a luxury left over from the time when the Back

Bay had been a pleasant, safe part of the city. Now it was neither; fights and muggings and curses echoed nightly over her wooden fence. But——there was the garden, and a tiny redwood sundeck that overlooked it. She worked frantically, jabbing her spade with the rapid-fire rhythm of a jack-hammer, or a machine gun. "Slow down, Rachel," Don said from the sun-deck, a drink in his hand. "Slow down, you don't have to plant Eden in one afternoon." She scowled at the image from ten years ago and hoed the ground around her tomatoes as if rescuing them from strangulation. "Take it easy," the image said. "All that storm and strife could kill you."

At night she dreamed of fixing a pipe. She could feel her hands grip the wrench as it tightened on the joint collars. She woke screaming.

After a few weeks the gardening ran out. There was only so much to do. The beans had all been propped on poles; the cigarette butts and beer cans passersby had tossed over the fence had all been cleared out; the flowers had all been pruned. Rachel's neighbors, made uneasy by the fierce order of her marigolds and the harsh measure of her scowl, left her alone.

She sat up later and later. All the curtains were drawn tightly and pinned over closed windows. She did not trust herself to even smell the summer night, heavy with lush promise——instead she watched TV news shows, hospital shows, old space dramas and even older Westerns. People were laser-fried by aliens and died. People fell off horses and died. People contracted odd strains of mutated viruses and died. Rachel watched it all, wrapped in an old hand-knitted afghan, glaring at the TV. Contestants won refrigerators, diplomats made the shuttle trip to the moon, patients fought off the odd mutated viruses and lived. Once, during a news segment about a spectacular transplant operation, she glimpsed Don in the background of the O.R., looking small and exhausted. Not even that made her turn off the TV. She let it all wash over her, staying with it right to the early morning sex shows, wanting only to stay awake, not to sleep, not to dream the calm, ordinary, useful dreams.

"MorMedic Campbell?"

"Nurse Ferrier."

"May I come in?"

"No."

Susan Ferrier blinked, whether at the rudeness or Rachel's appearance, Rachel couldn't tell. She knew how she looked. Soiled bathrobe, uncombed hair, pasty skin with dark circles under the eyes——hadn't missed a cliché, had she? The whole theatrical repertoire of panic. Touched all the bases. At the absurdity of this flash of perverted vanity, Rachel smiled sourly and Susan, mistaking the smile, walked in.

"It's about——well, about Don. I see him around the hospital, and he always looks so tired. Just spent. I know I probably shouldn't interfere, MorMedic——Rachel——"

"MorMedic."

The girl flushed. "Working alone is just too *much* for him. It's really none of my business——"

"No. It's not."

"——but he can't find another assistant, and frankly, I'm worried about him. He needs another assistant. He really does. But there aren't too many of——of you."

Rachel walked to the stove. She was out of coffee. A mug lay on its side, the last dregs soggy in the bottom. Three brown bags of garbage rotted in the sunshine from the window. She had just not been much interested in removing them. Through the glass, she could see a dented beer can caught in the rose bush.

"Of us what?"

"I beg your pardon?"

"You don't have it. Not too many of us what? Death rats? Decay-diddlers? Infidels? Frauds? What exactly do you think MorMedics are, Nurse Ferrier?"

"Mental healers," Susan said quietly. Rachel saw what she had missed before: dignity. The girl was timid, washed-out, bland, but she had dignity.

"Faith healers. But not *their* faith——ours. Does Don know you're here?"

"No. But——"

"Presumptuous, then, isn't it?"

"I just thought——"

"No. You didn't."

Susan drew a deep breath. Her oily skin mottled with red. "I'm not going to fence with you. I don't know what you're so angry about all the time, anyway. I don't know why you never relax, never——but Don lost three this week. All of them should have made it. One was an eight-year-old boy."

Rachel sat down. She lowered herself into a chair slowly, back straight, as if something were fragile.

"Tell me."

"The first one was on Tuesday. My head nurse said it was a gastric tumor, and the surgeon——"

"Not *that*. What was Don using with the kid."

Susan hesitated. "I don't know, exactly. He wouldn't talk about it afterwards, even though he was really upset. But somebody said it was something about a cliff."

She could feel it. Hauling the child in a rope-sling up the sheer face of the mountain, the body groggy but not completely inert, so that it flailed and groaned at the end of the rope. An eight-year-old would be heavy, on those thin shoulders. Because he was Don, it would be cold. The snow would whip past his goggles, sometimes blinding him to the ledge above, that safe ledge which, if he only could reach it, would let him keep the kid safe——let him put the small body in the back near the rocks, under the overhang, and shield it from the wind with his own body. Would let him pull off his gloves and wipe the blood off hands raw from hauling on ropes and hammering in spikes for hours. It would have been hours. And then the unexpected shift of the rope, the child sickeningly light for the blind moment before the snow gusted and Don could see the fall, slow and unstoppable as the fall of night. At the base of the cliff, in the waiting room, the parents who had hired Don would lift their eyes from unread magazines, to scan his face as he walked toward them. And he would have to tell them.

"MorMedic Campbell?"

"But Carl D'Amato is selling *life* insurance!"

"Who?"

Rachel closed her eyes. When she didn't answer Susan squirmed a little, an abortive half-moment that in another girl might have been a shrug, or a shoulder-flick of impatience, or a plea for attention.

"The third case was O.R. A knife-fight victim. Actually, the patient came through the surgery and we thought he would make it, but Don was still with him in post-op, and he was using the——"

"No. Don't tell me."

NIGHT WIN

"Rachel——"

"Don't *tell* me!"

Sunshine streamed in the window. Susan stood still, waiting. Rachel fidgeted, stacking the salt shaker on top of the pepper, ringing both with torn bits of advertising circular, making and unmaking frenetic designs her intent eyes did not even see. The child fell from the cliff.

"All right. I'll see your psychiatrist."

"Oh, Don will be so——"

"Yes. Set it up for tomorrow."

"Maybe today the doctor could fit in a——"

"*Tomorrow.*"

The girl nodded. They looked at each other across the littered table, Susan smiling uncertainly, Rachel fierce. There was nothing else to say. They might have been two different species, circling each other warily around the water hole of Rachel's shabby kitchen. A fly buzzed monotonously across the sunlit silence.

"Well, I guess I better be——"

"What is death to you?" Rachel asked abruptly, and waited. She expected an evasion or an embarrassed stare, something that would justify her dislike. But again Susan surprised her. She answered promptly, meeting Rachel's eyes directly, her uncertain smile gone.

"The enemy."

"Always?"

"Of course." The girl's eyes widened suddenly. "Isn't it always too——"

"Go home, Nurse Ferrier."

"But—"

"Go *home.*"

Now even watching TV was impossible. Her mind skipped crazily, missing whole chunks of plot, entire countries' worth of news.

"——and now the NBS newsbreak. Fighting had intensified along the Niger-Barmou border, with losses estimated as high as 4,000 men, women and children. A high official in nearby Mali, who declined to be identified, confirmed reports that both sides in the conflict have employed genetically altered bacteria in an attempt to gain control——"

Control, Rachel, control. You might be an initiator if you could just keep your own needs out of the metaphor.

And the great Don might be decent in bed if you'd just let any of yours in!

That wasn't called for.

"——called for an end to the death and destruction in a Security Council Meeting earlier today. Locally, purse-snatchings and muggings in the downtown area——"

Of course it hurt. What sort of question is that? No, don't touch there, it's still tender.

Don——what did you feel when the mugger pulled the knife?
I felt afraid.

Is that all? Nothing more complicated, more—mixed?
Of course not.

"——return you to the Himalayas and NBS coverage via telesatellite of the death-teasing struggle of seven American mountain climbers to climb the——"

Turn it off.
I want to see it.
Good God, Rachel, why?

I don't know. It's beautiful. No, it's not. It's outrageous, dangerous, big—I don't know. Don't you ever think that if you weren't a MorMedic, you might have lived that way? Pushing life to the limit?

Never. What's the point?

Does there have to be a point? Maybe they're just trying to escape all this endless cramped discontent that the rest of us live in!

I don't feel either cramped or discontent.

God, I hate your self-righteousness!

Do you?I'm sorry. But adolescent longings for some vague passionate grandeur don't interest me.

Self-righteous, mundane, limited——

"——limited to four days more of food and water, before facing a lingering death on this lonely Himalayan slope battered by winds of up to——"

Rachel turned off the TV. Silence filled the apartment. Hunched in her chair, pulling closely around her shoulders a shawl pointless in the summer heat, she stared at the blank screen. Beyond the drawn curtains she could feel the night, curling around the city like a sleek, stretching cat.

NIGHT WIN

• • •

She dreamed she was building a new frame for the kitchen window. She chose the nail; under her fingers it felt cool and solid. She held it straight and drove it in with clean blows, her hand bringing the hammer down over the exact center of the nail head, again and again. The kitchen filled with steady, balanced pounding and with the clean smell of new wood. The windowsill was nearly finished; it lay to one side on the floor, sturdy in the sunshine. She woke screaming.

The pounding went on.

It was the wind, fiercely blowing over the vast deserted plain outside her window, pounding at the apartment. Rachel tore open the locks on the barred grill and ran out onto the sundeck. Below her the garden lay crystalline in starlight. Beyond the fence a group of boys went by on Commonwealth Avenue, insulting each other in Spanish. A beer can was tossed over the fence, but just before it hit the dahlias the wind screamed and Rachel dropped to the deck, grabbed the railing, and hung on. She was out on the plain, alone in the howling wind. The few cottonwoods on the plain were twisted by the wind into grotesque knots. Tumbleweeds slammed into rocks that were themselves crumbled into tortured deformities by centuries of wind. A cottonwood crashed over, raking the air with branches, and the wind wailed and screamed. She would be swept away, she would be torn in half by this wind that could not exist. Not here, not at this distance, not without any contact or agreement. Not even Don could initiate such a metaphor——but it had to be Don's, he was the only one teamed to take her In at all. But how, and why? Whom was he rescuing? Who was dying?

A sudden gale force gust slapped her from behind, hurling her hair forward over her face, blinding her. Flat on her stomach, she grabbed handfuls of the tough prairie grass and tried to raise her head enough to see where the twister was. Dirt and grit blew into her eyes, then tore at her lips and tongue when she screamed.

A night moth fluttered gently over to the dahlias, folding pale wings.

She was crawling against the wind, looking for Don. She could move only a few inches at a time, grabbing fistfuls of grass to pull herself along. The grass came up at the roots; most of it was torn from her hands by the wind. Her hair jerked abruptly away from her face and pulled at the scalp so hard it hurt. Weeds and grit howled overhead, making a tearing gray sky only inches above her head.

"Don! Don!"

He was ahead of her, a dim shape in the shrieking gloom, trying to stand up. Rachel could see his body, naked to the waist, rise a few feet above the plain. Even as she raised her head to call again he was knocked to his knees, then spun sideways a few feet and slammed to the ground. She felt rather than heard the sharp crack of the bone at the left elbow. A second later he was trying to stagger to his knees. What was he trying to do? Where was the patient he was rescuing?

Crawling forward, Rachel reached up and pulled Don down by his belt. Instead of grasping her hand or shouting to her what was going on, Don twisted his body and clawed at her face with his one good hand. Rachel gasped and beat his hand away, finally pinning his wrist behind him. He jabbed upward with his knee but she was quicker, throwing her large body full length on top of his. Her right elbow came down on his broken one; even over the demonic wind she heard him scream. Their faces were inches apart, but when he spat at her the spittle whipped away horizontally.

"Listen! Don!"

He wouldn't hear her. Rachel's body, ten centimeters longer and twenty kilos heavier, couldn't hold his. The wind was lifting him from underneath, gusting up from the earth itself like some live, demented spirit.

"What the hell are you doing? The metaphor doesn't go like this!" Rachel screamed. Don's face strained beneath her, blank with concentration. They were three inches off the ground, locked together like rammed galleys, when Don's head fell backward; he closed his eyes and smiled as the wind slammed him in the face. Rachel hit him in the nose. Blood spurted out and was blown by the wind. She leaned over and tried to snatch at the whipping grass, and when her fist finally closed over a clump, she pulled hard. They tilted forward, her body riding his, until the grasses tore and their heads shot upward. Don's body slid sideways under Rachel's and she rolled off him, landing hard on the ground.

Free of her weight, Don rose another few inches. His broken left arm flopped like a puppet's. Rachel rolled under him and grabbed upward; her arms and then her legs wrapped around

NIGHT WIN

Don, dragging him down to her and tightening like a vise. The hair on the back of his head lashed at her mouth, tasting of sweat. He tried to flail backwards at her with his right arm, but she was beyond her reach, and he began prying at her hands clutching his chest. She locked her fingers and squeezed until something under them cracked.

At first her weight pulled them toward the ground, but then the impossible wind again began to blast them from underneath. It was warmer now, a warm raging wind as solid as tropic rapids. At three inches they began to rotate, but Rachel couldn't see through the flying hair and grit whether Don was using a twister in his senseless battle with——what? What the hell was he fighting her off to do? And where was the patient in this hellish metaphor? Above her Don gave a long, low sound: not a moan or a cry but a drawn-out breathy keening of such yearning and hope that Rachel tightened her hold until skin and blood jammed under her fingernails, and then she understood.

Don was the one dying. Dying not as a passive construct in somebody else's metaphor, but as an active participant in his own, both initiator and victim. He wasn't being tossed by the wind, he was *riding* it. Voluntarily mounting it higher and higher, back to the beginning, back where the wind blew from, flowed to, fell from the side of the cliff, slow and unstoppable as the fall of night. Night——night was there, mysterious and passionate and terrible enough to fill all those aches and yearnings that the glare of sunlight only exposed——

"No, damn it!" she screamed into his bloody hair. "Not you! Not *you!*"

Night. He was going to night, on top of the sky, above the wind. He was going to night, to the warmth and throbbing as the crimson blood rushed into her breasts, between her legs. Crimson flaring out like a nova spreading engulfing the longed-for, half-remembered temperature, blood-warm, salty dark——

Throwing her head forward, Rachel closed her teeth on Don's right shoulder. Blood filled her mouth, rushing in with outraged scream. The jerks of his body as he tried to rip free of her teeth tilted them crazily to the right, but not enough to flip over their locked bodies and leave her on top. The wind from beneath became stronger and louder; they were rising faster. Rachel spit out Don's shoulder—he had stopped the keening—and screamed "Fight it, damn you! You told *me* to fight it!"

There was no sign he heard. She tried to make the wind colder, harsher—hail, sleet, blowing sand—anything but this seductive warmth, cleaner by the moment, lifting them higher and higher. She succeeded in lowering the temperature a few degrees, but then the demented howling began to sound more regular, swelling and pulsing and mounting to a crescendo of power that was music and thunder and orgasm, that held her transfixed, no longer fighting.

They were being blown upward and northward, at an angle, towards the night. The plain unfolded below them, tattered and unimportant. Ahead the sky throbbed black and crimson, never wholly one or the other but a passionate, relentless blending, flashing lightning—under her legs, clamped around Don's, Rachel could feel the force of his erection. The wind sang past them, hot and alive. Rachel cried out, didn't hear herself, and closed her eyes, smiling into the night as the night flowed into her, and then blackness came.

The first thing she became aware of was her neck. It ached; the muscles were cramped and tense. Awareness of the rest of her body followed. There was no part of her that was not bruised and battered. Slowly, Rachel opened her eyes. At the same second, she realized that the wind had stopped and the air hung as still and heavy as she and Don were hanging.

They were in the branches of a huge cottonwood. Other trees, unseen before in the dust of the twister, dotted the prairie. Don lay pressed against the cottonwood's trunk, circled and pinned by Rachel's arms. Next to the trunk her hands clung to two of the branches; it was her hands that had held them in the tree. Rachel tried to open the fingers. At first she could not, so desperately were they knotted around the solid wood. When she had forced open her scraped and cramped hands, Rachel spread them in front of her, shifted Don's weight slightly so he would not fall out of the tree, and then stared at her spread hands. She turned them over and back, palms up and palms down. It was as though they belonged to someone else, as though she had never seen them before.

Hands. Driving a nail, picking a bouquet, stirring the rice, painting a window frame. Holding on for dear life, even when the mind desired otherwise. For dear life.

In front of her spread hands, Don moaned softly.

NIGHT WIN

• • •

The moth left the dahlias. It hovered over the beer can, flew to the deck, and settled on a fold of Rachel's nightgown. She sat up, looking at her hands. The moth flew away, wings pale in the moonlight as any ghost.

"Awake?"

"Yes."

"Rachel—"

"Don't." She put her finger to his lips. He looked exhausted, white ridges sagging on either side of his mouth, but whole. Irrationally, she had half-expected to see the broken arm and bitten shoulder. But there was only the old scar on his chest, and the new lump on his forehead where the gun butt had come down.

"It was a mugger," she said. "Just another stupid, greedy mugger. You must look like an easy target. He gave you a concussion, and you went into severe shock."

"I know. Susan Ferrier told me." His voice was flat, stretched like taut canvas over the pain underneath.

"So now you get to be a medical-first. After all, nobody else has ever initiated his own metaphor to finish killing himself. You'll be a celebrity, a real psychiatrist's dream. 'Metaphoric Death Wish Among the Metaphoric Healers: A Reverse Phenomenon.' Still want *me* to see the Freud-fly?"

Don didn't answer. After a moment Rachel looked away and said, "I'm sorry. God, I'm sorry. I didn't mean that."

"I had it coming," Don said. "All these weeks—all these weeks I thought it was *you*. Mrs. Angstrom. Shapiro. I thought it was *you*. But you must have been picking it up all along from me, some crazy repressed fascination with death I didn't even know I had—"

"From you?" Rachel said. It was a new idea. But then she thought of the calm, ordinary dreams that brought her awake screaming, of the delicious blood-warm water, of the wind mounting upward under her. "No. No, I don't think it was only you."

"What then?"

"I think," she said slowly, "I think it was both of us. There might have been something I was picking up from you, something you couldn't express directly—*control*—but then I—it wasn't all you. No."

Don reached up and fingered the bruise on his forehead. He deliberately pushed it, Rachel saw, hard enough to hurt, and she closed her eyes.

"Don't Don. Don't blame yourself."

"I could have killed us both. Only I didn't even know you were going to be there, in the metaphor. How did you get In? I didn't call you."

"Yes. You did. You must have, or the prairie metaphor wouldn't have reached me . . . wait. I was asleep, I was dreaming. Your trance reached my dream."

Again Don put his hands to either side of his head. This time the touch was tentative, probing; in his gray eyes brimmed a strange light, fascinated and horrified. "I wanted to die. I *wanted* it. I constructed a metaphor to hurry towards it, not to stop it—"

"I know," Rachel said. "I know. But you also reached out to me, or your trance did. And you must have known, at some level, that I would stop you."

"Why did you?Why *did* you try to stop me? You tried to get there yourself, before—with Mrs. Angstrom. With Shapiro. Why stop me? Why didn't you join me from the beginning?"

"I don't know," Rachel said. "Why did you stop *me* before, and this time want to go on yourself?"

There was a long silence. In the corridor footsteps passed. Somewhere a phone jangled softly. Don squeezed his eyes shut. "I'll have to see a psychiatrist, if I'm going to work again. We both will."

"No!"

"Rachel, I *have* to. If I don't talk about it, if I let it go, it will *grow*, don't you see? It will grow, and next time—"

"Then not to me. Don't talk about it to me."

"Ever?"

"No."

"It would help you."

"No. It would help *you*, because for you the important thing is to get it out, bring out whatever—once you get it out in the sunlight, you can take it apart and label all the parts and make each one just another tool. Then you won't be in danger of giving in. But I don't work that way. I can't."

Don chewed on his lip. A long moment went by, and Rachel held her breath.

NIGHT WIN

"If you can't," he said finally, "then you can't. But maybe if I can understand what *I'm* doing, how whatever need in *me* starts you changing the metaphor—if I can get my end under control—Rachel, I need to work with you. It has to be you, now. You're the only one who would know what's happening and would stop me if—"

"Hush," Rachel said. "Hush. We'll stop each other."

Don groped for her hand. She held it, feeling the scrawny wrist bones and the blood in his pulse and the callus on the third finger where he held a pencil. Her fingernails dug into the bony knobs of his knuckles. She could feel there, in the veins and nerves and delicate bones of his hands, the question he hadn't yet asked, and she waited.

"The night in the metaphor," he said, finally, "the Night. Death. Is it really as beautiful as I felt? As desirable?"

"Oh, God, Don. How do I know? The only other one who has seen it is you, and you were linked with me. How can I tell if it's really that beautiful, or if it's just that I—that *we* need it to be like that?"

Don's hand tightened on hers. Rachel gripped it hard, grateful for the blood and bone and flesh next to her palm.

"We'll stop each other," Don said. "Rachel?"

She nodded. Unsmiling, they looked at each other. Both were careful to keep their eyes focused, to stare straight ahead at the other's face, to avert their heads from the parted yellow drapes fluttering at the sill, from what lay beyond the yellow drapes.

Their two hands clasped desperately. For dear life.

Outside the window, night came.

"FOREVER,"
SAID THE DUCK

Jonathan Lethem

" 'Forever,' Said the Duck" was purchased by Gardner Dozois, and appeared in the December 1993 issue of Asimov's, *with an illustration by Karl F. Huber. Jonathan Lethem is yet another of those talented new writers who are continuing to pop up all over as we progress into the decade of the 1990s. He works at an antiquarian bookstore, writes slogans for buttons and lyrics for several rock bands (including Two Fettered Apes, EDO, Jolley Ramey, and Feet Wet), and is also the creator of the "Dr. Sphincter" character on MTV. In addition to all these Certifiably Cool credentials, Lethem has also made a number of memorable sales in the last few years to* Asimov's Science Fiction, *as well as to* Interzone, New Pathways, Pulphouse, Universe, Journal Wired, Marion Zimmer Bradley's Fantasy Magazine, Aboriginal SF, *and elsewhere. His first novel is coming up, and he has already sold a second. He lives in Berkeley, California.*

In the wry and razor-sharp story that follows, he invites us along to a wild party in a decadent future where nothing is as it seems, and the guest list features quite a few surprises. . . .

Pearl O'Hennies was in the corner, talking to Notable Johnson. "Can you *believe* her gall, calling everyone up like this?"

"But, my dear, that's exactly what *he* did," said Notable. "They're the only two really here. *We're* all samples."

They were talking about their hosts, who were in another of the blank, featureless rooms.

"What is it, a contest?"

"A contest, you mean to see who had more *lovers*? I think they're above that. They've known each other all these years—"

"Why don't they just call each *other* up, then? Why all this?"

"Well, they could be with each other, of course. In the real world, instead of this blank virtual space. But then *we* wouldn't all be here. It is about *us*, you see. Even if they won't talk to anyone but each other."

"I heard they've got games planned, for later."

"What, spin the bottle?"

Cambert Moid stepped over to where they stood. "Have you ever seen anything like it?" he asked.

"Hello, Cambert," said Pearl crisply.

"Hello, Pearl. I suppose I should say, long time, no see. But"— he mimicked a southern accent—"I don't rightly know if that's true. I suppose our real selves could have warmed up to each other by now. Besides, this is hardly 'see,' now is it?"

"You talk too much, Cambert," said Pearl.

"I'll let you two catch up," mumbled Notable Johnson, and he slipped away. He was en route to the monitors where guests were punching up drink simulations when he ran into Caitlice Frisman.

"Caitlice!"

"Oh, Johnny." She put her arms around him. "Nice, nice, nice. But what, excuse me, what the *hell* are you doing here?" She leaned in close. "You sleep with that remorseless pussycat?"

"I take it you refer to our host."

"Yours, not mine," she corrected.

"FOREVER," SAID THE DUCK

He nodded his shameful assent to her question.

"Well, a party like this is what you *get*, what you deserve, for a glitch like that—but enough. You're in charge of your own regrets. Just tell me when it happened."

"You're humiliating me, Cait," he said affectionately. "Two years—how should I count it?—two years after us, after you and I—"

"Then you know how we've been, and you must tell me. Because I—this copy here is from right after we broke—you weren't even *talking* to me, Johnny. But you're from later, and so you know how we've been, out there, in our real selves."

"Oh, fine, Cait. Nothing could keep us from—coffee every Monday."

"Ah."

They both fell to a moment of sadness. Then Caitlice said flippantly: "So am I magnificently fat now?"

"Oh, no, you still look terrific. But that reminds me, Cait, listen; Gavin Urnst is here, a very early sample, and last I knew he was in the hospital, quite sick—"

"We mustn't tell him here," she said quickly. "Ruin his time, when he couldn't do anything. Any more than you would tell *me* if I *was* fat. Do you think he—"

"Died? I can't know. Anyone, I mean, you or I—"

"Shh."

They were quiet again for a minute.

"Cait, if this thing goes long, let's find each other. I mean, it could get unbearable. I've heard they're hoping we'll all pair—"

"Shhh. Say no more. It's a date. Save the last dance for me. And now I must mingle, darling."

Notable nodded. Caitlice turned and attached herself immediately to a group containing Millard Heron, O.K. Tinkers, and Wendy Airhole.

"This is such an indignity," Wendy said. "I was only with him as a favor, just stayed long enough to qualify for the copying. I wanted him to have me to *access*, but not for this fucking *party*. I remember thinking that I shouldn't, just out of pity for my poor copy—that is, *me*, now, *here*. God!"

"Hmmm," said Millard Heron. "He told *me* it was the other way. That *he* only slept with *you*—"

"Oh, Millard, what do *you* know?" Wendy breathed out in a weary rush. "The things women have to tell men just to keep them from imploding with insecurity, just to keep their dicks hard long enough to be *entertaining*—and then to think they go around repeating it to each *other*—"

"Hey, we're at a party," said Caitlice, singingly. "Make the best of it, there's no harm done here. You, *real* you, doesn't care about this, doesn't object, won't recall it. You and I, real you and I, might be having *our very own version of this same party right now*—"

"I would never," said O.K. Tinkers. He shuddered. "Oh, I would *never* want to see them all, all in the same place—"

The four laughed, resentment suddenly abolished.

"This *could* be a sort of nightmare for them," Wendy speculated merrily. "If we somehow joined forces—"

Caitlice took her by the elbow, tsk-tsking. "Excuse us, boys. Come for a drink simulation, Wendy."

"You think I should lighten up, Cait, don't you?"

"I think you could be having fun." Caitlice steered her away from O.K. and Millard.

"My kind of fun is darker than yours, Cait. Doesn't the, the *smugness* of it just creep you out? But I'll have a drink if you like. It'll just get me bitchier. They made a mistake calling *this* particular lady out of storage."

"Stop vamping," said Caitlice, delighted. "I know your act too well."

"I'm just warming up. I'm going straight to the source tonight, Cait. And you're right, I should have a drink."

"Straight to the source?"

"They *think* they're here together," Wendy said, lowering her voice.

"Who?" But Caitlice knew.

"Our hosts, the 'real' ones. But I'm going to get *between* them. Take him 'home' at the end of the party."

At the console, they each tapped up a drink's worth of process distortion.

"Here, stand still, let me check something." Caitlice reached over and dug in Wendy's pocket, and pulled out a green ticket.

"What's that?" said Wendy.

"All the samples at this party have a ticket in their pockets, green or red. A little extra our hosts wrote into tonight's program. Red means you're *his* guest, green *hers*."

Wendy didn't speak, but her smile fell.

"FOREVER," SAID THE DUCK   157

"I guess anyone they *both* had copies of, they had to choose whose version to bring," said Caitlice, "because they wouldn't want *two* of people, you know—"

"That was a one-time thing, a kink. I should be here with *him*, it was me and him that really had any kind of—"

"Hey, don't be defensive." Cait turned out her pocket to reveal a ticket: green.

"You, we both—" Wendy giggled.

"I always liked her better."

"Well, I'll be."

"It's interesting, isn't it, the way in our scene we all pride ourselves on going both ways, but it's the male-female things that go public and get all historicized, and the same-same stuff stays under the table, doesn't become the official version. It still makes us blush."

Wendy put her hands on her hips, instantly convinced. "I *know*. Really. Look at me, even, backpedaling. What closeted wimps we are! God, doesn't that really burn you up?"

"No, dear, it burns *you* up, like everything else. I just said it was interesting."

"Oh!" Wendy put her wrist to her forehead, exaggeratedly. "You are just *so* superior. Hey, are you a plant?"

"What?"

"You're with *them*, aren't you?" Wendy poked Caitlice between her breasts. "You're *real*, you're with them, a plant, to facilitate the party."

"No, no, no. I'm a sample, like you."

"*Cait*—"

"On my honor."

Wendy pursed her lips. "Well, okay. Let's go, then."

Arman Danzig stepped up from behind them, his cigarette in a long holder. "Go where, ladies? Is there somewhere to go?"

"We have to get to *them*, Cait," said Wendy, ignoring him. "The real ones. Where the action is."

Caitlice shook her head, and trembled slightly. "I want to be at the party. There are people to meet, people I haven't seen in a long time." She grabbed Arman's elbow, though she didn't like him. "Lovely, funny people in a ridiculous situation. I don't need—"

"This *is* interesting," said Arman.

"People *not* here is the situation," said Wendy. "Including you. People not meeting, a total and complete lack of anything *actually* happening. The only way to be *real* is to affect *them* somehow—"

"No. You. I don't need to do that. That's for you." Caitlice lightened suddenly, smiled, having convinced herself. "But I'll sneak up and watch, later. I'd like to see you do it."

"Think of it," Wendy continued, inspired. "The only way to even know any of this happened would be to make such a splash, such a big dent in their evening, that they're so shaken that they have to come and *talk* to you about it, I mean the *real* you. 'Wendy, listen, I can't get *her* to talk to me any more because of what your sample and I did at the party,'—he'd have to confess all about this sick little party—'and I want you to go talk to her about it' and then I'd say 'look, dear, *my* ticket was *green*, I was never *your* guest at all.' That would be something."

"Yes, and if you did a good enough job, you could have them *both* coming to you afterward with confidences, pleading their individual cases," mused Arman.

"Have we met?" said Wendy.

"I'm sorry," said Caitlice. "Arman Danzig, Wendy Airhole."

"And what color is *your* ticket?" said Wendy.

Arman's lip twitched around the holder. "I believe that's a personal question, Ms. Airhole."

"I'll show you mine—"

"What if I said I hadn't bothered to wonder the color of yours?" said Arman. "Or check the color of mine?"

They were enchanted with one another.

"Look at what you've let slip," said Wendy. "You've suggested you'd have to *check* to know—that they've both got copies of you. But can there really be that many of us?"

She turned to Caitlice, but Caitlice had tiptoed off.

"Don't look now," Arman stage-whispered, "but it's our quarry." He jabbed backward over his shoulder with the holder. Their hosts were passing through the room.

"They're mobbed," said Wendy. "It's disgusting."

"Sycophants all. Harmless. Just—traffic. A hedge we must clamber over."

Wendy liked him better and better. "Then let's."

Arman nodded and stepped sideways into the little crowd. "Oh, hello," he said to Darth Gatsby, who stood on the fringe.

"FOREVER," SAID THE DUCK 159

"Hello, Arman," said Darth miserably.

"Are you having a wonderful time?" Arman asked, openly staring past Darth, at the hosts.

"Yes, of course," Darth moaned.

Arman noted with approval that Wendy was inserting herself on the other side of the group, working her way into a conversation with Fran Krapp and Hella Winkie.

Arman nudged past Darth to where Candy Bale stood listening to her host expound.

"—there are wrinkles in the program," he was saying. Candy wavered toward him, rapt. "There are side rooms in this space, for instance. You just have to find them. So if you start to notice that people you saw earlier aren't around—"

"Like a game of sardines!" Candy blurted.

"Right," he said.

Arman reached down and fondled Candy's realistic buttock as he pushed between the two of them. She gave an exaggerated gasp and opened her mouth at Arman.

"Sardines indeed," he sneered at her. "Or guppies." He twitched his cigarette and performed a slight bow. "I'm sorry. Do go on with what you were saying."

"Hello, Arman," said their host.

"Hello. But please. Don't let me interrupt. I am—we're both, obviously, hanging on your words. What other 'wrinkles' are built into tonight's program?"

"Well, I can't go into it all, but you'll find a few things revealing themselves over time anyway. But here, this is one trick nobody's picked up on. If I stick my tongue in someone's mouth"—at this he took Candy by the waist and put his mouth close to hers—"my drink or drug load is transferred." He kissed her, and Arman watched as her eyes closed, then opened again, wide.

She staggered backward as he released her.

"I'd had two drinks," their host explained.

"But I'd already *had* two," said Candy.

"That makes four, then, doesn't it?"

"Oh," said Candy. "—Hic—".

"I see," said Arman. "Could she return it, now? By putting her tongue in *your* mouth?"

"I shouldn't tell you everything. But the second kiss of any kind doubles the load, and distributes it evenly. We'd then both be carrying four drinks, for instance."

"So you share the intoxication of anyone you seriously take up with," mused Arman. "No hope of sloughing yours off unless you kiss and run." He stood on tiptoe and made an insinuating face at Wendy, who had worked into a group with her hostess.

"Here, Arman," giggled Candy, lurching toward him, mouth open. Putting his cigarette holder back in his mouth, Arman stepped deftly to one side and took her by the arm.

"Look," he said, lifting her chin with a finger. He pointed at Darth Gatsby, who'd been squeezed out of their group and was standing looking wan. "Go. Fetch."

Candy exploded toward Darth, and away from Arman.

"But now you're sober," Arman said to his host. "That can't be any fun."

"True enough. Join me?"

They moved toward the console together, and away from the crowd that ringed Wendy and her host. Arman caught a sly smile from Wendy as he turned away: they'd separated the hosts.

"So tell me," said Arman, "what *do* you have planned for tonight? Is it true that you want them all to pair up?"

"It's a party. People can do what they want."

"While you and she pull the strings, you mean."

"Every party includes random factors, determined by the hosts. But the *outcomes* are unknown—"

"Ah. But is *your* outcome unknown?"

"I don't see why not—"

"Then let's take that tramp Candy and find one of your little sardine rooms, yes?"

Arman caught his host's nervous glance back over his shoulder.

"What?" said Arman. "Can't be separated from your 'real world' buddy? This isn't summer camp. Come on." He prodded gently at his host's elbow.

"I might just—"

"It's a *party*," Arman said menacingly. "Don't be all impossibly coupled. It's too early for that. I *know* you, I know what you're capable of—"

"Yes, and I know what *you're* capable of, Arman." Sighing, his host reached into his pocket and brought out a little pearl-handled revolver.

"What," Arman scoffed. "The coward's way out? Am I disinvited?"

"FOREVER," SAID THE DUCK 161

"No, no. I would never do that. A guest at my party stays as long as he likes, spends the night, whatever. You're not disinvited. But you are dosed with MDMA and on the other side of the party—"

—and when his host pulled the trigger Arman found himself to be exactly that. He was several rooms away, wedged behind a conversation between Pearl O'Hennies and Omidan Rosengreen, and burdened with an irritatingly benign and rosy worldview.

"Feh," he muttered, and grabbed Pearl O'Hennies from behind. He twisted her around and planted his tongue in her mouth, then pulled away, wiping his lips, and stalked off angrily into the crowd.

"Seems you have an admirer," said Omidan.

"Goodness," said Pearl, still astonished, her mouth wide.

"Or was that that drink thing?"

"Something—not just a drink, I'm not sure—"

"Well, he certainly had quite an effect on you, one way or another. People are behaving strangely at this affair, but I suppose some of us haven't 'gotten out' in quite a while."

"You, uh, get called up very much?" asked Pearl in a small voice. She struggled to flatten out her perceptual processing. It seemed to her that as a program she ought to be able to prevail over this influence. Then she noticed that Omidan was talking, answering a question which presumably she, Pearl, had asked, though she couldn't now recall what it was.

"Oh, Omidan," she interrupted, "don't you feel sorry for them, resorting to this, wanting to spend time with *us?*"

Omidan, eyebrows arching, said: "That's an interesting way to look at it," then paused, and looked at Pearl intently. "What *are* you on?"

"I don't know," said Pearl. She pursed her lips, wide-eyed, then began giggling. "Maybe I should kiss *you*," she said. "You can tell me what you think."

A figure materialized in the corner behind them: Wendy Airhole. She blinked at them in astonishment for a moment, then scowled.

"Where did you come from?" asked Omidan.

"I was exiled to the margin," said Wendy sourly.

"For what reason?"

"Why is anyone ever exiled to the margin? For threatening the center."

"You should adopt the outlook that a party, by definition, has no center," said Omidan. "We certainly don't feel on the margin ourselves here. Something quite extraordinary has just befallen Pearl."

"You're the second person to lecture me about my attitude here tonight," said Wendy philosophically. "What happened to Pearl?"

"Arman Danzig kissed her, not at all in a friendly way. Now she's tripping or something, she's got processing trouble."

"For instance," said Pearl, giggling, "you just turned into Dizzy Duck, I think, or is it Douglas? With the hat? This is just getting stronger and stronger."

"It's Douglas Duck, with the hat," said Omidan, "and I see it too. Wendy just blinked away, as fast as she came, and now here's Douglas Duck, with feathers and a bright orange beak."

"It's still me," said Douglas Duck in Wendy's voice, angrily.

"This is new," said Omidan, not hearing. "There wasn't anyone fictional here before. There isn't any way that either one of them could have—*slept* with Douglas Duck, is there?"

"I don't know. I wish I could think—look how pretty that duck's hat is, Omidan. Can I touch your hat, duck?"

"It's *me*," said Wendy again, louder. "I'm just in a Douglas Duck body."

"Oh, how nice. I never saw a real cartoon before. Can I touch you?"

"Maybe she doesn't want to be touched," said Omidan. "She probably needs to get used to her new body."

"We're all real cartoons, here," said Douglas Duck, annoyed. "In a manner of speaking."

"But not with such—bright, glowing colors," said Pearl.

"Am I the only one?" Douglas Duck hopped up, trying to see over their heads into the crowd.

"No," said Omidan. "Look, there's an Arnold Schwarzenegger. I wonder if everybody will change eventually? There's a Bumpy the Cat, talking to the alien monster from that movie, whatsitcalled. And Alfau the Alligator! Oh, I love that show. I wonder who got to be Alfau the Alligator—"

"This is the last straw," said Douglas Duck. "Their respect for us is nil."

"It would seem so," said Omidan.

"They love us," said Pearl. "They want us to be happy."

"FOREVER," SAID THE DUCK   163

"I thought they wanted us to pair off," groused Douglas Duck.

"Do you have genitals?" asked Omidan politely.

Douglas's white gloved hands pulled at the elastic waistband of his pants. "Sort of."

Notable Johnson and Deconstructor Dawg came up to them. "Hello, Pearl," said Notable. "Have you seen Caitlice?"

"Notable! Uh, no, not for a while, but—"

"I'm having trouble spotting her," he fretted. "She must have taken on one of these characterizations."

"Yes, it makes it hard," said Omidan.

"You look unhappy," said Pearl. She threw her arms around Notable's neck and thrust her lips against his. "Mmmph."

Deconstructor Dawg introduced himself to Douglas Duck. "O.K. Tinkers," he said.

"Hello, O.K.," said Douglas. "It's me, Wendy."

"Wendy! I heard about your plan, to get between them—"

"Let's not talk about it."

By the time Notable Johnson located Caitlice Frisman, who was hidden in the body of a Philip Guston self-portrait complete with one eye, one booted foot, facial stubble and an enormous, gnarled cigar, he himself was incarnated as the health-food vampire, Count Granola.

They reclined together in near-total darkness on a large couch in a small side room.

"Oh, Cait," said the Count. "I was afraid I wouldn't find you, when everybody was suddenly creeping off—"

"Nonsense," she said, tousling his slick hair with her clubby, clownlike fingers. "I promised we'd be together. It's just that— you know how I feel about parties."

"Yes," he said, a little sadly.

"When Darth Gatsby gave Fran Krapp all his drinks—"

"Cait," he interrupted, "you and I could never have stayed together. I mean, for real, out there."

"Of course not, silly," she said. "That's why this is so nice. Such a treat."

In another side room, on a mattress on the floor, Douglas Duck and Albert Einstein lay on either side of Candy Bale, each idly caressing her body as she lay unconscious. Candy was one of a handful of guests whose form had remained constant throughout the party. Douglas Duck had taken off his hat and pants, and

Albert Einstein wore only a shirt, and was smoking a cigarette in a holder.

"Well, Arman," said Douglas. "They really had their way with us, didn't they?"

"Yes, darling." Albert drew on his cigarette. "Everyone had their way with everyone. Everyone always does."

"I—for all the, for everything—it really *was* a party, wasn't it?"

"Yes, darling."

The duck cocked his head and opened his bill as if to speak, then suddenly stopped.

"What?" said Albert.

"I wish it could go on forever," said the duck.

SYNTHESIS

Mary Rosenblum

"Synthesis" was purchased by Gardner Dozois, and appeared in the March 1992, issue of Asimov's, *with an interior illustration by Gary Freeman. Rosenblum made her first sale, to Asimov's, in 1990, and has since become a regular at the magazine, with more than a dozen sales to her credit—and we are happy to say that we have a number of new stories by her in inventory; her linked series of "Drylands" stories have proved to be one of the magazine's most popular series. A pleasingly prolific writer, she has also sold to* The Magazine of Fantasy and Science Fiction, Pulphouse, *and elsewhere, and her first novel,* Drylands, *appeared in 1993 to wide critical acclaim; it was followed in short order by her second novel,* Chimera. *A third novel,* The Stone Garden, *is coming up soon, as is her first short story collection, and she is already at work on a fourth novel.*

In the vivid novella that follows, she takes us to a high-tech future for an intricate and powerful study of some very old kinds of family relationships. . . .

165

Mary Rosenblum

A graduate of Clarion West, Mary Rosenblum lives with her family in Portland, Oregon.

Standing on a rock in the middle of the Pre-Cambrian ocean, David Chen raised his arms like a conductor. At his feet, the primordial sea responded, swelling up around the barren crag on which he stood, rich with the potential of life. Sticky, yellowish foam clung to the lava rock, stuck to David's bare feet. His virtual program translated the touch of foam on his palms with low-level electrical stimulation, suggested the damp breeze, but this one was a Net piece. You didn't *smell* the ocean, or feel the damp, briny caress of that breeze.

In a stationary piece, he could add complex sensory input: the cold touch of foam, the tang of the rich sea. He could make this piece *live*. David suppressed a sigh. You had to have a gallery to get a stationary showing. Chen BioSource did very well on the Exchange, but the family firm didn't do well enough that he could afford to put on his own stationary shows. This piece would get its opening on the Net. Tomorrow. That was a big enough triumph, he told himself.

Tomorrow. Tension stirred in David's gut. He had managed to bury that deadline, but now it surfaced, ticking in his brain like an antique clock. He frowned at a plume of volcanic ash twisting across the pale sky. Was it out of balance, or was this just a case of pre-opening jitters? Wind moaned across the sea with the lonely voice of woodwinds, prophesying change. David stretched a virtual arm to tweak at the ash plume. Better. Not a bad prologue, he told himself and counted down; three, two, one, *now*.

The sea heaved, pregnant with life. Creatures writhed, swarmed, coalesced and divided in a frenzied symphony of evolution. David stepped into the troubled sea and let himself sink. The silty water swirled around him, and the sense of motion was vivid enough to make David a little seasick. Good. Nothing for the nit-pickers to bitch about here. He had researched every species, down to the last cell. David climbed back onto his rock, allowing himself to savor a tentative anticipation. *Creation*, he'd called this piece; his

SYNTHESIS

biggest to date. And it was . . . good.

Yes, good. All around him, swimming motes grew legs, feeder fronds, fins that became jointed swimming legs. The Earth writhed and shuddered with the spasms of birth and death. Music soared accompaniment as mountain peaks thrust up from the seething water, piercing the yellowish sky. . . . David stiffened as an ominous darkness spread slowly across that sky. It dimmed the sun, cast a threatening shadow across the landscape. A breeze riffled the water, and the suggestion of cold raised goosebumps on David's neck. On the rocky shore, the first hesitant swimmer was flopping and struggling its way into the intertidal zone, gasping with rudimentary lungs.

That wasn't supposed to happen. "Pause," David snapped and the scene froze. "Goddammit!" He searched the motionless landscape of sea swell and breaking waves. "Where the hell are you, *this* time?"

A pointy, canid face peeked at him from behind a thrust of black lava rock. American red fox. *Vulpes fulva*, and you could see every hair ripple in the wind, David thought grudgingly.

Red-furred, prick-eared, the fox grinned a white, toothy grin. Its green eyes glinted with mischief and it made a very human, very rude noise.

Enough! David stretched out his hand. The pistol appeared in his fist, a vintage western-style revolver with a pearl handle. The fox flicked its white-tipped tail, laughed a boy's laugh, and streaked across the static sea. It vanished into thin air as David fired. For a long moment, he scowled after it. Then he tossed the revolver into the air. It blinked out of existence. "House?" he said. "Did I make contact?"

I'm sorry. House's voice whispered over his audial implant. *The intruder was able to withdraw from the program before the security trace connected.*

David grimaced, a headache nibbling at the back of his brain. He had changed the program entry codes again only yesterday, had thought that he'd seen the last of his pesky ghost for awhile. This piece opened *tomorrow*. Damaged or not. "Eraser," David said between clenched teeth. He snatched the oversized chalkboard-duster from the air and raised his hand to sweep away the fox's added shadow.

But it contributed something to the theme of the piece—a hint of trouble to come. An ominous warning. David tapped his toe on the frozen sea. He frowned at the ancestors of land life, caught in their struggle to crawl up onto the muddy ocean verge. Earth would never be the same again. The shadow . . . fit. Oh hell. "Save," David commanded. When the scene had been safely stored, he wiped away the fox's darkness with sweeping, angry strokes.

Excuse me, the House program interrupted him. *You are due at your father's apartment in one hour.*

David sighed and disappeared the eraser. He wanted more time, wanted to run every moment of this piece through his virtual fingers, reassure himself that his elusive ghost had done no more damage, that texture, shading, and tone were exactly what he had intended.

He did *not* want to meet with his father this evening.

David sighed again. "Store and exit." He closed his eyes against the momentary disorientation of the collapsing virtual.

His virtual lab took shape around him; three by three meters of carpeted walls, floor, ceiling. He stood in the middle of the floor, lanky and naked except for his singlet. The silver threads of his intradermal Kraeger net glittered in the subdued glow of the strip lights, covering every square centimeter of his skin. David wrinkled his nose, smelling his own sour sweat. His hair had come loose from its braid and it stuck to his neck. Resisting the temptation to recall the piece and blame a glitch in his House program for his tardiness, David went to shower and dress.

His father refused to use virtuals. He wouldn't even put on a suit of virtual skinthins, although he had had David netted before birth. Typical, David thought as he hesitated in the atrium outside his father's apartment. His father might detest the technology, but a Kraeger was the last word in power dressing in the business world. So Fuchin had had David netted. To benefit the family. "We Chinese are obsessed with family," David murmured. He brushed a nonexistent wrinkle from his tunic, wishing that the old man wasn't so stubbornly intransigent about the technology. He would be much easier to deal with in virtual.

"*Bù yâu*, don't preen for me," his father said when David finally entered the room. He was speaking Mandarin. "Save such actions for a future bride's attention."

Not that subject again. "Hello, Fuchin." David inclined his head stiffly and settled into the indicated chair. His father went

SYNTHESIS 169

in for antique lacquer chairs and a profusion of colored fabrics. Calligraphied scrolls hung on the walls, praising virtue. An antique writing set—ink box, carved jade chop, inkstone, and brushes—was laid out neatly on a carved desk. The antique clutter made David feel claustrophobic. "How are you feeling?" he asked his father. "Shau Jieh told me that you were having trouble sleeping."

"*Ching ni*, speak Mandarin, please. Use English for business. Your youngest sister worries too much." David's father waved his hand. "She is a good daughter." He reached for the porcelain pot on the table at his elbow and poured two cups of pale tea.

His father looked classically southern, David thought. His face might have been lifted from an antique Guangdong scroll. David's own features were more diluted; the product of his mother's mixed caucasian blood. His eldest half-sister, Dà Jieh, liked to remind him of his mother's mixed blood. David's mother had been something of a scandal, a very late and very young second wife. She had given him her own father's name, but David didn't remember much about her. He regarded his father's stark profile, lips tightening as he read the signs of anger folded into the brown, aged skin. What had he done *this* time?

"How is Yu Hwa?" his father asked.

"We aren't seeing each other anymore. We got mutually bored. Middle sister *is* about to give you your third grandson," David said. Èr Jieh had opted for selected gender again—to please Father, he was sure. David sighed. "Fuchin, if we have to fight, can we at least fight about the real issue and not about my childless status?"

"Try one of these Phoenix-Eye dumplings. They're made with shrimp. Wild-harvest shrimp, not artificial paste. A gift from Shau Jieh." His father sipped his tea. "You have no child. Can't you think of your family? Who will carry on the name? Who will light incense for me?"

"This is not fifteenth century China." David declined the proffered dumplings with a shake of his head. "Chen BioSource is a family company, not a dynasty."

"Your short-sightedness tires me to death." His father's frown deepened. "I understand that you have been dealing with a representative of the Tanaka corporation. Why didn't you ask me first?"

170 *Mary Rosenblum*

Aha. "My job is to deal with company representatives so that *you* don't have to." David spread his palm so that the silver threads of his net caught the light. "Have I misunderstood?"

"You exceeded your authority. I am the head of Chen BioSource and I am the majority stockholder."

"I only talked to Mr. Takamura this afternoon. Less than five hours ago." They had met in a plush Tokyo office; in virtual, of course. Mr. Takamura had worn the virtual face of a popular Japanese media star; the latest in power dressing. "I was going to bring it up in conference, tomorrow." After he finished *Creation*. After the opening.

"That is not appropriate." His father's palm slapped down on the lacquer table, making the pot shiver. "I am to be consulted before *any* such dealings. We will not do business with Tanaka."

"Fuchin." David hung on to his temper with an effort. "Have you discussed this with the rest of the family? Have you talked to Dà Jieh, to Eldest Sister? Half of the genetic templates we market are for improved strains of commercial sea-life. I gave you the report on the upcoming revision of the Antarctic treaty. Japan is rumored to be the winning bidder for harvest rights in the antarctic waters. Tanaka is the largest Japanese firm involved in serious aquaculture. They will benefit. They made us an outstanding offer."

"I risked everything to create Chen BioSource." His father rose stiffly to his feet. "I did it for our family; for you and your sisters, for your children's futures. I did *not* do it to benefit Tanaka. I am sick to death of hearing about Tanaka. You would throw away everything that I have worked for, give it away to strangers. You have no sense of family."

"And I wonder about your sense of business," David said in English. He clenched his fists on his knees. "I was not selling out the firm. Tanaka is interested in a long-term contract, that's all. I thought our intention was to make a profit."

"There is profit and there is profit."

"And Tanaka is Japanese." David met his father's disapproving stare. "Prejudice is an antique and expensive luxury, Fuchin."

"And loyalty is beyond price. Your eldest sister agrees with me. Tanaka is a danger to our independence."

"Does she?" David's laugh hurt his throat. "That's a new tune, considering that her last three designs were targeted specifically

SYNTHESIS   171

for Tanaka's Pacific fisheries—*with* their direct input." He should have expected this. Dà Jieh was always ready to stick a knife into him, where their father was concerned. "If I'm so incompetent and disloyal, then why don't you fire me and hire someone else?" he demanded bitterly.

"Do you want to waste your life playing your expensive games?" His father's lip curled. "You are my son. You are *Chen*. Chen BioSource is *your* heritage."

"And *your* dynasty." David flushed. He got to his feet, stared down at his father. "I'll meet with Mr. Takamura and reject his offer. I hope the *family* firm doesn't regret this."

"Er-dz!"

David wanted to ignore his father's command, but his muscles obeyed out of lifelong habit, pausing David at the door, turning him around to face his father.

"I have decided to retire. Two months from today." His father's face might have been a mask, carved from dark, bitter wood. "On that day, Chen BioSource will become your responsibility. On that day, you may do as you wish."

David turned on his heel without bowing, without speaking. He strode through the anteroom, out into the large atrium that his father shared with David's youngest half-sister. She was waiting for him, sitting on an upholstered bench beside a small pool of water-lilies. Her hair was pulled back smoothly from her wide face, braided into an intricate knot at the base of her neck, and she wore a floor-length tunic of jade colored cotton.

"Come sit with me," she said in Mandarin and patted the bench. "Fuchin is feeling very threatened today."

"By what, Shau Jieh?" David dropped onto the seat beside her.

"It's because he's old. He knows that he is starting to make mistakes and it terrifies him."

"He didn't seem very terrified. I got the impression that *I* made the mistakes." David nudged a polished pebble from the rim of the pool. It fell into the crystal water with a tiny splash. Gold and white koi fled, trailing diaphanous fins.

"Fuchin sees himself in you—perhaps too clearly." She smiled at the widening rings on the pool's surface. "How does that *work*? I can't tell that the water is a holo unless I try to touch it."

"There's a chip inside each pebble." David nudged another bit of agate into the holographic pool. "The program senses it and generates the ripples."

172   Mary Rosenblum

"It's a wonderful job, Little Brother. What are you working on now?"

"A piece called *Creation*." David let go of his anger. Shau Jieh was only four years his senior, and the only sister with whom he had been close as a child. His middle and elder sisters had been adults—disapproving adults—to his young eyes. Only Shau Jieh had been willing to play tag and fly kites with him. "It's about the origins of life on Earth," he told her. "Sort of a symphony of evolution. It shows on the Net, tomorrow."

"Wonderful." She clapped her hands with delight. "I'll Net into it. Did you tell Fuchin?"

"Tell him what?" The bitterness rose in David's throat again. "He doesn't approve of my *games*. And you—you're throwing away your life here, Shau Jieh. You don't have to be his servant. Why don't you move out, or move in with someone who'll appreciate what they've got?"

"I like living here." She blushed. "Fuchin didn't mean it. About your art." She touched David's arm lightly, tracing the silver threads of his net with her fingertips. "Chen BioSource has eaten him," she said sadly. "It's become his immortality, and lately he's been feeling very mortal. You care about your art, and that frightens him."

"You protect him too much." David smiled to take the sting out of his words. "Chen BioSource would have fallen apart years ago, if you weren't here to keep us all speaking to each other. Sometimes, though, I wish . . ." He shook his head impatiently, at a loss for words. What *did* he wish? That his father would enter one of his pieces? Approve of it? How childish, David thought. Father wouldn't even step into virtual to deal with an important client. "As long as you're playing mediator, ask Eldest Sister to leave me alone." He tugged at the thick braid of his hair. "I have enough trouble without her encouraging our father's prejudices."

"Don't be angry. Dà Jieh cares about her genetic designs as much as you do about your virtuals. She gets . . . jealous."

"Of *what*? Surely not of *me*, her incompetent little mongrel brother?" He laughed, but his sister looked troubled. She was taller than he when she stood up, but sitting down, her enormous eyes gave her the look of an anxious child. David bent down and kissed the perfectly straight part on top of her head. "I'll try not to get into another fight with her," he promised, dropping back into English. "But I wish she'd lay off. I make plenty of trouble

SYNTHESIS

for myself without her help. Why can't we get along?"

"What's bothering you tonight, Younger Brother?"

"Does it show so much?" David looked down at her hand. Those thick, blunt fingers looked so clumsy, could communicate such warmth. "Fuchin told me that he's going to retire," David said slowly. "In two months. Shau Jieh, I'm confused. He accuses me of betraying the family with one breath, tells me that he's turning the company over to me with the next."

"Fuchin thinks that you do a very good job," his sister said in a low voice.

"Does he? I'd like to hear that from *him*. Just once." David stood abruptly. "I have a *game* to finish."

"Don't be angry."

"I try," David said through tight lips. "I really do, Shau Jieh. Good night."

"Good night," his sister said, but her eyes were sad. Frowning into the depths of the holoed koi pool, she didn't look up as he left.

David took a cab to his tower, caught the lift to his mid-level floor. Beyond the transparent walls of the tube, the spilled jewels of LA's lights sank downward into darkness. For decades, the city had waited for The Quake. The Big One. It had never arrived. David imagined the spangled city-scape shattering, blossoming into flame and ruin. Seen from this height, distanced and abstract, it would be a beautiful and terrible image. Powerful. The lift stopped at his floor and David pulled himself away from the view.

David maintained a single room beside his lab. It was sparely decorated, the opposite of his father's cluttered space. A few cushions lay scattered around a single low table, and a futon on a platform served as bed and sofa. His excess income went into the purchase of Netspace for his virtuals. David ordered himself a cup of tea from the kitchen-wall, feeling slightly disoriented, as if the room had changed subtly in his absence. He had never been truly able to imagine himself as the executive of Chen BioSource, even though he had known that it would happen someday. David stared into the golden depths of his tea. His father's retirement had seemed as real and as unreal as the predicted Big Quake; a threat that hovered forever beyond the horizon of tomorrow.

But tomorrow had arrived.

174   *Mary Rosenblum*

David left his tea on the table, went into his lab. He stripped off his tunic, tossed it into a corner. Light rippled across the silver threads embedded in his skin. You had to be netted *in utero*, during early fetal development. Those threads translated every twitch of muscle, every biochemical shift, to his virtual programs. An intradermal net gave you the ultimate range of interaction in virtual.

Ironic, that it had enabled David to practice virtual art. Father certainly hadn't spent Chen money on it for *that* purpose. It had been an investment for the business, for the family. Food and family, David thought sourly. Our cultural obsessions. "Studio," he commanded, and spread his arms.

The walls shimmered, became the off-white walls of his virtual Studio, soaring two stories to a multipaned skylight. An easel stood in one corner. A half finished painting of Van Gogh's *Sunflowers* stood on its paint-spattered shelf. A green plant spread lush, tropical leaves in one corner, and a black and white cat washed its face contentedly on an antique steam radiator. Dust motes glittered in a shaft of sunlight that found its way through the skylight, and soft dulcimer music filled the air.

In here, in the virtual sanctuary of his Studio, neither his father nor Chen BioSource existed. David walked over to a rack of canvases that stood against one wall. He picked out *Creation*— green water and black rock painted with heavy, confident brush strokes. It was his strongest work yet. David pulled on the canvas. It stretched in his hands, lengthening, widening, until it was door-sized. It *became* a doorway, opening onto heaving waves and a small lava crag. No sign of fox prints. David started to step through the doorway, paused as a two-toned chime rang through his Studio. Only a few friends knew the entry code. "Come in," David said and sighed.

A door appeared in the Studio wall, a smooth panel of hand-rubbed birch. It swung open to reveal a tall, slender man with spiked blond hair and the face of a breathtakingly beautiful boy.

"Hello, Beryl."

"You're working, dear heart?" Beryl wandered over to the canvas-door, moving with languid grace. He peered in and shrugged. "Your stuff's good, but it's too subtle for me. I like a little raw violence stuck in here and there."

"Thanks." David snapped his fingers and a white curtain dropped across the Pre-Cambrian scene. Right now, he did not

SYNTHESIS

want to listen to Beryl's deft needling, or a dose of the latest gossip. All he wanted to do was to walk through that door into his piece, lose himself in it. "What's up?" he asked shortly.

"I've got a little present for you." Beryl reached and a padded chair appeared under his hand. "No charge, for a friend." He curled into the chair, smiling.

Beryl's body language reminded David of a cat. A supple, purring leopard. David wondered what Beryl looked like in the flesh—in flesh-time. "You charge for everything," David said. "Even if it doesn't always show up on my Exchange account."

"You wound me." Beryl didn't look wounded. "Who are BioSource's enemies, dear heart?"

"Enemies?" David blinked. "We've got plenty of rivals in the field; Antech and Selva Internacional are probably our biggest competitors. Why?"

"Someone is buying Chen BioSource security codes on the Net."

"*What?*"

"When did you lose your hearing, dear heart?"

Sabotage? Piracy? The possibilities buzzed in David's head like biting flies. He wanted to doubt, but Beryl hadn't acquired his reputation by selling flawed information. "We're not a high-end operation." David shook his head slowly. "We're not big time. Who the hell wants to pirate gene-templates? It would be cheaper to *buy* them."

"I told you what I know." Beryl yawned. "Find out who's buying and ask *them*."

Troubles, troubles. He would have to warn the rest of the family and spend time reviewing Security for cracks. It would mean upset, a flare of tempers and accusations. His father was going to throw a fit. David's earlier headache had come back. How long before he spent his every waking moment worrying about Chen BioSource?

"I'm off. Edith is throwing a hot party tonight. Are you coming?" Beryl's chair vanished as he stood. "No? Too bad. Well, if I hear any whispers about Chen codes, I'll let you know."

"For a price."

"Of course. Wasn't my information on the Antarctica treaty worth the investment?"

It would have been, if his father had been willing to listen. David balled his hand into a fist as the birchwood door closed behind Beryl and vanished. No time for *Creation*, now. He windowed into BioSource Security, called up a quick overview of the last ten days. No one had tried to enter. David purchased an extra level of protection, wincing at the cost. He chewed his lip, considering. He should call Father. But his father would want to know David's source, and he did not approve of freelancers like Beryl. So the family would get into it, spend the night in a frenzy of argument, and nothing more would be accomplished, anyway.

If someone already had the codes and tried to use them, the extra layer of security he was installing should alert David. If they'd already been into Chen filespace, it was too late.

Who wanted to spend that kind of money to swipe a handful of genetic designs? *Someone* did. He would have to ask Eldest Sister about it. Tomorrow would be soon enough. In fact, it would be too soon.

Near midnight, David finally windowed out of Security. Tired, but too tense to even contemplate sleep, he swept the curtain aside and plunged into the surge of the Pre-Cambrian ocean. Life formed and reformed around him, evolution in full song, a dance of eternity. David watched it from his rock, a cold sinking in the pit of his stomach. It had looked good, this afternoon.

It didn't look good to him now. It looked flat and over-ambitious, like a kid trying to copy the Mona Lisa with crayons. Technical perfection with no soul. A three-D video game. A flash of rusty color caught his eye and David spun.

The fox sat on its haunches on a stretch of muddy beach, its head tilted, eyes quizzical.

"You little sneak." David clenched his fists. All the jagged bits and fragments of this night balled up in his stomach, ignited into rage. "You damn Network ghost! Stay the *hell* out of my pieces!" He leaped off his rock, staggering in waist-deep water. "I'll trace you. I'll *kill* you, do you hear me?" Panting, he struggled for the beach.

The fox flicked its white-tipped tail and fled.

"Bastard!" David yelled after it. He stumbled, fell to his knees in the mud, palms slipping, spilling him flat on his face. Rage popped like a bubble inside him. He'd done too good a job on his beach. If he hadn't made the mud slippery, he wouldn't be on his face in it. That irony wrung a laugh out of him as he picked himself up. The fox had vanished. David erased the virtual mud

SYNTHESIS

from his skin and continued to run the piece through. There were no signs of any more fox prints.

The effects he had tried to achieve—the harmonies and dissonances, the subtle contrasts in textures and atmosphere—were still there. But he couldn't recapture the excitement he had felt as he created them. David sat down on a rocky headland, fatigue a dry ache behind his eyeballs. Opening jitters, he told himself, but it was more than just jitters. There was a dusty feeling in the back of his brain, a sense of futility. "Beginning," he commanded the program with a sigh. "Run."

Once more, the sea swelled with diversifying and proliferating life. Once more, the ugly, questing snouts of the air breathers poked at the intertidal mud. David frowned at the sky. "Pause." He retrieved the fox-marked scene from storage, overlaid it. Yes. The shadow *improved* it. What the hell, David thought, and merged the overlay in.

This would be his last piece, his last show. In two months, there would not be enough time for this. It would become a hobby, a pleasant diversion. If he did it at *all*. David ran through *Creation* again and again, not satisfied with it, not able to let go of it. In the early hours of the morning, too numb with fatigue to feel *anything*, he downloaded it into the show's Netspace.

"I haven't any idea what they're after." Thin, tall, radiating suppressed energy, his eldest sister crossed her arms on her desktop. "Security is *your* problem, isn't it?"

"It is." David forced a smile. When had Dà Jieh started to seriously dislike him? A cloudy memory stirred in his mind— a formal family dinner with some honored guest or other. David remembered cushions piled beneath him so that he could reach the table, remembered his father's hand on his head as he boasted of David's progress with his tutorials. He remembered his eldest sister's eyes, as she sat silently across the table from him.

At age twenty, she had taken a dual degree in biochemistry and genetics, had done so with the highest honors. Had his father told their visitors *that*? With a child's narcissism, he hadn't remembered. David shook his head. "It would help me if I knew where to start looking," he said. "What have you got under development?"

"If you are making the executive decisions for Chen BioSource, it is advisable to pay attention during conferences."

David swallowed a groan. Shau Jieh had spilled the beans. "You do a great job of keeping us informed." He dropped into English. "But what about projects in the theoretical stage? Things that you haven't officially begun to develop yet? Have you seen any signs of entry into your filespace at all?"

"No. Nothing is complete enough to steal. I hope your Security is as tight as you claim. Have you discussed this with our father?"

"Not yet. We're at an impasse, unless we can discover who is after us." David sighed. They were meeting in his sister's Office virtual. It was a packaged job, standard and plastic. He had offered once to design her something more interesting. He wouldn't make that mistake again. "What about the new line of cod that you're working on?" he asked.

"Tanaka's the only company doing open-sea farming on any scale." She frowned down at her desktop, ran her long fingers through her clipped-short hair. "They've already contracted for it. Why steal it? No. I would guess that your pirate is after the high-yield strain of oil-producing corn cells we've targeted for the vat-culture industry. It will out-perform anything on the market."

Her expression was earnest, but David frowned. She was dealing with him in realtime and her Office wasn't editing her body language. There was . . . evasion in her posture. "Dà Jieh, Eldest Sister, I didn't know about Fuchin's plans before last night." He groped for the words he needed. "I'm not . . . happy about his decision. I don't think that I'm ready to take this on yet. I'll do the best I can, but I need your help," he said. "I need the whole family's help."

"Perhaps you should tell our father *ni bù néng*, that you can't do it." She had reverted to Mandarin, her tone coldly formal.

"I promised Shau Jieh that I wouldn't fight with you."

"You'd rather play your precious games."

Father's words. "They're not *games*," David said.

"Oh, yes. *You* call it *art*." His sister smiled coldly. "You remind me so much of your mother. Shau Jieh tells me that she's somewhere in the Colorado Preserve. Heli-skiing with her latest lover. She only liked to play games and spend Chen money."

"I'll give you the status report on Security as soon as it's complete," David said. He bowed, turned on his heel and stepped into his Studio. "What does she *want* from me?" he said. "Damn it!"

SYNTHESIS

The cat blinked at him from its perch on the radiator, jumped down and arched against his ankles. David reached down to scratch its ears absently. Yes, his mother was in Colorado. He wondered how Shau Jieh knew—wondered if Youngest Sister was keeping track of her. She had made a complete break with their father when she had left, but unexpectedly, David had received a call from her. It had come a month ago, on his thirty-first birthday, a barely remembered voice from a barely remembered past. She had left his father—and David—when he was two.

Reality and unreality. David gave the cat one last pat and straightened. Special lenses in his eyes let him see a cat. He stretched out a hand and visual suggestion made his nerves interpret low-level electric stimulation from his net as warm flesh and fur. So he petted a cat and it comforted him. You could make love in virtual, to a perfect, unreal partner. You could fight an enemy. Your body could go into shock from a virtual wound. A month ago, he had sat in the virtual of a plush resort livingroom across from a petite woman with fine pale skin, a Chinese face and reddish hair. His mother had looked thirty-five, no older. She had smiled at him with a sad, slightly puzzled expression, as if she couldn't quite remember him, or couldn't believe that he was actually her son. They had drunk coffee together and she had asked about his art. *I couldn't live in your father's world,* she had said, as if she was answering a question. *I tried, but I couldn't. I am sorry, David.*

I didn't ask, David thought. I've never asked her why she left. He watched the cat leap back onto its radiator. The thirty-five-year-old woman on the virtual sofa had been as unreal as this cat. In fleshtime, his mother would be in her late fifties. That young woman on the sofa had been more real to David than the dim memories that sometimes haunted his dreams.

The boundary between the real and the unreal was a fragile one. David rubbed his eyes, remembering that family dinner again, and how he had beamed in the spotlight of his father's pride. Once again, he tried to remember if Fuchin had praised Dà Jieh, but all he could summon was a vision of her cold, angry eyes. "Access Hans Renmeyer," David said, and sighed. "Semi-formal mode."

The square, blunt features of his agent appeared in the air in front of David. "David." Renmeyer smiled, visible only from the waist up. "I was going to call you. *Creation* has accumulated the greatest share of access-points of any piece in the MultiNet show this past twenty-four hours."

"That's great," David murmured. This wasn't a realtime conversation. Renmeyer's body language was just a hair off. You could always tell a sim from a realtime interaction.

"The Show committee has offered you a further three days of exhibition," Renmeyer's sim announced. "They'll download your royalty statement to your personal account at the conclusion of the show. It's the standard contract. I have it ready for your signature, if you agree."

So *Creation* was a success. Absently, David scanned the oversized document that appeared in front of him, laid his palm against the signature box. Such a success might conceivably bring a gallery invitation. David wandered into his living room, ordered up a bowl of noodles and bok choi that he didn't really want. He should feel triumphant. Fulfilled. *Pleased,* at least.

He felt tired.

David spent the morning windowed into Security, reviewing reports, double checking for unusual currents in the daily informational flow. Nothing presented itself to him. If anyone was probing Chen security, they were too good for him to detect. Thoughtfully, he called up the file on the company's current projects—Dà Jieh's projects. She was the creative genius that powered Chen. She was the one who found the backdoor means to ends that other engineers had given up on.

She knows what our pirate is after, David thought, and then wondered why he thought so. You could attach a dozen negative interpretations to her hostility. Some day, he would ask their youngest sister about it. Shau Jieh would know. Shau Jieh had worshipped her as a kid, had followed her tall, brilliant sister like a shadow.

David finally exited Security in mid-afternoon, spent a hurried couple of hours reviewing the day's reports. Chen BioSource was down on the Exchange and there was no reason for it to be down. He scowled. Rumors of the pirate interest? He would have to ask Beryl. The Studio waited for him on the other side of the wall. David could feel its breathing presence as he dumped his uneaten noodles into the recycler and drank a glass of water. *Creation* was a success, with an extended showing to its credit. Enough to interest a gallery? Enough to get it a stationary showing?

SYNTHESIS 181

It didn't matter any more.

The walls squeezed in on him. David banged his glass down on the counter. It tipped over, rolled off onto the carpeted floor. It didn't break and he didn't pick it up. Grabbing a jacket from the closet, he went out into the hall, down the lift and out into the street.

The city streets always depressed David. Crowded, littered with a human spoor of food wrappers and trash, they made him think of cracks in the city reality, accumulating dirt and debris. Black-market vendors hawked food, chemicals, and information from carts and coat-pockets. Public terminals and virtual booths clustered at every corner.

People in the street shuffled past in a faceless river, on their way from *here* to *there*, flesh brushing flesh, making no eye contact. We are at our most isolated in the street, David thought— although lately, he had felt as if someone was following him every time he left the tower. He never noticed any particular person when he turned to look, but the feeling haunted him. He didn't feel that shadow's presence today, though. Shoulders hunched, David threaded his way through the crowd, welcoming its grimy, claustrophobic crush. He couldn't think down here, and he didn't *want* to think.

A crowd filled the small square at the end of the block, thronged around some shouting evangelist, or revolutionary, or entertaining crazy. Pedestrian traffic stalled, backed up, and spilled over into the street. David let the crowd pressure push him into a narrow alley between two old office buildings. A small shop opened into it; a custom clothing designer. The expensive holo decoration and squalid site suggested that it was the peak of chic . . . for the moment. The holos were mediocre. David eyed them, then noticed three figures crowded into the shadowy recess of a sealed-up doorway.

Two youths held a kid between them. They wore black skinthins and tattoos on their hairless scalps. The boy looked about twelve; street-kid ragged. This was just another city reality, ugly and everpresent. People walked, hurried, or strolled past. There were fewer here than in the main thoroughfare, but they were equally blind; as if they were walking inside separate virtuals. Light from the storefront holo shone on the kid's face, warm as afternoon sunlight. It made his green eyes glitter. David hesitated. Skinthins peeked from beneath the kid's dirty clothes. The way he tilted his

head and hunched his shoulders against the hands that gripped
him looked . . . familiar. David mentally overlaid red fur on that
thin face, adding pricked ears. The boy's lips drew back from his
teeth, and David saw a fox face, a ghost face that had laughed at
him with glittering green eyes.

"Hey," he said, and stopped.

The taller of the youths turned to stare at David. His pale eyes
looked like glass marbles in his expressionless face. His posture
suggested that David was no threat. With unhurried grace, he
turned back to the kid, seized his wrist with a long-fingered hand,
and twisted it.

The kid screamed.

Still unhurried, the two of them let go of the boy, stalked
past David, and disappeared into the main street. David stared
after them, stunned by their casual violence. Quick movement
at the edge of his vision jolted him out of his trance. He turned
in time to grab hold of the kid's grubby tunic. "Not so fast."
The virtual skinthins beneath the filthy clothes were expensive,
state-of-the-art. David shoved the boy back against the concrete
wall, eyes narrowing as the kid's chin came up. Yeah, it was *him*.
The fox-ghost. His body language gave him away. "What the hell
have you been doing in my pieces?" he demanded.

"Nothing, man. Leggo! You're crazy."

"Don't give me *nothing*." David shook him. "You damn van-
dal! You've been all *over* the place! Did you think it was fun? Did
you get a kick out of screwing around in my pieces and messing
things up? Was that it? *Was it?*"

"No," the kid gasped. "I went in because you're *good*. You're
the best."

"Bullshit," David said between his teeth.

"No shit, man. I'm an artist. Like you." The kid looked up
through the tangle of his dirty-blond hair, his fox-eyes glittering.
"I'm good. But you're better. For now."

"So work your own pieces."

"Netspace costs. And I wanted to see how *you* did stuff."

Something unsettlingly like veneration gleamed in those green
eyes. David scowled. The kid was thin. His bones pushed sharp
edges against his pale skin. He was cradling the hand that the
youth had twisted, and there were pain shadows at the corners of
his mouth.

"That guy hurt you," David said.

SYNTHESIS
183

"I went into this jerk's abstract. What a piece of shit." The kid's lip curled. "But he's got better security than you do. I guess word got around that I was haunting your stuff, so they looked for me here."

"You've been following me, haven't you? In the street."

"I wanted to see you. It's just a thing, you know? Realtime flesh, I mean—I just like to do that. *You're* the same," he said. "You don't put on a Self when you're working."

"Why bother?" David looked away from those glittering eyes. He felt a twinge of recognition for the *hunger* that he saw there. That shadow *had* added just the right touch to *Creation*. David sighed. "Someone needs to look at your hand," he said. "Come on."

The kid didn't say a word on the way to a nearby clinic. David half expected him to bolt, would have been relieved if he had. The boy's body language suggested flight. He walked tense and wary, poised. But he didn't bolt. At the clinic, at David's request, a receptionist ushered the boy into a treatment cubicle. He hunched silently on the bench, a cornered fox, ignoring David. He didn't make a sound as a bored medical tech set his broken wrist with a single twisting pull, but his skin went dead white and beads of sweat glistened on his forehead. The tech put a cast on his wrist, handed him two orange capsules for pain, and left.

David ran his own card through the terminal for payment. Outside, the kid followed him blindly, as if he was sleepwalking. The plastic cast encased his hand and part of his forearm. The boy cradled the hand in his good arm, carrying it as if it were a piece of wood. At the entrance to David's tower, he hesitated, and a shadow of his earlier wariness stirred in the green depths of his eyes.

"It's all right," David said, because the look in the kid's eyes demanded *some* kind of reassurance.

The wariness didn't go away, but the kid nodded and walked through the door into the entryway, as if David had extended a formal invitation.

David felt a growing uneasiness as the lift carried them upward. Slanting beams of afternoon sun touched the soaring new towers and the old office buildings, gilded the city with light the color of hope. He hadn't meant to do this—bring the boy home. His father's impending retirement cut him off from this kid with his hungry eyes. David had simply meant to pay for the medical treatment, repay that moment of veneration. Well, whatever he had meant or not meant, the kid was *here*: wide, drugged eyes focused on the expanding cityscape, filling the cramped lift with the thick, sour smell of unwashed flesh. David wrinkled his nose.

Feed him and send him home.

In his apartment, David ordered the kid a sandwich from the kitchen-wall, and sat across from him at the small table, mildly repelled by the ravenous manner in which the kid devoured the food. "What's your name?" David asked as the kid licked the last crumbs from his fingers. "Where do you live?"

"I'm Flander." Uninvited, he helped himself to coffee from the kitchen-wall, perched himself on the corner of the table. The glaze of shock was fading from his eyes and he swung one foot, restless and a little tense. "I live around," he said.

"On your own?"

"Shy-Shy kind of keeps track."

"Who's Shy-Shy?" David asked. He didn't really want to know, wanted this kid out of his apartment, all accounts settled and closed.

"She's a cool lady I know. I hang around with her a lot." Flander picked at the slick plastic of his cast, frowning. "*Creation* did real good on the Net today. What are you going to work on next?" And then: "You left it in. The shadow."

"It was a good touch. Valid." David prowled across the room, aware suddenly of how *small* it was. "I . . . don't know what I'm going to work on next." I'm hedging, David thought. He wasn't ready to put it into words yet—that he was through—not to himself, and certainly not to this fox-child.

"What about that volcano piece? I liked it and I haven't seen if for awhile. I can't get at your stuff when it's in storage."

"Don't sound so apologetic," David growled. No, that hunger in the kid's eyes wasn't for *food*. "I'll show it to you." He pushed his chair back. Let this be the closing act, he decided. Let the kid muck around in the piece; David had been blocked on it for months, and it didn't matter anymore now anyway. Then he could send him home to his friend with the weird name, Shy-Shy. David went into his lab. The kid followed, pulling a virtual mask down over his head, tugging a glove over his uninjured hand. "Studio," David said and watched the walls stretch and pale. "Not the fox again?" He glowered at the prick-eared creature. "That was quick. You know all my codes, don't you?"

SYNTHESIS

"Not all of them. I told you—I can't get into your storage." The fox lolled its tongue, grinned. "I like this Self. There are people who want to know what I look like in fleshtime."

"Sure of yourself, aren't you?" David reached for the racked canvases. "What would those two have done if I hadn't interrupted them?"

The fox didn't answer that one. David stretched out the volcano canvas, stepped into it. The fox was there ahead of him, nose in the air, as if it was sniffing the breeze. It was limping, David noticed, holding its left paw clear of the ground. The feel of the piece washed over him, and he frowned. He had started with rage, poured it out in the billowing ash and thick remorseless streams of glowing lava. Then he had tried to reshape it with a gentle moonlit sky and the lush leaves of surviving tropicals. All he had achieved was the flat realism of a travelogue, and the nagging feeling that it *could*, damn it, work.

Scowling, David muted the hot glare of the lava column, added steam where it touched a small stream, turned the steam opalescent in the moonlight.

"You're lucky you're netted," the fox said in Flander's voice. "It's tough to do the really fine stuff in skinthins. Who paid to fix you up?"

"Our company."

"Shy-Shy's netted." Flander/fox darted past him, loping three-legged into the blackened desolation beyond the creeping tongue of lava. "What about this?" He nosed the gray ash, and tiny leaves unfolded.

Yeah, you could do it that way . . . maybe get the right effect. David chewed his lower lip, wandered back along the cooling lava flow. Try this. . . . He planted sprouts and cracking seeds. Small animals scuttled through the ashy wasteland, burrowing, mating, living. Beyond rage, hope . . . Yeah, it was a nice contrast, if he could get it into balance, give it some *focus*. He shaped, vanished what he had just done, swore, and tried something new. Life in the aftermath of devastation? Hope sprouting in the ashheap of despair? It could work, yes, it *was* working. Excitement seized him, flowed like molten gold through his veins. David reached, made and unmade, twisted and shaped the fiery world in a frenzy of creation.

Hours later, fatigue finally stopped him. David put down the virtual boulder he was holding, mildly surprised by the tremor in his muscles. He wondered what time it was. He felt good, fine. He hadn't felt like this since *Creation* had started to come together. His knees quivered and the muscles between his shoulderblades ached, but it was a good tiredness, a welcome one. "Store," David rasped, dry-mouthed. He looked around for the fox. He had lost track of it some time ago. "Exit Studio," he said, and staggered as the lab reappeared around him.

The kid—Flander—was curled up in the corner, head pillowed on his arm, the plastic cast a white blot in the muted light. He was asleep. "Hey," David said.

He didn't twitch.

The floor kept trying to tilt beneath his feet. David shrugged and stumbled to the other room to drink glass after glass of water. Outside, in the grimy reality of the streets, it would be getting light. Before he fell across his futon, David carried an extra quilt into the lab and draped it over Flander.

It seemed as if only minutes had passed before the House woke him. It nagged him out of bed with subsonics and unbearable jokes about family, business, and the demands of a schedule. David felt like shit. He was not in the mood for jokes this morning, wondered what the *hell* had possessed him to design such an adolescent wake-up. Tea seemed like a good idea, but it pooled like molten lead in his stomach.

He had let himself forget about the kid.

David stopped dead in the doorway to the lab. Flander was still asleep, tangled in the quilt, his injured arm sticking out as if it didn't quite belong to him. David groped for a solution to this situation, found nothing ready to hand. With a sigh, he sat down in a realtime chair, called up his office, and put the kid out of his mind.

There was plenty waiting for him on the slab of polished jade that was his desk. A major supplier, Chem Suisse, had unexpectedly failed them. During the night, Chen BioSource had fallen even farther on the Exchange. David wiped the depressing reports from the jade with a sweep of his hand, frowned as glowing red letters reappeared in their place. It was a message from his father announcing that he was on his way over to see David. In person, of course.

Your father has arrived, House announced.

David groaned and went to let his father in.

SYNTHESIS   187

"*Ni hǎushiang bìng*. You look sick," his father said as David opened the door. "What did you do? Drink all night?" He marched into the room.

Eldest Sister was with him. She gave David a smooth smile, walked primly across the room to seat herself at the table.

Their father clucked his tongue disapprovingly at the dirty dishes piled beside the kitchen-wall. "Can't you at least offer me tea?"

"May I offer you tea, Fuchin?" Resigned, David ordered pot and cups from the kitchen-wall, carried them to the table. "This is my *room*. It isn't an office."

"Your hospitality is as lacking as your attention to family affairs."

"Fuchin, I have spent a large part of the past thirty-six hours dealing with family business." David noticed his sister's expectant expression, flushed, and got hold of his temper.

"Your new Security costs us a fortune."

"Surely you reviewed my report on the piracy threat. Would you rather have someone in our filespace?"

"The expectation of theft is yours, not mine." His father glared at David. "Our margin of profit will be severely strained by the extra Security cost. I am here because we are about to default on our contract with North America Aquaculture. Dà Jieh tells me so."

"The report is on your desk. You haven't gotten to it yet?" His sister's tone was demure. "The contract depends on a specific delivery date. As you surely know. Since Chem Suisse can't fill our order for amino acids, we won't meet the deadline."

"What are you going to *do* about it?" His father's hand slapped the tabletop and David jumped.

"I plan to contact other suppliers." David turned his tea cup between his fingers, struggling to organize his sluggish thoughts. "We can probably get what we need from European Pharmaceuticals."

"We don't have much of a margin," Dà Jieh interposed smoothly. "If we get too far behind, we won't make the deadline, and North America can legally decline the order."

"They won't do that." David banged his cup down. "They've given us leeway on deadlines before."

"You should have thought about this," his father interrupted harshly.

The supply failure had been a matter of bad luck and bad timing, but Fuchin was never willing to blame luck. He *was* willing to blame David. Anger sat like a stone in David's chest, but beneath the anger was a cold awareness that his father was partly right. If he had considered *all* possibilities, he could have lined up alternate suppliers ahead of time.

I didn't consider the possibility of The Quake happening tomorrow, either, David thought bitterly. He lifted his head suddenly, caught his sister's eyes on him. Hatred? David felt a small jolt of shock, but her face smoothed so quickly that David wondered if he had imagined it.

"If I receive the required supplies within a week, I can push our production schedule," she said. "Perhaps we will make the deadline."

"I hope that you will not be so lax again." Father stood. "I expect you to be competent. At least that." He looked over David's shoulder, frowned at the doorway that led to David's lab. "You cannot play your games and do a good job for your family."

"I have never let my *art* hurt Chen BioSource," David said as he ushered his father out of the room.

The words sounded weak to David, a petty defiance without real dignity. He clenched his teeth and bowed to his father. When the door had closed safely behind them, he stomped into his lab. He had intended to call up his office, start querying suppliers, but a virtual was already open. David staggered as his net automatically popped him into a familiar landscape of lava and struggling greenery.

The fox lay on a patch of black loam, licking its injured paw. "Wow, man." It snapped its jaws. "You really did a fine job on this last night."

"Thanks." David struggled with leftover temper. "Go play with it. It's all yours, okay?" He called up a door, opened it into his office.

"What do you mean? I thought we were working on it?" The fox limped after him, ears pricked. "That old boy sounded like he was bugging you. How come you didn't tell him and the bitch to take a hike?"

"Eavesdropping is rude. The old boy happens to be my father *and* my boss. The bitch is my sister. Go play."

"I wasn't eavesdropping. I don't speak the lingo, and don't give me *play,* man. You still should've told him to take a hike."

SYNTHESIS

The fox leaped three-legged onto the corner of the jade desk. It stretched out a paw, hissed a quick patter of commands. A tiny, perfect image of David's father appeared on the desktop, hiked stiffly across the smooth surface. Its face looked thunderous.

It was a marvelous caricature. In spite of himself, David smiled. "You *are* good." His smile faded. "It's a long story, Flander. I . . . don't have time for this anymore. The volcano's a throwaway." He looked away. "If you want to do something with it, go do it."

"You're crazy, man." Flander's voice skidded up half an octave. "You're *good*. You can't just *stop*. Some gallery'll offer for you, for sure. That piece is no throwaway. Man, what you *did* to it, last night. And I was *asleep*." The fox flattened its ears.

Flander was right. The volcano piece *wasn't* a throwaway. Not anymore. David closed his eyes, remembering last night's magic. "I've got work that has to be done," he said. "Give the fox a rest, will you?"

"So do your work. I'll hang around till you're done." Fox metamorphosed into a fur-covered boy-shape, shed fur all over the desktop to become Flander. He looked up at David through a fringe of dirty hair. "I don't want to screw around by myself," he said softly. "I want to see how you made that piece *work* like you did."

How do you say no to veneration? David looked away from the kid's glittering, fox-ghost eyes. He didn't *want* to say no. "What about this Shy-Shy?" He fired his last shot. "Isn't she going to worry?"

"I called her from your Studio." Flander grinned. "She said you sound like a good guy, that I was lucky as hell that I met you, and I should say thank you about a hundred times. Thank you," he said.

David sighed. "I've got to deal with this business stuff first. Go take a shower. You stink."

David spent the morning in his office, using Security to scour Chen BioSource filespace. He came up clean, but the cost made him cringe. Better he should have found evidence of a break-in. Father was going to scream, and that wouldn't help their shaky position on the Exchange. He tracked Beryl down in one of his virtual lairs, quizzed him about that mysterious shakiness.

Rumors, Beryl told him. He was a willowy youth with a shaved scalp today, but his leopard-slink gave him away. *It's floating*

190   *Mary Rosenblum*

around that someone is out to shaft Chen BioSource. Sorry, dear heart. No names, just intent.

"Don't send me a bill for *that*," David told him sourly.

He tracked down an alternate source for Eldest Sister's amino acids, and turned the details over to his middle sister. Er Jieh handled that kind of thing. If they didn't run into trouble in development, Chen BioSource would make the contract deadline. Barely, but they would make it. David stretched, grimacing at the gritty ache of tension in his neck. He needed a shower, he decided, and exited his office.

Instead of exiting to his lab, he found himself standing in his volcano piece. Flander—in human form, this time—was sitting crosslegged in a patch of scorched and wilting fern, chin in his hands, staring moodily at a blackened tongue of cooling lava. "I can see what you changed," he said. "I can't figure how it makes the piece work."

"I don't know, either. It just *felt* right to me." David lowered himself to the ground. "That's new," he said nodding at the ferns beneath Flander.

"I didn't feel like sitting on rock. That's all."

"Sure." David examined the clump. Every crushed or bent leaf was perfect, right down to the smeared film of ash on the green fronds. Flander was showing off. "You have an incredible talent for detail," David said. "But those ferns don't belong there."

"I know. I'll wipe 'em when I get up." The boy tilted his head, eyes bright. "Are you done with the office stuff? Can we do this for awhile?"

"Yes," David said, because he needed to forget the Exchange, his sister's hostility, and his father's eternal dissatisfaction. Hell, why *not* play with this kid?

They worked together. At first, David cloaked himself in the memory of the boy's venerating eyes and tried to assume the role of Teacher. That didn't last long. The kid was good in his own right, quick and perceptive, with an off-beat point of view that somehow resonated with what David tried, sent him off into paroxysms of inspiration. Before long, they were arguing over details, changing and erasing, reshaping the entire piece.

There were fox-prints everywhere.

"Hey, we've got to quit," David said finally.

"Why?" Flander tossed a handful of pebbles into the air, turned them into a flock of small, jewel-toned birds. "I'm not tired."

SYNTHESIS

"You ought to see your face. Have you eaten anything today?" Reluctantly, David shrank the piece to a virtual canvas again, racked it. "I know you haven't."

"Neither have you." Flander scratched beneath the edge of his cast. "It's not that late."

"I can't do another all-nighter. I have a business to run." David exited the Studio, propelled the boy into the main room. He ordered sandwiches and fruit while Flander stripped off his hood and glove. "Eat this," he said, handing a plate to the boy. Shadows stained the skin beneath Flander's eyes, made them seem too large and too bright. "Then go home and get some sleep."

"How come your dad wants you to quit doing art?" Flander bit into a pear, wiped juice from his chin.

"I didn't say he did. It's my decision. I can't just *play* at this," David said slowly. "It matters too much to me. I'm not going to have the time to do it the way I want to do it."

"So you're just going to quit? To do what?"

"To run a family dynasty." David took a huge bite of sandwich. It tasted like sawdust.

"Huh." Flander peeked into his own sandwich, put it down. "I don't know. I probably would've gotten into something dumb if it hadn't been for Shy-Shy—doing sex virtuals for the X-parlors, or shoot-em-ups, or something like that. She kept bugging me all the time, telling me that I had to remember what I *wanted* to do."

There was understanding in his tone, sympathy. This skinny, half-starved street kid was forgiving David for making a bad choice. David choked on his mouthful of food, caught between insult and laughter.

"You're lucky to have her around," he said when he could finally talk. "She gives you a lot of support."

"She does that," Flander said soberly. "She's the cracker and she's *hot*. She's the one who got me into this artist's Netspace the first time. She's always there for me—I can't remember anybody before Shy-Shy. I wouldn't have made it without her."

The expression in Flander's eyes silenced David. He picked up his plate, hiding an unexpected pang of envy. What would it feel like, to have someone look at you like that? David wrapped Flander's untouched sandwich in a piece of plastic, handed it to the boy. "Eat it later," he said. "If you want to come back, we'll finish this piece." Let this one be the last, instead of *Creation*.

He had a little time yet. "Call me from the tower entryway and I'll let you in."

"I'll do that." Flander grinned. "Thanks." He darted out of the apartment, quick as a fox streaking for cover.

David had planned to let Flander do most of the work on the volcano piece, but he couldn't stay out of it. The piece was coming alive, promising to be more powerful than *Creation*. David worked on it whenever he could snatch the time, putting off sleep until he was stumbling with exhaustion. Using Flander's flashes of crazy inspiration as a springboard, he catapulted into soaring flights of invention. The Milky Way fell down into the seething cauldron of the volcano in a cascade of cold light, as if the universe was folding in on itself, coiling back into primordial fire.

Even Beryl should like this one, David thought, and laughed out loud. He had reached a new level in his work, and it felt good. Flander was part of it, too. A big part. David had stopped sending Flander home in the evenings. He let him sleep on the cushions in the main room. It had finally dawned on David that the kid lived on the street. This Shy-Shy might provide emotional sustenance, but Flander's bodily needs were his own business. David nagged him to eat and a little flesh began to hide Flander's bones.

"How come you don't live with her?" David asked Flander one afternoon. The cloud he was working on looked like a pile of oatmeal. "Doesn't she worry about you sleeping on the street?" David scowled at the cloud, erased it with an angry swipe.

"She lives around, okay? She doesn't hang out in any one place very long. You know, you're too stuck on reality." Flander retrieved the cloud, combed it into a glittering comet tail. "Shy-Shy and I take care of each other, and we do just fine."

"Easy. I wasn't criticizing." It sounded as if this Shy-Shy was one of Beryl's cohort, dealing in blackmarket information. You kept your realtime, fleshtime self out of sight, in that trade. David muted the fiery comet-tail to a whisper of ice crystals.

The communication chime interrupted his thoughts. "Come in," David said, glad of an excuse to stop struggling with comet-clouds.

Hans Renmeyer's torso took shape in David's virtual doorway. "David." He bowed from invisible hips, in realtime, this visit. "I apologize for the lateness of the hour. I'm interrupting your work."

SYNTHESIS

"That's all right." David exited into his Studio, noticed from the corner of his eye that Flander had reverted to fox shape. "What can I do for you?"

"I hope you're going to have something new for me soon. In the meantime, I have some good news for you." Renmeyer cleared his throat, pausing portentously. "I've received a query from the Roberts Gallery, in London. They are interested in giving your piece *Creation* a stationary show."

A stationary?

"It's not a large gallery." Renmeyer spread his hands apologetically. "But it's relatively prestigious. In my opinion, as your agent, the invitation is well worth your consideration."

Out of the thousands of artists who showed on the Net, only a handful showed stationary. A very small handful.

"I . . . accept," David said.

"Good, good." Renmeyer's smile grew wider, warmer. "I'll review their contract and have something for your signature tomorrow. I wish you continued success," he said, bowed again, and exited.

Fox feet hit David in the small of the back. He turned around and nearly went down flat as Flander, boy-shaped again, threw himself into David's arms with realtime mass and force.

"I told you, man," he yelled gleefully. "I *told* you they'd come after you. You're so good. You're so damned *good*." He sobered suddenly, looked up into David's face. "You're not quitting now. Right?"

"No. I'm . . . not." David drew a long breath. "We're good. *We'll* be great."

"Your old . . . your Dad's going to be pissed, isn't he?"

"I'm not sure that he will ever speak to me again." David exited the Studio, shivered as the lab appeared. A part of him had been shaping this decision as he and Flander had shaped the volcano piece. "Chen BioSource is his universe," David said heavily. "My father designed a son to fit into that universe. The David Chen that he sees is a virtual—the son he believes in, the one that doesn't really exist. I'm not sure he will ever see *me*, or understand who I am."

"That's tough, man." Flander put a hand on David's shoulder in a surprisingly mature gesture of comfort.

"Yeah, it is." David's voice wanted to crack. He put his arm around Flander, squeezing warm, realtime flesh. "I meant it about the *we*," he said. "We do good together."

"We do that." Flander grinned, fox-eyes dancing. "Wait till *this* piece hits a gallery. What are we going to call it, anyway?"

"I don't know. I haven't come up with a title yet." David tossed his loosened braid back over his shoulder and sighed. "Let's go get some dinner," he said.

The House program interrupted them as they celebrated with buns stuffed with real chicken. *Excuse me*, it intoned apologetically. *You have an urgent call from your youngest sister. She says it's an emergency.*

An emergency.

Father. David knew it, even as he stretched a virtual hand to open a door to her apartment.

She wasn't there. A pale, stylized carp with flowing fins—his sister's personal sigil—answered him. "I'm at the hospital," it said in her voice. "Come right away, David. Selva Internacional filed a piracy suit against us, and Fuchin had a heart attack. Please come."

David blinked as his apartment re-formed around him. His arms and legs felt numb, without sensation, as if he had been sitting at the table for hours without moving. The room seemed to be shrinking, closing around him like a fist. David pushed himself stiffly to his feet, breathing too fast as the shrinking room squeezed his ribs, compressed his lungs.

"What's wrong?" Flander pushed his chair back as David started for the door. "What was she saying?"

"Nothing," David said, and walked blindly out of the apartment.

David stood close to Shau Jieh at his father's bedside. He had spent a sleepless night at the hospital, sitting in a barren little waiting room that reeked of disinfectant while a million slow eternities crawled past. He had waited there, trapped in that barren cube, because it would have been wrong to wait at home, to visit the hospital in virtual. Wrong. Fuchin wouldn't even wear skinthins.

Tubes went into his father's nose, into the veins that writhed like blue worms beneath his crepey skin. Orange blobs of remote monitors clung to his head, chest, arms, and legs. Every synaptical flicker was being recorded and evaluated and responded to.

SYNTHESIS   195

Medicine inflicted the ultimate lack of privacy, David thought dully. His father looked shrunken, shriveled, as if the tubes were draining his blood, as if the monitors were alien leeches, sucking away life and substance. David put his arm around his sister's waist, felt her tremble slightly. At the foot of the bed, their middle sister sniffled audibly and predictably into a tissue.

Dà Jieh stood behind her. She raised her head, looked coldly at David. "If you had spent more time attending to business, this would never have happened."

"That is *enough*." Shau Jieh's tone made them all blink. "We will *not* fight at our father's bedside."

Dà Jieh shrugged and pressed her lips together. Silence filled the small room.

That silence felt like an accusation. David bowed his head, eyes on the pitiless white of the hospital sheet. If he had been in his office yesterday evening, he might have seen the brief before his father had discovered it, might have been able to deal with it, or at least prepare him. Might have, might have . . . David clenched his hands into fists.

Whoever had bought Chen codes had gotten in and out without tripping Security. They had duplicated his sister's developmental records on her new strain of cod, and they had destroyed some of her files. Now Selva Internacional was claiming that they had developed the template first, that the identical nature of the Chen template indicated piracy. Chen BioSource no longer had the developmental records to disprove Selva's claim.

It had been a very clever bit of espionage. If Selva won their suit in entirety, Chen BioSource would have to file for reorganization. It was not likely that the company would survive it. I should have caught it, David thought bitterly. I shouldn't have taken my sister's word for the untouched state of her records.

When the suit had been filed, he had been in his Studio with Flander. Playing *games*. David turned away from the bed.

"Er-dz? My . . . son?"

The dry whisper sounded faint as the rustle of an insect's wings. "Fuchin?" David bent over the bed, squatted beside it when his father's eyes didn't seem able to focus on his face. "I'm here," he said. "We're all here."

"Save us," he whispered. His withered fingers twitched, touched David's hand. "Chen BioSource will die. The family will die. Don't let it die!"

"Fuchin, it's all right." David took his father's hand and squeezed it gently, frightened by the weakness of that spidery touch. "It's just numbers, Fuchin. How many years have you been playing with numbers?" He forced a smile, tucked his father's hand back onto the bed. "I'll play better than Selva, and everything will be fine."

"It *must* be." His father's withered lips trembled. "It *must* be all right. Please promise me . . . ?"

Death lurked in his father's eyes. David could see its shadow. His immortality, Shau Jieh had said of Chen BioSource. No, David thought. It is his *life*. If it dies, he will die. "I promise," David whispered.

Èr Jieh crowded in beside him, weeping openly now, and David used the moment to slip out of the room. There were public terminals at the end of the hallway. Renmeyer's face looked grainy and lifeless on the flat screen.

"I don't understand." The poor resolution couldn't hide his shocked expression. "David, *why* do you want to cancel the gallery show?"

"I don't have time to do the sensory effects," David said woodenly.

"It can't require *that* much time. I don't understand. The contract I presented to you was more than reasonable."

"It's not you. It's not the contract. Look, I'm sorry." David exited the connection abruptly.

It was more than a lack of time that had made him cancel the show. *Sorry.* Who had he been apologizing to? Renmeyer? Flander?

Himself?

Shau Jieh caught up with him at the lift. "Younger Brother, wait." She grabbed his arm, forced him to stop.

"You stay with him. I can't." David ran his hand across his face as her eyes filled with hurt. "He *created* me, do you realize that? I'm not sure that I'm even real."

"Stop it. He loves you. He does." Her voice was full of pain. "We Chinese are so obsessed with sons. Fuchin is obsessed with it—I know that, and I know that it's not a good thing. But don't hurt him." She clung to his arm. "Don't walk away from him, Little Brother. Not now."

"It's ironic." David raised his arm slowly, turned it so that the silver netting caught the light. "It's ironic that he bought this for me."

SYNTHESIS   197

"*He* didn't net you." His sister looked surprised. "Your *mother* did. I remember them arguing about it. She used to design virtuals. Before she married Fuchin. I thought you knew."

"I didn't know." David felt numb. I never asked, he thought. She didn't exist for me. Was that what she had been trying to tell him in her awkward, birthday visit? "Don't worry," he said bitterly. "I'm part of our father's private virtual. I can't walk away." David turned his back on her tears and fled.

His apartment seemed unfamiliar to David, as if he had been absent for months, instead of merely hours. David glanced into the lab. Flander was obviously inside some virtual or other. Stripped to his skinthins, hooded and gloved, he sat crosslegged on the floor, eyes fixed on the far wall, unaware of David's fleshtime presence. His good hand twitched as he did whatever he was doing in his invisible universe. David watched him for a moment. Everyone had their own personal virtual, he thought bitterly. Their personal reality.

What is *mine*? he wondered.

David's hand clenched into a fist. He went back into the main room and entered his office. The jade desktop waited for him, covered with neat lines of flowing script. It was the digest of Selva's suit, as reported by his office attorney. The projected outcome looked bad for Chen BioSource, whether they settled or not. Selva had them. It was simply a question of how badly Selva wanted to hurt them and how much they were willing to spend to do it. Corporate espionage and piracy were being prosecuted fiercely in the international courts. David stared at the words until they blurred into meaningless loops and squiggles. Their message didn't change.

I was good, David thought. I have that. I was *good*.

A door appeared in the wall of David's office. "David?" Flander's voice. Virtual knuckles rapped on virtual wood.

Go away, David thought, but he sighed and opened the door. Flander wasn't alone. A tall woman stood beside him. She had silvery hair pulled into a stylish club at the base of her neck and a square, strong face. She was netted.

Shy-Shy. It had to be. I've seen her before, David thought, but the connection slipped away from him.

"Hello." Her voice was low and warm. "I'm sorry to bust in on you like this, but Flander doesn't know the meaning of the word patience." She rumpled Flander's hair gently.

Flander grinned back and the absolute *unity* of that shared moment made David look quickly away.

"I asked her to come in," Flander spoke up. "Shy-Shy's *hot*, man. She gets me in *anywhere* I want to go! She can find out who dumped that suit on you. She can find out who is working the levers, no problem."

David felt as if his mouth was hanging open. "What did you do?" he managed finally. "Translate my sister's private message?"

"Sure. You were *way* upset, man. I don't speak the lingo, but the library does." He lifted one shoulder in a casual shrug.

David grimaced, fighting an outraged sense of *invasion*. This was the fox, he reminded himself. The ghost who had slipped in and out of his pieces. Flander was a street kid. Nothing was sacred to him. David sighed, tired beyond belief. "You've been into everything, haven't you? Even my office?"

"Don't blame him too much." Shy-Shy's hand tightened on Flander's shoulder, but the shake she gave him was a gentle one. "You've been good to him and he was really worried. He wouldn't take no for an answer." She laughed softly and pushed a wisp of hair back from her forehead. "I *am* good," she said. "I can find out what you need to know. *If* you want me to. *He* gets to decide," she said to Flander as he opened his mouth. "It's his business, even if you've been into it up to your eyebrows."

"I'm sorry, David." Flander's eyes were anxious. "You didn't tell me not to look."

"It's okay," David said. Shy-Shy was waiting, one casually possessive hand still on Flander's shoulder. She was *dressed*; real-leather boots, natural fiber tunic, fiber-light embroidery. The works. Street-power chic. She wasn't dirty, she wasn't skinny. Why the hell doesn't she take *care* of him? David thought resentfully. "I'd . . . appreciate your help." He forced the words out. "For my father's sake."

David remained in his office while Shy-Shy and Flander worked the Net. They worked together, and he didn't want to watch. Instead, he caught up on the orders, the supply problems, and the reports; all the dreary details of running a business that went on—that *had* to go on—in spite of personal tragedy. He dealt with what had to be dealt with, and kept on working, sorting through

SYNTHESIS

the low-priority bits and pieces that had accumulated like dust in the corners of the business. He was obsessing, knew it, and didn't care. In the private hospital room, monitor-leeches tethered his father to life. David could feel the numbers, the projections, and the worries closing around him like fingers, solidifying like the walls of a newly-opened virtual.

When Flander blinked into existence in front of his desk, David started convulsively. "Use the door," he snapped.

"Sorry. I forgot." Flander grinned at him. "Man, I was *right*. I *guessed*. Shy-Shy said it would've taken her twice as long if I hadn't tipped her where to start."

So the power-dressed wonder-woman had cracked Selva. David stretched, feeling his vertebrae crackle. His muscles ached, and the clock on his desk shocked him. Hours had passed. I was hiding, David thought. "Show me," he told Flander.

"You bet, man. Shy-Shy got it down cold. Because I guessed part of it." Flander was still grinning, pleased with himself, full of pride for this prize he had brought to David. "Just watch," he said.

David blinked as the lights dimmed. One whole wall of his office shimmered and became a screen. A movie was playing on it, a flickering kaleidoscope of antique cinemascope color. Rows of red velvet seats lined the floor in front of it. Popcorn and crumpled candy wrappers littered the floor and a couple necked passionately in the front seat. David wondered irritably how long it had taken Flander to design these details. His gaze shifted to the screen and he went cold.

Up there on the screen, in gritty two-dimensional passion, Beryl and his eldest sister writhed in a tangle of black silk sheets.

"He records *everything*, man! You ought to *see* what Shy-Shy and I had to wade through." Flander wriggled like a puppy. "But it's there. She hands him some stuff—hardcopy—and after she leaves, he runs it under his scanner. He thinks he's got *some* security, man. He's never run into *Shy-Shy*!" The enormous bed vanished, replaced by white sheets of hardcopy, lined up neatly.

David stared at the scrawled numbers and symbols. Sickness gathered in his belly as he recognized his sister's handwritten notes.

"I saw her face, when she was here. She *hates* you, man. Shy-Shy said that a slick piracy job would cost mucho. If big money wasn't part of it, maybe it was *personal*. That made me think it was an inside job, and your sib seemed like a natural. So Shy-Shy boosted me into her virtuals. Your sister doesn't check for ghosts." His lip curled. "She went to see this guy this evening—while you were doing business stuff. I thought maybe he had something on her, but she looked pretty happy to see him. So we went into his filespace and found the stuff you wanted. She's a real bitch, isn't she?"

Dà Jieh. Eldest Sister—proud, disdainful Dà Jieh. All this time, *her*. She had played him like a puppet, and he had let her, because she was *family*. He had been as blind to reality as their father, but it had been their father who had paid the price. David had thrown his gallery show away for nothing. If Dà Jieh wanted to destroy Chen BioSource, nothing that David could do would save it. Some part of him had guessed. Maybe that was why he had buried himself in business this afternoon. He had been hiding from the truth that Flander's wonderful Shy-Shy would dig up for him.

David clenched his teeth until his jaw ached, struggling with a deep resentment against the stranger who had walked into his father's life and casually pointed out the ugly cracks in the foundation.

"David?" Flander touched his arm, realtime flesh warm behind those virtual fingers. "I'm sorry. I'm really sorry, man."

Realtime, fleshtime comfort, and this Shy-Shy didn't even keep him *fed*. "Thanks," David whispered. There was nothing he could do. "Beryl's the key. He trades in information and levers." It didn't matter. "I need to talk to Beryl." It didn't fucking matter. . . . David turned his back on Flander and plunged into his office.

He spent the rest of the night hunting Beryl, chasing him through a virtual maze of social and business connections, hopping from party to party, from shrug to knowing shrug.

I don't know. I haven't seen him around.

Don't know where he lives. No one does, man.

Get real, Chen.

Beryl didn't want to be found. Not by David, at least. In the early morning hours, David gave up. He exited the dregs of the party that he had dropped in on and found Flander in his office. He was sitting on the floor, arms clasped around his drawn-up knees, watching David. David had a vague memory of seeing

SYNTHESIS   201

him in just that position every time he had dropped back into his office.

"You look like shit," Flander said softly. "Go sleep, man."

"Shy-Shy," David said. The word came out as a dry rasp. "Get Shy-Shy for me. She can find Beryl."

"Give it some *rest*, man." Flander sounded anxious. "He'll be around. Don't kill yourself, okay?

"Now!" David clenched his fist. He *had* to find Beryl, had to hunt him down and confront him, because if he *didn't* . . . he'd have to confront Dà Jieh. "Get her," he said.

Shy-Shy didn't look as if Flander had waked her. She looked fresh, solidly unruffled, as if she'd been up for hours, or all night, or maybe she just didn't need to sleep at all, David thought sourly. Again, that twinge of familiarity—stronger, this time. He could almost remember. "Beryl," he said, struggling with the fog that kept filling up his head. "The guy my sister . . . met. He's hiding from me. I need his address."

"His security must have picked up a trace from my ghosting. Maybe he guessed it was you." She nodded. "No problem. I downloaded his address into your office filespace after I got out of there. Sorry. I thought you'd find it." Shy-Shy touched his arm. "You look like shit," she said softly. "Go sleep, man."

Flander's exact words of a minute ago, spoken with Flander's phrasing and syntax and inflection. In spite of his exhaustion—or perhaps because of it—David heard it. Differences in timber and pitch misled, but the mechanics were . . . the same.

Familiar. Shy-Shy was so damn *familiar*. Cold trickled down David's spine, raised gooseflesh on his arms. He looked at her closely, with an artist's eye this time, *seeing* her. Change the gender, the hair and eye-color, add thirty years of aging, and she looked . . . like Flander. She could be his mother, or his sister. You could change your self in virtual, but you moved the same, thought the same, talked the same. The cold spread, filling David's belly with ice. *She* was power-dressed, but *Flander* scrounged to live. Flander slept on the street. Where did Shy-Shy sleep?

Now that he knew to look, it was *there*. Shy-Shy *was* Flander and . . . she wasn't.

David shivered, his teeth rattling briefly together. She was a *simulation*, an autonomous virtual persona. She had to be, and she *couldn't* be. *No one* could create that kind of autonomous body language. She was right here, in the same office with Flander, but her every twitch was independent and *perfect*. *No one* had that kind of talent.

Flander's fingerprints were all over her. David knew his style well enough by now to recognize them.

Even knowing, she still seemed *real*.

David didn't have the kind of talent that it would take to do something like that. He would *never* have it. Numbness was seeping out to the ends of his fingers, up into his brain. "Shy-Shy's a sim," David croaked. "My God, you *made* her."

"No way, man." Flander's body jerked, but he laughed. "Shy-Shy, listen to him!"

David feinted suddenly at Shy-Shy's face, watched her involuntary jerk of reaction, watched her eyes widen, her pupils contract. *Perfect.* You couldn't tell. It made Renmeyer's expensive sim look like an automaton.

I thought *I* was good. David stared at Shy-Shy's face, watching her get angry, seeing Flander's body language in the tightening of her lips, the tension in her shoulders and the curve of her spine. That knowledge that he had talent, *major* talent, had been a talisman for David to keep forever.

Flander had just taken that away.

Showing off. Flander was *showing off*, like he had showed off with his clump of ferns. The kid had been sitting here, watching him *bleed*, laughing up his sleeve because dumb David couldn't even tell a sim from a realtime virtual. "You little shit," David breathed. "You goddamn *punk*." His fist caught Flander on the cheekbone—realtime flesh bruising realtime flesh.

Flander tumbled backward with a cry, sprawling at David's feet.

"Knock it off!" Shy-Shy dropped to her knees beside Flander, angry face turned up to David. "What the hell's the matter with *you*?"

"The game's over." Fists clenched, breathing hard, David stood over Flander. "You *made* her. *Look* at her! You can see the touches. The way you color skin. The way you detail every hair and every wrinkle. She's controlling her own movement— but that's *your* body language. I could run a side-by-side; it's the same, down to the last twitch. Did you think that I was *completely* stupid?" he said bitterly. "Yeah, I thought she was real. Did you

SYNTHESIS 203

get a kick out of watching me make a fool out of myself? You little street punk! You think you're so damn clever!"

"I didn't do it." Flander scrambled to his feet, eyes wild, shaking so hard that he could barely stand up. "She's *real*. She takes *care* of me. Always." On her knees on the floor, Shy-Shy clasped her hands, her eyes as wild as Flander's. "She's real!" Flander screamed. "You hear me? She's *real*!"

The image of Shy-Shy popped like a soap-bubble. Flander gave a hoarse, animal cry, and vanished from the office.

"Flander?" David yelled. Silence. It seeped into David's flesh as the seconds ticked by, chilling his anger, turning it into a cold sickness. "Flander?" he called again. "Come *back* here!" He exited the office, premonition prickling his skin like gooseflesh. The lab was empty. So was the living room. The exterior door stood open.

I wouldn't have made it without her, Flander had said of Shy-Shy. There had been love in his eyes when he had looked at her, and she had loved him back. She had been dressed in street-power clothes. What kid would clothe a hero in rags? David looked down the wide empty hallway toward the lift. Was it even possible? he asked himself. Could you create a virtual persona that complex and complete, and then *forget* that you had done so? The answer scared him. You would have to be insane. Seriously insane.

Perhaps. Or perhaps you had to be so lonely that such a creation made you *sane*. If you were talented enough, you could invest that persona with all the love and comfort and safety that didn't really exist anywhere in your fleshtime world. In a way, you could bring that creation to life. Until someone made you see what you had done, anyway.

Reality and unreality. Where did one end and the other begin? I *killed* Shy-Shy, David thought, and sudden grief twisted him. He looked down at his hands. They were clean. Not one trace of Shy-Shy's blood soiled them. He wiped his palms on his tunic and went back into his empty rooms to keep his promise to his father.

The address that Shy-Shy—that Flander—had left on file led David to a decrepit brick building. It stood on the edge of the burned-over scar that had once been the L.A. Barrio, and it looked as if it had been consistently neglected for a century at least. Old earthquake damage had flaked away the concrete façade, and black cracks zig-zagged through the weathered bricks. There was no lock on the entryway. Inside, it smelled like piss. David breathed shallowly. The *Out of Order* placard taped to the lift doors looked about as old as the building. David climbed the stairs. Dust sifted up from the mud-colored carpet and hung in the air in his wake, glittering like gold in the shafts of sunlight that made it through the grimy, steel-netted windows on the landing.

Beryl lived on the third floor. David stood outside on the landing for a few minutes, catching his breath, waiting for his heart-rate to return to normal. *No major security*, the file notes had told him. *He's safe, 'cause no one knows where he lives.* Shy-Shy's words. Flander's voice. David bent to examine the locks. They were mechanical. As old as the building. Good cover, David thought coldly. What thief would bother? He slid the thin blade of the smart-key into the first lock. One by one, the locks clicked. David turned the handle, pushed, and walked in.

The squalor inside stopped him on the threshold. The cramped room smelled worse than the hallway; a mix of dirt, unwashed human flesh, and spoiled food. Crusted dishes and clothes lay scattered everywhere. A rumpled bed, a table, and a chair took up much of the floor space. Dust filmed the tabletop, tracked with indecipherable smears. Beryl sat on the edge of his bed, stark naked, his eyes wide and glazed.

Like David, he was netted. Light glittered on the silver threads in his skin. David felt a dull sense of shock. The Beryl he knew was all feline grace, beauty, and sneering self-confidence. The virtual Beryl. The *fleshtime* Beryl was short, with soft, flaccid muscles, a layer of fat around his waist, and drooping shoulders. His skin looked translucent in the glare from the overhead lights, sickly pale, like some cave-dwelling insect.

Beryl shivered as he exited his virtual, and his face tightened into an expression of surprise and fear. "What the *hell* are you doing here? Get out," he said in Beryl's silky voice.

David looked at the dirty cotton sheets on the narrow bed, remembering black silk and his sister's smooth shoulders. "It was a *virtual*," he said. "Flander was right. This wasn't blackmail." *Why?* David shook his head slightly. To get *him?* Had she been willing to risk the company just to make David look like an incompetent? It wouldn't make any difference, he thought bitterly. Their father wouldn't stop believing in his virtual son,

SYNTHESIS

no matter what Dà Jieh did. He took a step closer to Beryl, another.

"Hey, man." Beryl backed up fast, grunted as the table-edge stopped him. "No need for violence, okay?" he stuttered. "Look, let's do this in comfort. How about in your office?"

"I think I prefer fleshtime." David took another step, hands at his sides. Perspiration gleamed on Beryl's face, and David could smell the rank, sour odor of his fear. He is afraid of *me*, David thought. Not because I might hurt him, but just because I'm *here*. "So, tell me." He leaned closer, breathing in Beryl's face. "Tell me all about it."

"Sure, man. What's to tell?" Beryl was bending backward, away from David, hands braced on the tabletop. "It was just a little business deal. A sweet set-up, if you want to know. Your sister is a sharp lady. An operator." He flinched, although David hadn't moved a muscle. "She fed me the stuff," he said breathlessly. "All I did was pass it on to Selva—I know someone there—and settle the details with them. Look, *she* designed the scam. I was just the runner. That's the *truth*, man."

Yes, it probably was the truth. More or less. "You're going to call Selva off," David said softly. "They're going to drop the suit."

"No way." Beryl's voice went up half an octave. "They're going to make *bucks* taking a bite out of Chen BioSource. They're not going to walk away from that."

"I know where you live." David didn't smile. Beryl shuddered. "I have copies of the pirated data, so their bite isn't such a sure thing anymore. I'll kick in some money, and you come up with the rest of the price. You'll find something to trade. You have one hour," he said. "Then your address goes public."

"All right." Beryl's arms were trembling. "All *right*, you bastard."

David sat down gingerly on the edge of the upholstered chair. Something more or less yellow had spilled on the arm and dried. It looked like vomit. David looked away, watched Beryl as he went into virtual.

Now he could see the Beryl he knew. The man's body language changed. The muscles in his face firmed. On the other side of an invisible, electronic wall, he tossed his beautiful head, sneered, slunk like a grinning leopard through someone's day. His body mimicked those movements. Which is *real?* David wondered

206   *Mary Rosenblum*

suddenly. *This* Beryl, or the *other* one? David felt dizzy. The
smell in the room oppressed him, and a dry finger of nausea
moved in his belly.

"It's done." Beryl finally exited. Arms crossed, back against
the wall, he glared at David. "Check your mail. Selva is with-
drawing their suit. Now get out."

David checked. The withdrawal was there, filed and legal. He
got to his feet, looked into Beryl's flaccid, twitching face, and
left. Outside, the dingy city streets felt like paradise. The nausea
still sat coiled in David's gut. Beryl would have to move. His
invisibility had been compromised. David imagined him walking
through the crowded streets, trapped in realtime as he relocated.

Beryl would get his punishment.

David hailed a cab and gave it the lab address.

His sister was waiting for him. Beryl had called her, of course.
She greeted David serenely, and ushered him into her private
apartment, up on the second floor of the building that housed
her lab. The spotless, almost spartan decor jarred with David's
memory of Beryl's squalid clutter. He looked at his sister's profile, smooth and perfect as porcelain, wondering what needs had
brought her into Beryl's virtual bed. Sex only? Or something
more?

"I didn't expect you to discover my little plot." She set a tray
down on a low lacquer table. "I expected you to be misled
by the pirate rumors we planted. Tea?" She handed David a
delicate cup.

The glaze was a depthless, gleaming black. A tiny, illusory
pearl seemed to glimmer in the bottom. "You did this just to make
me look bad," he said. "You came within a hair of destroying
Chen BioSource." Of destroying Father. "I haven't told Fuchin,"
he said. "Yet."

"Don't try to lever me with our father. I am weary to death
of him *and* of you." Her eyes gleamed, hard and depthless as
the glaze on the cup in her hands. "You don't care about Chen
BioSource. It's a burden to you, a distraction from your so-called
art, Little Brother." Her lips twitched. "I *am* Chen BioSource. *I*
design the templates we sell. I care about the company more than
our father ever did. But I am merely a daughter. So Fuchin had
to find a brood mare and make himself a son. I have spent my life
making Chen BioSource work, and he is going to give it to *you*.

SYNTHESIS 207

Because you are his *son*." Her voice trembled. "Tanaka wants a new krill I'm developing. They value me for what I *am*. They have offered me a position as head of their aquaculture design unit and I am going to take them up on it. Fuchin will still have a company to give you, but it won't be worth much without me. Tell him whatever you wish, Little Brother. I don't care."

Dà Jieh. Eldest Sister. David looked down at the cup in his hands, remembering her eyes as their father boasted of his *son's* achievements to that forgotten visitor. The illusory pearl gleamed in the bottom of his cup. His sister and their father shared the same passion, the same virtual. Chen BioSource: Immortality. Dynasty. Life. But Father could only visualize it through a *son*.

David set his cup down very carefully. "I *am* self-centered," he said to his sister. "I didn't understand. I am sorry."

He left her sitting there, the black cup in her hands, wary surprise on her face.

David's apartment rang with quiet. He prowled the empty room, peered into the lab. He peeled his tunic off over his head, threw it into the corner, and entered his Studio. One by one, he pulled out the racked canvases. No sign of new fox-prints. David pulled out the volcano piece, stretched it out. Flander was woven into every nuance of the piece. David saw his signature in the delicate shadows cast by grassblades, in the gleam of light on a bit of smooth stone. Stars cascaded into the caldera, dying in shimmering light.

The piece was a masterwork.

Because of *Flander*—crazy, talented kid, gone now, maybe forever. What would happen to him, without Shy-Shy? Maybe he could recreate her, somehow convince himself again that she was real. Maybe he couldn't.

"Erase," David cried in a shaking voice. "Delete all storage." The dying stars trembled.

Are you sure you want to do this? his Studio program queried.

David opened his mouth, closed it. This is what my sister did, he thought, and felt dizzy. Jealous, hurt, and angry, she had tried to smash what she loved. David touched a fern-frond, noting the tiny cinnamon spots of the spore-cases on its underside. I was going to destroy this, he thought, because I am hurt and because I am . . . jealous.

Jealous. He would *never* be as good as Flander. Sooner or later, the world would know it.

208   *Mary Rosenblum*

"Cancel the erase," David said. He squeezed the scene back down to a canvas, racked it carefully.

"New canvas," he said and picked the white rectangle out of the air. It stretched in his hands, blindingly empty. "Azure," David said and wiped sky across the expanse of nothingness. He muted it to twilight blue, shaded darkness over it; nightfall seeping into the weary end of day.

David worked on into the night in a frenzy of creation. He sculpted Shy-Shy's image, remembering the weathered angles of her face, the love and warmth that Flander had put into her eyes. He added the furtive, driven traces of a fox, melded it all into a symphony of love and hope and compromised dreams, of darkness and light. He put his father into it, too, gave him blind, all-seeing, virtual eyes and a grieving face. Reality and unreality twisted together, became a skein of human hopes and fears and desires.

Sometime well into the next day, David passed out. As he fell, limbs drifting toward the floor in slow motion, the entire piece unrolled inside his head. It was good. David felt one piercing moment of triumph, and then the floor touched his face and darkness swallowed him whole.

They all came by to see Father on the day that he was released from the hospital. They brought gifts, delicacies of fresh fruit or wild-harvest seafood, and he basked in their attentions. He looked better than he had in months. This was Family, operating as it should. Chen BioSource in the flesh. The virtual was intact. David stayed at the periphery, aware that Shau Jieh was keeping an eye on him. His eldest sister nodded to him, and her porcelain face betrayed not one echo of their interview. If she was worried that David would betray her part in the lawsuit, it didn't show. Her bit of espionage had been the smashing fist of an enraged child. Her withdrawal to Tanaka was the calculated destruction of an adult. In either case, Chen BioSource would die.

Die was the appropriate word. Fuchin *was* Chen BioSource. David had understood that in the hospital, when he had made his promise to his father. David sighed. You could kill in virtual. In the illegal parlors, you could kill the body with drugs and unreal weapons. You could kill the soul. David tried to banish the image of Flander's face as Shy-Shy vanished from his life. We surround ourselves with unreality, he thought. Not just the Beryls, who had

SYNTHESIS   209

retreated from the physical world, but people like his father, who
had surrounded themselves with an illusory reality shaped to fit
their needs.

His middle sister had finally herded her boys out of the room.
Only Shau Jieh remained. David went over to the bedside. He
knelt down, took his father's hand in his. "I'm glad you feel
better," he said in perfect, careful Mandarin.

"You did what I asked. You got Selva to drop the suit. I am
proud of you, Er-dz."

David looked away from the approval in his father's eyes. A
part of him would always long for that approval. A part of him
had been willing to give up everything for it. David took a deep
breath. "Selva decided that the suit didn't justify the expense.
Fuchin, I am leaving Chen BioSource. I can't work for you
anymore."

"What are you saying to me?" His father struggled higher on
the pillows, his cheeks quivering. "You talk nonsense. What will
you do? Walk away from your family? Turn your back on us?"

"I don't want to walk away from you," David said gently. "I
am still your son, I am still David Chen, but I can't manage the
company. I don't want to do it."

"*Wanting* has nothing to do with it. You have a responsibility.
To me. To the family."

"I do." David stood. "I know that there are people who will do
a better job than I can. I *am* thinking of the family."

"You think only of yourself." His father's tone dripped bitterness. "Like your mother did."

Father had never spoken of his mother to David before. There
was hurt in his voice. David held out his arm, watched light
run across the silver threads embedded in his skin. Had she
been implanting a hope, or an echo of her own failed dreams?
I'll ask her, he thought. I *need* to ask her. "*Dwèi bu chi,* I'm
sorry, Fuchin." David reached out, touched his father's shoulders
gently. "What I do is for the best. I hope you understand that
someday."

His father turned his face to the wall, his expression closed,
hard as stone.

"Fuchin?"

His father gave no sign that he had heard. David looked down
at his hands. They were trembling. He closed them into fists and
turned away. Dà Jieh was still in the atrium. She was sitting on the

210   *Mary Rosenblum*

bench beside the holoed pool, staring at the gold and white fish.

"Reality and unreality are not so easy to tell apart." David stopped beside her. "Sometimes the unreal has as much power as the real. Maybe more."

"Are you trying to be a philosopher now? I thought you were an *artist?*" Her tone was acid.

"I transferred my company shares into your account." David watched the graceful flick and swirl of the kois' trailing fins. "That gives you a strong majority."

"What are you saying?"

Her expression was wary, as if she expected a trap. In a way, it *was* a trap. David sighed. "I can't stop you from going to work for Tanaka. I can't stop you from destroying Chen BioSource. If you stay, Fuchin will have to listen to you. I don't think he'll like it, but I've quit. That might change his attitude a little."

"You're going to walk away? Just hand over all your shares, with no strings attached?"

"Check your account. It's done. I can't change it now." Those shares were the chains that would bind her forever. She cared about Chen BioSource as much as their father did. David dropped a pebble into the water, watched rings form and expand, chasing each other across the still surface. Flander was right. He was too stuck on reality. David lifted his head, met his sister's black, porcelain eyes. "I wish that I had as much talent as you do," he said softly.

Something flickered in those depthless eyes and she bent her head. "If what you tell me is true," she said, "I will probably reject Tanaka's offer."

"I hope so." David walked away.

Shau Jieh was waiting for him beside the lift. She said nothing, but her eyes were sad.

"Our *sister* is the son that Fuchin wants," David said to her. "Gender has nothing to do with it. Do you think he can ever understand that?"

"I don't know," she said. "I'm sorry."

"Me, too." He had destroyed the David Chen that his father had believed in. He had done it to keep Chen BioSource alive, destroying the smaller illusion to preserve the greater one. There was no way to heal the hurt that he had left behind in his father's bedroom. Part of David would always grieve for that lost father.

SYNTHESIS

211

David lifted his sister's hand gently from his arm, kissed her, and stepped into the lift.

"Your piece, *Synthesis,* is remarkable. Your use of the volcano theme is masterful." Hans Renmeyer paced across David's Studio, hands clasped behind his expensively clad back. "I take it that you have settled whatever was . . . troubling you? Never mind, never mind." He spread his hands, smiling. "Your access-point rating is still high after seven days on the Net. I haven't seen anyone get such a lengthy showing for months now." He coughed delicately. "Perhaps another gallery will be interested. I have heard some . . . rumors."

"Good." David reached out to stroke the black and white cat. I am afraid, he thought. After the payoffs to find Beryl, the bribes for Selva, and his stock transfer, he didn't have much money left. He had never done this for the money, as a means to stay off the street. "If you present me with an offer, I'll accept it," he said. "I give you my word."

"Good, very good. Tell me—" Renmeyer paused, his hand on the Studio's virtual door. "Why did you choose the name *Synthesis?* I'm just curious."

The piece had named itself. It *was* a synthesis, a merging of himself and Flander, or reality and unreality. "Because of fox prints," David said to Renmeyer's uncomprehending face, and ushered him out of the Studio.

Alone, he took the canvas of Shy-Shy and his father out of the rack, stretched it open. He hadn't worked on it since his night of frenzy. David ran through it slowly. It *was* good. Not perfect, but good. "*Grief,*" David said. "That's what I'll call this one." It was a hymn of grieving for what was, and for what couldn't be. And for what might have been.

A flash of red moved at the edge of his vision. David turned slowly, heart leaping. The red fox sat on its haunches in a sweep of stars. *Vulpes fulva*—and you could see every hair ripple in the wind. It cocked its head, green eyes wary, ears pricked.

"You're very good," David said. "You're going to be better than me."

The fox flattened its ears, curled its lips back in a snarl.

"*Together,*" David said softly, "we can be great."

For a long moment, the fox didn't move, and David found himself holding his breath. Then it opened its jaws, lolled its red tongue over its pointed white teeth, and trotted into the center of the scene. It flicked its tail and scattered shards of light across the piece.

David opened his arms and Flander walked into them; grubby, skinny street kid whose ragged clothes covered state-of-the-art skinthins. He needed a shower. David watched the glittering droplets of light settle over his father's face and Shy-Shy's, like shed tears, like forgiveness.

It was the perfect touch.